THE DUKE'S SWORD

The Duke's Guard Series,
Book One

C.H. Admirand

ARE YOU SIGNED UP FOR DRAGONBLADE'S BLOG?

You'll get the latest news and information on exclusive giveaways, exclusive excerpts, coming releases, sales, free books, cover reveals and more.

Check out our complete list of authors, too!

No spam, no junk. That's a promise!

Sign Up Here

www.dragonbladepublishing.com

Dearest Reader;

Thank you for your support of a small press. At Dragonblade Publishing, we strive to bring you the highest quality Historical Romance from some of the best authors in the business. Without your support, there is no 'us', so we sincerely hope you adore these stories and find some new favorite authors along the way.

Happy Reading!

CEO, Dragonblade Publishing

Additional Dragonblade books by Author C.H. Admirand

The Duke's Guard Series
The Duke's Sword

The Lords of Vice Series
Mending the Duke's Pride
Avoiding the Earl's Lust
Tempering the Viscount's Envy
Redirecting the Baron's Greed

The Lyon's Den Connected World
Rescued by the Lyon

Dedication

For Tara Nina, author extraordinaire and my critique partner. Who else would call you before coffee to tell you she was awake at 3 am and had a thought about the plot in your current wip?

For Scott Moreland, my fabulous editor, who encouraged me to write this series about *The Duke's Guard*—men who were not titled, nor did they have the wealth that more often than not went along with a title. They are the men who stand in front of the Duke and Duchess of Wyndmere and their family, men who have vowed to protect them with their lives. The O'Malleys, Flahertys, and Garahans would die to keep that vow.

Author's Note

There are bits and pieces of my life in every book I write. Sometimes it's a story passed down a few generations, or something that happened to me. I usually don't mention it, but as I was writing the opening scene in Chapter Eighteen, I remembered sitting in my grandmother's rocking chair tracing the line of our infant daughter's brow, and then the other, watching her eyes slowly close. FYI, it didn't work on our sons. She has used this soothing motion on both of our grandsons. And though she might not admit it, to this day, if I quietly traced the arch of one of her eyebrows and then the other, she would close her eyes and drift off to sleep.

PROLOGUE

"Y E WANTED TO see me, Yer Grace?"

The Duke of Wyndmere stood in a small copse of evergreens near the perimeter of Wyndmere Hall. "Aye."

O'Malley ducked beneath the low-hanging branches, knocking freshly fallen snow down the collar of his greatcoat. Ignoring the icy chill, he met his employer's gaze, and his gut clenched. "Ye've received another threat."

The duke's eyes hardened to an icy blue. "Against the twins."

O'Malley fought to contain the surge of anger inside him. The duke depended on him to remain calm. "When?"

"Just now."

"Is the messenger still here?"

The duke nodded. "In the kitchen."

"I'd like to speak with him, if ye don't mind."

"Eamon was on hand when the man arrived. You were patrolling the perimeter. I've asked him to keep the man company."

"Me cousin will keep the man talkin' until I get there," O'Malley stated.

The duke glanced around him before adding, "There are a few leads, but nothing definitive."

The fact that they yet existed increased O'Malley's worry. The duke was a fair and generous man. He'd come into his title upon the death of his older brother—who was the anthesis of the current duke…a man who had enemies who sought revenge beyond the grave.

"Bleedin' bastards, every last one of them," O'Malley grumbled. "What kind of men would threaten the lives of yer babes?" Not waiting for the duke to respond, he added, "Defenseless infants only a few weeks old!"

He mulled over which of the duke's enemies would make such a threat. Was it from a source unknown to them? A glance at the duke had him setting those thoughts aside. The duke was obviously trying to calm down before he spoke to his wife. "Have ye sent word to Gavin King?"

"King sent the missive. Our friend on Bow Street assigned a group of runners to make discrete inquiries."

"Will he be notifyin' the rest of yer guard?"

"King has been in touch with Captain Coventry. By now the men stationed at my town house in London have been informed. Those in Sussex—at Lippincott Manor and Chattsworth Manor have also been made aware."

"What about Summerfield Chase in the Borderlands? Penwith Tower in Cornwall?"

"King's missive advised a messenger was dispatched to Cornwall."

O'Malley nodded. He would have sent out multiple messengers if he were King. "And the Borderlands?"

"King's messenger advised he'll be leaving within the hour to continue on to Summerfield Chase."

"Yer Grace," Patrick hesitated, unsure if he should speak up, but he and the duke had a rapport that extended beyond O'Malley's working situation. "Do ye need me to go to London to meet with Coventry and King?"

The duke declined. "Not at this time. I expect your men will have formulated plans to increase their protection."

"Aye, mayhap addin' to their number."

The duke frowned. "You know I depend heavily upon you, Patrick."

"Aye, Yer Grace. If ye change yer mind, I can leave as soon as I saddle me horse."

The Duke of Wyndmere's expression relaxed. "Between you and Captain Coventry, you've trained my personal guard to what it is today...the envy of my contemporaries. Bare knuckle champions, crack shots with a pistol or rifle—"

"Don't be forgettin' our skill with a blade."

The duke slowly smiled at the man dubbed *The Duke's Sword*. "One would think that every jackman of you grew up fighting."

O'Malley's silence had the duke shaking his head. "Forgive me. I did not mean to make light of the situation in Ireland, Patrick."

O'Malley let go of the breath he'd inhaled. "Of course, Yer Grace. Ye aren't like the others who believe we're a people who cannot be trusted to own or work our land without interference from the lords sent to oversee our lives."

"Indeed."

When he paused, O'Malley asked, "Is there anythin' else I need to be knowin'?"

His Grace sighed. "Coventry is sending another candidate for the position of nanny."

The head of his guard reminded him, "Ye know between the O'Malleys, the Garahans and Flahertys, we will protect yer little ones with our lives."

"It's the only reason I'm able to sleep at night—when Richard and Abigail aren't crying to be fed."

O'Malley knew without question the subject of hiring another nanny was foremost on his employer's mind. "Do ye want me to listen in on this meetin' like I did with the others?"

"Yes, though I know it doesn't fall under the list of duties we discussed when you agreed to take on the position as head of my guard."

"Ye know we will do whatever is required to see to it everyone in yer family, and extended family—at Wyndmere Hall and yer other estates, will be protected."

"Thank you."

Going over the latest rotation of the guard in his head, he asked, "When do ye expect her to arrive?"

"Mid-week."

"It'd be an honor to assist ye in this regard. I'll be lettin' the men know. We won't let ye down."

"You've had my back, and more than held up your end of our bargain. I'm the one who is honored to have you and your kin guarding my family."

Their gazes met and held. With a nod, O'Malley left to do the duke's bidding.

Watching him go, the duke paused to offer a brief prayer of thanks for the men in black who guarded his kith and kin—*Patrick O'Malley—The Duke's Sword...and The Duke's Guard.*

CHAPTER ONE

P ATRICK O'MALLEY, THE head of the Duke of Wyndmere's personal guard, stared at the earth-toned vision stepping down from the duke's carriage. The dimpled smile she bestowed on the footman assisting her from the carriage punched him in the gut.

She was breathtaking!

Eyes the color of the finest Irish whiskey widened. In their amber depths, he saw pain, sorrow, and anticipation. Drawn to the swirling emotions, he paused. The woman blinked, and only determination remained. A lock of peat-brown hair slipped from beneath the drab bonnet perched on her head and caught on her long, dark lashes. She swept it out of her eyes with her small, gloved hand.

O'Malley's gaze drifted from her entrancing eyes to the curve of her cheek and below to the no-nonsense, mud-brown traveling gown she wore. Nothing could conceal the lush curves God had bestowed upon this petite beauty. He froze, rooted to the ground like a veritable oak as images sliced through him.

Tangled sheets.

Flickering firelight.

Silky brown tresses spread across the white of his pillow.

Air snagged in his lungs, and his heart began to pound. Light-headed, he blinked and would have embarrassed himself if not for the vise-like grip his cousin had on his shoulder. The lightning-quick squeeze broke the spell the woman had woven around him from the moment he'd laid eyes on her.

"Welcome to Wyndmere Hall, Mrs. Alexander. O'Malley at yer service." With a nod to the man beside him, he added, "Me cousin, Garahan."

She inclined her head. "A pleasure to meet you Mr. O'Malley. Mr. Garahan."

His cousin groaned. "Just Garahan, if ye please." Before O'Malley could say the same, Garahan added, "The same goes for me cousin, O'Malley here…and the rest of the duke's guard."

Her eyes widened. "Of course. Mr.—er…is *Just* your given name? I have worked for a number of families with unusual names."

Garahan snorted to cover his laugh of disbelief. "Nay, 'tis Darby." With a glance at O'Malley he added, "He's Patrick."

O'Malley ignored his cousin's response to study Mrs. Alexander. Her husky voice added another layer of temptation to the beauty standing before him. She was a little bit of a thing—no taller than the middle of his chest and not a woman to be ignored. Her whiskey-colored eyes and dangerous curves had knocked the breath clean out of him. Praise God, his cousin had been there to bring him back down to Earth with a punishing grip on his shoulder. It had done the trick as his cousin had meant it to.

Grateful it hadn't been the duke joining him to greet the latest in a series of women hired and interviewed, O'Malley swept his hand toward Wyndmere Hall. There had already been two nannies that the babies didn't take to and several others interviewed. "This way if ye please. His Grace is waitin'."

"Thank you, Mr. O'Malley." Her obvious discomfort was a surprise as she quickly amended, "I do beg your pardon. Force of habit, you know," she explained. "I will make it a point to address you, and the rest of the duke's guard, by your last names as requested going forward."

He nodded and walked beside her toward the rear entrance.

Normally a man of action and not words, he struggled to keep the conversation going just to hear the sound of her voice. "How was yer trip?"

"The last leg of the journey was a bit longer than I'd anticipated."

Most women would have kept talking—well at least the women he'd been acquainted with. Was she too tired to speak? Mayhap she was not accustomed to speaking to the hired help...*she* would be the hired help if the duke and duchess engaged her services.

Bloody hell! Was he losing his mind? To keep his thoughts from circling back around to the tempting curves he'd best ignore, he blurted out, "Given the time of year and the weather, I'll not be doubtin' it. Merry will show ye to yer room so ye can settle in before I escort ye to meet with His Grace."

"Merry?"

"Aye, the housekeeper."

She stumbled and would have landed on her knees if not for O'Malley's quick reflexes. "Easy now," he soothed, slipping his arm around her waist. She stiffened, and he immediately shifted his arm to link with hers. Was it his touch that bothered her, or did she have an aversion to men?

Deciding to err on the side of caution, he apologized, "Beggin' yer pardon, Mrs. Alexander. I meant no offense, was only tryin' to steady ye. I did not want ye to fall and injure yerself."

"Er...thank you for your assistance, Mr. O'Malley. I must be more tired than I realized."

Her worry surprised him. Before he could comment or ask what she was concerned about, she rushed on to say, "I'm normally quite sure-footed and would not have you thinking otherwise. It is essential in caring for those precious little ones in my charge."

He inclined his head, waiting for her to finish. She released a breath she must have been holding, waiting for him to respond. "'Tis me duty and pleasure to help ye." He opened the door to the kitchen and explained, "'Tis the quickest way to enter the duke's home and lettin' Constance, the cook, and Merry, the housekeeper, know that ye'll be requirin' a bit of rest before ye meet with His Grace. The duke and duchess treat their staff like family. Most of the staff comes and goes through whichever route is the most expedient."

She bit her bottom lip, and his brain simply shut down as need clawed his gut, tearing at his control.

"There is no need to stand on ceremony with me, O'Malley. I don't want to keep the Duke of Wyndmere waiting."

O'Malley stared at her. Her amber eyes widened, and he had to lock down on the desire to yank her into his arms. The temptation to sip from her sumptuous, rose-tinted mouth battered the walls around his heart, threatening to weaken it after all these years. *Would she taste of sweet summer berries or tart cherries?*

Struggling not to give voice to his thoughts, he quickly regained his iron-clad control to advise, "His Grace is a fair man and would not want ye to be collapsin' in the middle of yer interview."

"He most certainly would not," an older woman proclaimed from where she stood by the cookstove.

"Constance," he said with a smile. "Mrs. Alexander has come to meet with His Grace about the twins. Constance is His Grace's cook."

"His Grace is a man to be respected, not feared," another woman remarked from where she stood at the entrance to the kitchen.

"Ah, and Merry is his housekeeper," O'Malley acknowledged with a nod. "Mrs. Alexander."

Merry smiled warmly. "We've been expecting you. His Grace will be most upset with us if we do not take good care of you. After all, you are going to be taking care of his precious babes."

Seeing that the housekeeper had a firm handle on the situation, he bowed to them. "I'll be lettin' His Grace know ye've arrived and will require a brief rest."

Chin high, eyes flashing, Mrs. Alexander disagreed. "I'll thank you not to put words in my mouth, Mr. O'Malley."

Used to being obeyed, his shock must have shown on his face—given the snort of muffled laughter coming from where Constance stood tending a pot on her stove. Inhaling slowly, he dug deep to keep from biting out the reflexive response. Doing so would only embarrass him when called to account for speaking sharply to the prospective nanny—*it didn't matter that he'd earned the moniker of The Duke's Sword...he would suffer the fires of hell before letting his pride get in the way of his job—protecting the duke, his family, and his staff.*

"I wouldn't dream of it, Mrs. Alexander."

She smoothed her skirts and inclined her head. "Then we understand one another."

Unable to keep from pricking her delightful temper, he remarked, "I cannot see that we do."

Her expression changed from irritation to surprise.

"Ye have yet to address me as me cousin advised—no 'Mister', just O'Malley."

Her eyes narrowed as she stared up at him. He could not help but wonder if it pained her neck to do so. She was such a tiny thing—in stature...not in form. God help him, her form had his hands itching to pull her against him and plunder her sweet mouth. *Time to move on, O'Malley.* "If ye'll excuse me, I'll leave ye in the excellent care of Merry and Constance."

Without waiting for a response, he spun on his heel and retraced his steps. Outside, he stood on the path where it branched off in three directions and whistled loudly.

An answering whistle had him striding forward on the path that led to the outbuildings. He caught up to his cousin, Eamon O'Malley, by the building they'd commandeered as their headquarters. "What have ye learned?"

His cousin frowned. "'Tisn't a rumor."

Patrick forced the lid shut on the emotions and temper

threatening to boil to the surface. *The duke was counting on him.* "'Tis what we feared. The nightmare doggin' his heels since His Grace accepted the title has resurfaced. With the help of King and Coventry, we'll get to the bottom of this latest threat."

His cousin agreed. "We've increased patrols, but this will be requiring more men."

"Aye. His Grace mentioned hirin' from the village."

Eamon's eyes widened. "Are ye sure that's wise? How do we know they'll be trustworthy? Won't it take time for Coventry or King to make the trip and meet with them?"

Patrick motioned for his cousin to walk with him. Side-by-side as they had been growing up, they took the path to the stables. "We don't have time to wait. The duke trusts his staff. We'll have to keep an eye on the new recruits."

"Humphries has been in his role as butler since His Grace's father held the title," his cousin remarked. "No doubt he knows everyone in the village."

Patrick agreed. "Although Stames, his valet, accompanied the duke from London, His Grace has trusted Stames to deliver urgent messages to both Coventry and King in the past."

"We'll add him to the list." Eamon stopped in the middle of the path.

Patrick scanned the area before asking, "Problem?"

His cousin took one last look around him and rolled his shoulders. "'Tis a feeling is all."

Patrick had come to count on his family's inherent intuition. All of the O'Malleys had it in some form or another. "Someone sneakin' up behind ye feelin'?"

"Aye."

"We'd best speak to the duke as soon as he returns from his daily perimeter walk."

"I don't think this can wait," Eamon warned.

"Let's divide and conquer then," Patrick suggested. "I'll start with Humphries and Stames while you speak with the steward and the stable master."

His cousin stared at the buildings that comprised the duke's stables. The two long buildings housed the stalls where the duke's stallion, carriage horses, and horses with various temperaments—to suit any number of visitors to Wyndmere Hall—both male and female, were cossetted. There was no other word for the way the stable master cared for his equine charges. Primped and treated like the royalty they were, given their bloodlines.

The largest of the buildings housed the duke's collection of conveyances. Two town coaches with the Wyndmere crest on the side, a phaeton, a curricle, two large wagons used to haul supplies for the household to and from the village, along with the spare parts necessary to keep those carriages in top working condition.

Eamon stared off in the distance again before stating, "'Tis a lot of ground to patrol, given the threat."

"We'd best get to it then."

The men parted. Eamon walked toward the main building, where the stable master would be at this hour of the morning. Patrick retraced his steps, taking the path back to the house.

He stamped the snow from his boots and entered the warmth of the cook's domain. Drawing in a deep breath, he smiled recognizing the scent. "Cream scones."

The duke's cook laughed. "And berry tarts."

Patrick grinned. "Would ye be savin' one for me then, Constance?"

The older woman beamed. "I have another tray in the oven. Seeing as you and your men seem to enjoy them."

"Thank ye. I need to have a word with Humphries and Stames. Has Mrs. Alexander recovered sufficiently to meet with His Grace?"

Constance nodded. "Though Merry had to practically sit on the woman to get her to rest briefly."

He snorted. "Stubborn woman, ye'd think she had the blood of me ancestors in her."

The cook slowly smiled. "Well now, it seems that she does.

11

Her maiden name is O'Toole."

He paused in the doorway leading to the other side of the house. "Is she related to the duke's London cook?"

Constance beamed. "Distantly. The connection is a few generations back."

"Well then, I'll have to amend me first impression of the woman now that I know she wasn't being difficult because she was exhausted...'tis her fine Irish roots." He grinned. "She's got more than a bit of grit to balance the feisty temperament that will see her through whatever fate tosses in her path."

He was chuckling to himself as he opened the door leading to the main part of the house. "Humphries!"

"What can I do for you, O'Malley?"

"A word in private, if ye will." Patrick counted on the fact the butler knew everything that occurred within the duke's household and would be ready to assist however he could.

Humphries ushered O'Malley into one of the smaller receiving rooms. "Is this about the kidnapping threat?"

"Aye. I've spoken with Eamon just now and will be speakin' to the others as soon as they return from their patrols."

"I shall do whatever you need, you have but to ask."

Relief eased one of the knots holding his gut hostage. "The duke has asked me to sit in on his meetin' with Mrs. Alexander. Afterward, we'll be meetin' with His Grace to suggest men to be added to our outdoor patrol of the grounds, the perimeter, and the road into the village."

"Has the duke hired men? I hadn't heard."

"Nay," Patrick advised. "We'd like ye to suggest a number of men from the village to add to our number."

Humphries nodded. "I'll have the names ready for your meeting with His Grace."

"Thank ye. Might ye be knowin' where Stames is?"

"In His Grace's chambers."

Patrick was halfway to the duke's chambers when he heard soft voices coming from the nursery. He recognized the duchess' voice and, after a moment, the husky tones of the other voice. *Daft woman was supposed to be resting!*

Time to find out what the woman was up to. She should not be bothering Her Grace when she was caring for the twins. He knocked on the open doorway, immediately relieved to see that the duchess was smiling as she held her son while quietly speaking to Mrs. Alexander who held her daughter.

"Have you come to meet our new nanny, Patrick?"

O'Malley wasn't surprised often, but her comment managed to do just that. "I hadn't realized His Grace met with you, Mrs. Alexander."

The woman never looked away from the bundle in her arms when she answered. "I haven't had the pleasure."

A niggling suspicion filled him as the duchess sidled closer to him and whispered, so as not to wake her son, "Jared doesn't know yet. I've just asked—no," she qualified, "begged Gwendolyn to stay and care for our darlings."

He held his tongue, wanting to remind the duchess what she no doubt already knew. His Grace did not want to hire another nanny who would only stay for a few days. The job was a difficult one given that there were two babes. The twins were very particular about who held them by screaming their little heads off sounding their displeasure to all and sundry within a mile of Wyndmere Hall.

"Welcome then, Mrs. Alexander."

She blinked before responding, "Thank you, O'Malley."

He nodded at her use of his last name. She had listened and remembered. "I'll let the duke know."

The duchess shook her head. "I've just sent word that his presence is needed at once."

The sound of heavy footfalls on the stairs had her biting back her laughter as the duke burst through the doorway. "What's wrong? Is it Richard or Abigail?"

"Er…neither."

He tilted his head back and closed his eyes.

The duchess leaned close to Mrs. Alexander to advise, "I'm afraid I've worried His Grace."

"It would seem so," the woman agreed.

When the duke's lips moved, but no sound emerged, the duchess added, "He picked up the annoying habit of counting when vexed with me from my mother."

Patrick snorted, then cleared his throat to apologize. "I beg yer pardon, Yer Graces."

The duke ignored him in favor of his wife. "Persephone, we have had this conversation many times."

"I know. But darling, it was imperative that you came at once."

He raked a hand through his hair. "To see that our daughter is awake, and our son is sleeping?"

Her delighted laughter filled the room with happiness, warming Patrick's heart.

She sighed before asking, "Are you going to be difficult about this?"

"I'm afraid I am, my dear. You promised not to raise the alarm unless it was of the utmost urgency."

Patrick watched the expression on the duchess' face change from delighted to disturbed. She lifted her chin, turned her back on the duke and walked to the other side of the room where she gently settled Richard in his cradle.

Without a word, Mrs. Alexander did the same, gently placing the now-sleeping Abigail in hers.

"Persephone."

Patrick noted her name sounded like a warning. The look on the duke's face brooked no argument as he motioned for his wife to follow him. He wasn't surprised when she declined with a subtle shake of her head.

It took all of O'Malley's control not to burst out laughing at the agitated looks exchanged between the duke and duchess. There were bound to be fireworks at any moment. He knew without question that neither of them would want that to happen in front of Mrs. Alexander. It wouldn't if either had been thinking clearly. 'Twas up to him to intervene.

"Her Grace has something of import to discuss with ye."

The duke's head turned toward O'Malley. "I am well aware that it is something she feels is of importance. However, I highly doubt I share the same opinion."

A glance at the duchess revealed she was ready to ring a peal over the duke's head. If he'd been home in Cork, and it would have been his ma doing the speaking, his da—God rest his soul, would have listened. He smiled remembering the time or two his father hadn't and ended up with a lump on the back of his head. His mother had two favorite kitchen items she wielded with excellent aim. Her rolling pin and favorite cast iron frying pan.

Willing to step into the fray and take a direct hit from the duke or his duchess, Patrick asked, "Have ye spoken with Her Grace about the messenger?"

The silence was deafening. The duke cleared his throat before responding. "I have one more detail to see to before speaking with her."

"*She* happens to be standing between two men who promised not to keep anything of import from her."

When the duke glowered at his wife, Patrick decided he would have to take another risk that may not bode well for the future of his family's continued employment with the duke. "The messenger has only just arrived," he answered, stretching the truth to suit the situation and volatile tension in the room.

The duke cleared his throat. "You must pardon the confusing conversation, Mrs. Alexander. Our home is not always in such a state of upheaval."

The duchess' delighted laughter bounced off the walls, banishing the doom and gloom from a few moments before. "If Mrs. Alexander is to accept my offer of employment—which is what I felt was of sufficient urgency to have you summoned, then she will have to become used to our volatile discussions."

O'Malley was accustomed to the fact that Their Graces were

ofttimes at cross purposes trying to reach the same goals, but Mrs. Alexander was not.

The duke's manner changed abruptly. "I have not had the opportunity to speak with Mrs. Alexander, as I was informed that she needed to rest after her journey."

Stepping into the fray, Mrs. Alexander spoke up. "It was gracious of you to allow me the time to collect myself, Your Grace. It was a rather arduous journey, given the condition of the roads and the cold temperatures."

The duke inclined his head, accepting her explanation. Before he could speak, she continued, "I heard one of your babes crying and that was all it took to restore my energy." With a smile for the duchess, she added, "One should never let an infant cry for too long. Upsets their digestion, you know."

Patrick did not expect what happened next, though he had seen the many moods of the duchess while she was carrying. Her eyes welled with tears and, in a heartbeat, Mrs. Alexander enveloped the duchess in her arms and was comforting her before the duke crossed the room to do so.

Trained to observe, he noted the duke's unease. Having watched his mother's moods swing drastically after the birth of his younger siblings, he sought to redirect the direction of the duke's thoughts. "Do ye need me to speak with the messenger, or shall I wait for ye in yer study?"

The petite woman's gaze met his and there was no mistaking the compassion the woman felt for the duchess. His aunt had always managed to soothe his mother whenever she came to visit. The two often spent time in one another's homes after another of their babes were born. He and his brothers—as well as his O'Malley cousins, were like stairsteps in age—there was a bit of a gap before his sisters were born.

Satisfied the duchess was in good hands, he waited for the duke's reply.

It wasn't long in coming. "Persephone, would you care to rest while Patrick and I meet with Mrs. Alexander over tea?"

The duchess straightened to her full height and linked her arm through Mrs. Alexander's. "Our babes are sleeping peacefully—thanks to our *new* nanny. I would dearly love to rest my eyes for a bit, but do not wish for you to batter Gwendolyn with unnecessary and incessant questions."

"Unnecessary?" the duke grumbled.

"Incessant?" Mrs. Alexander inquired.

"Therefore, I will allow you to meet with her on the condition that the meeting go no longer than a quarter of an hour."

"How the devil am I supposed to ascertain whether or not her qualifications and personality will be what we require in the care of our most precious possessions?"

Patrick watched as the duchess slipped her arm free and glided across the room to stand before her husband. "They are most precious, my darling," she agreed. "Aren't they?"

The duke traced the tip of his finger along the curve of his wife's cheek before responding. "Without question." He lifted her hand to his lips, placing a brief kiss to the back of it. "If you would ring for Merry, she can sit with Richard and Abigail while we have our very brief meeting with Mrs. Alexander."

"Of course, Jared."

He bowed to the duchess and turned to Mrs. Alexander. "If you would accompany my wife, O'Malley and I will await you in my upstairs study."

"Yes, of course, Your Grace."

The first to leave the room, Patrick was waiting for the duke in the doorway to his study at the end of the hallway. "Do ye plan to ask the same questions as the others ye've interviewed?"

The duke snorted. "Why bother? My darling duchess seems to have her heart set on Mrs. Alexander."

"Do ye still need me to stay then, or shall I return to me post atop the roof?"

"I value your opinion in all things, Patrick, and would like you to stay."

"Of course, Yer Grace."

The women joined them a few moments later. The duke settled his wife in a chair by the fireplace where the heat would hopefully soothe the bit of exhaustion she tried to hide from him. He smiled, imagining her drifting to sleep during the brief meeting, precipitating the need to carry her to their bedchamber where he would—

"Jared, do stop woolgathering," the duchess urged. "Else you'll waste your precious quarter of an hour."

He opened his mouth to speak, then must have thought better of it. A glance was all Patrick needed to note the delighted expression on the duchess' face. The two were matched well and deeply in love. He briefly wondered what that would feel like. He thought he'd taken the fall before, but obviously the bewitching *Saoirse* had other ideas. True to her name, she'd needed her freedom. He had no choice but to give it to her.

His job as head of the Duke of Wyndmere's personal guard took all of his time and attention. The duke's life and that of his family, and extended family, were in his hands—and that of his brothers and cousins. There was no time to court a woman, let alone indulge in a brief dalliance with one of the willing widows from the village. He dismissed those thoughts to concentrate on the answers he knew the duke expected to hear. If he didn't, it would be up to O'Malley to ask.

With the duchess settled, he turned his attention to the duke and Mrs. Alexander. He noted a flash of pain, so sharp and so deep, it changed the hue of her eyes from warmed Irish whiskey to a dull brown. She blinked and the emotion was gone.

The duke cleared his throat—his signal that Patrick was to speak.

Alert, he mentally went over the last question the duke asked her. *Was there anything preventing her from staying on longer than the twins' fourth month?* Was that at the root of the pain he'd witnessed?

The duchess and the duke would need to know if there was anything that would prevent the woman from carrying out her duties. At the duke's nod, Patrick asked, "Have ye accepted another position that would prevent ye from stayin' on past the twins' fourth month? That only allows ye three months to care for them as they were four weeks old yesterday."

The woman's pain was tangible. Tears welled in her still-dull eyes, but she blinked them away. "I have not, as yet, but expect to. I was quite clear in my letter to His Grace." She turned to face the duke. "I only accept positions caring for infants from birth to four months old."

The duke inclined his head agreeing. "It was the only reason you were not our first choice of the candidates, Mrs. Alexander. We are hoping to hire a nanny who would stay with us for at least a year."

Patrick watched the woman's eyes clear. She must have waged an inner war with her emotions to do so. She rose gracefully. "Although I would enjoy working with Your Graces, and your darling little ones, I cannot accept a position that goes beyond the babes' fourth month."

"Do ye mind me asking why not?" O'Malley watched a hint of fear flicker in the depths of her eyes.

"I am afraid I do mind." She curtseyed to the duke and duchess. "Thank you for your time and for conveying me from London. If it wouldn't be too much trouble, would someone be able to drive me to the village, I'd like to secure a seat on the Mail Coach."

The duchess shot to her feet and reached for the woman's hand. "Please stay, Gwendolyn. I'd be grateful for the next three months if that's all you can spare us. Once my husband sees how utterly at ease Richard and Abigail are with you, he will understand why I simply cannot let you leave."

The other woman blinked, and a look of pure pleasure added the warmth back to her eyes, changing their hue to a warmed glass of the Irish. O'Malley found himself looking forward to a sip or two before heading back out into the cold.

The duke rose to his feet to stand beside his wife. "I have no doubt that you are correct, my darling. No need for me to observe her actions further before adding my plea to Mrs. Alexander to please stay."

Separately, the duke and duchess were forces to be reckoned with. Together, they were unstoppable. Pride filled him. He would alert the men to the fact that Mrs. Alexander...the fair Gwendolyn, would be caring for the twins for the next three months.

The duke turned to him, and the unasked question was there as Patrick expected it to be. He nodded, indicating he would send messages to Coventry and King immediately about Mrs. Alexander's odd insistence she only stay four months with each family. Though he knew for a fact that she had been vetted as had every other candidate. This time, they would dig deeper, given the discrepancies they'd discovered only after the first three candidates were engaged.

He would have to ask the duke if he intended to continue his search for a nanny immediately or wait another few weeks. For now, the twins would be in the woman's tender care. The vision of her cradling Abigail, soothing her with quiet words and feather-soft touches to the babe's brow and cheek returned. He agreed with the duchess, she was the right choice.

"If ye have no further need of me, Yer Graces, I'll be goin' back to me post atop the roof."

Mrs. Alexander's eyes widened. "Whyever would you need to go on the roof in this frightfully cold weather?"

He could not help but feel the hint of worry couched in her tone. "Ye'll soon discover workin' here that me men and I change shifts and positions around the duke's home, the perimeter, and the land surrounding it every four hours."

"But the rooftop?"

"Aye." With a glance at the duke, he added, "If ye wish to know anythin' further about me duties—or that of me men, ye'll have to ask His Grace."

She drew in a breath and shook her head. "I am quite certain that will not be necessary, but thank you for advising me."

"Me pleasure." He bowed to the duke and duchess, then Mrs. Alexander before taking his leave.

Using the servants' staircase, he rushed down the stairs and into the kitchen, relieved to find the messenger just finishing the meal Constance had prepared for him.

"His Grace needs to add to the messages he's already sendin' to Captain Coventry and Gavin King of the Bow Street Runners."

The messenger used his sleeve instead of the napkin Constance provided to wipe his mouth. "Thank you for the food. It filled the hole in my belly."

Constance beamed as she removed the empty dishes.

O'Malley waited for the man to rise. They walked outside to the stables together. "Here's what His Grace would like ye to add."

A short while later, satisfied that the messages would be delivered, and none of the staff had overheard the duke's additional request, O'Malley followed the path leading around the side of the house to the door that led to the roof.

The air was crisp, clear, and cold, but he didn't mind. He preferred it to being cooped up inside all day. Drawing in a deep breath, he let it clear his muddled thoughts and the mystery packed into a gown the color of fresh-turned earth.

When he realized where his thoughts were straying, he admonished himself, "She's not for ye lad, nor to be trusted until ye've heard from Coventry or King."

With the proper changes of his horse, and if the weather held, the messenger would be arriving in London and return with news in the next few days. *Lord willing.*

Patrick had the feeling he would be hard-pressed to keep his distance from the entrancing Gwendolyn.

CHAPTER TWO

G WENDOLYN HELD HER breath and then slowly released it. Five minutes after the irritating man left the room, O'Malley's presence remained. Tall, broad-chested, and with shoulders that were meant to be leaned upon, Patrick O'Malley had captured her attention the moment she'd descended from the duke's carriage, stumbled, and fallen into his arms. Even an hour after their meeting had ended, the man was still at the center of her thoughts, clinging to them like a burr stuck to a horse's hide.

She had anticipated her reputation preceding her when she arrived from London, but this was the first time any of her employers had sent a private carriage to collect her. Unused to such luxury, she had nearly insisted she find her own way to Wyndmere Hall in the Lake District. Common sense returned and she admitted, if only to herself, that it would be counterproductive. Therefore, she accepted the duke's generous offer of transportation, though rumors, and ridiculous reasons as to why the first few nannies engaged were let go after only a few days' time, circulated like mad through the *ton*.

She had no intention of leaving until her self-allotted time had ended. She never accepted a new post without insisting she would be leaving when the babe reached four months of age. Her heart stuttered in her breast remembering why, though she would never explain the tragic reason.

Woolgathering, she brought out the earth-shattering memory when she stepped down from the carriage, intending to thank the footman for his assistance. The bold green eyes of an impossibly handsome, broad-shouldered man, garbed in black from head to toe had nearly been her undoing. It was a startling contrast against his fair hair. The desire flickering in his eyes caught her full attention. They were the color of polished emeralds, reminding her of Beltane fires burning on the hilltops surrounding her home. The raw power of the man drew her inexplicably toward him—dear Lord, she craved the burn.

The heat of his body enveloped her, searing her to the bone. His lips captured hers—and she jolted. Immediately, she shoved those dangerously distracting thoughts aside. Gazing down at her tiny charges, she felt the subtle shift in the walls around her heart. *So perfectly formed, just like her son had been.* Angelic faces resting against tiny little hands while they slept. When she lowered her lashes, she could all but see their transparent wings fluttering as they breathed in and out.

Placing the tip of her finger near Abigail's open mouth, she felt the tiny puff of air against it. Relief speared through her as she turned to step over to Richard's cradle. Once again, she felt the tiny puff of air, immediately relaxing. Her charges were breathing easily and sleeping peacefully. Time to push the unreasonable worry aside.

Three positions ago, she'd been in Baron Wellsley's home long enough to place her carpet bag in her room, when a bone-chilling cry rent the air. She'd dashed toward the nursery, and burst into the room to find him cradling his newborn son to his chest. By the time she'd calmed him enough to take the baby from him, she realized what had happened. The baby had stopped breathing. She'd heard of such a thing, but this was the first time she'd experienced it. She stayed long enough to send word to her employer's sister, who came at once. Between the two of them, they made the arrangements for the interment of the painfully tiny coffin in the crypt next to his mother.

Had the babe's mother been inconsolable in Heaven?

Had the Lord needed another perfect little angel?

The memory was far too close to the one she dreamed of nightly. Gwendolyn tucked it away, burying it deep inside of her. Time to stop blaming the Lord for taking her husband and their premature son. Forgiving Him was another matter entirely. In the depths of her battered heart, she knew she would have to in order to move forward in her life. She was tired. She wanted a family of her own but was not sure she was brave enough to open her heart to the promise of love again.

There had never been any man but Jonathan. How could she even think to replace her husband or their son?

Her heart clenched as the memory tried to resurface. She tamped it down. The past is gone and could never be resurrected. That was why she chose to stay such a short time with each of her charges. To stay longer would run the risk of forming an attachment she could not risk when she knew ahead of time that she could not stay.

Her heart could not take it.

"There you are, Gwendolyn." The Duchess of Wyndmere swept into the room, all smiles. The energy emanating from the woman helped her to focus her attention on what mattered— taking care of the two beautiful babes entrusted into her care.

"Richard and Abigail are still asleep." She felt the smile move through her, lifting a tiny part of the heavy load of her past until she was once more able to handle the weight. "You and His Grace have been blessed."

The duchess agreed. "There are moments when one or both of us are not quite sure of the extent of that blessing."

Gwendolyn covered her mouth to keep from snorting out a laugh. She cleared her throat and softly replied, "Mayhap the two o'clock in the morning feedings interspersed with random unhappy tears of frustration?"

The duchess turned to stare at her. "How odd that you would put it that way. Do you think our darlings feel frustration as we do?"

Gwendolyn nodded. "Though they have not yet learned to communicate as effectively as they will when they are a bit older, I have it on good authority, and personal experience, that little ones do indeed feel frustration. Why else would they be crying when they are dry, fed, and tucked into a cozy blanket?"

Her Grace seemed to be mulling over Gwendolyn's words. She could all but see the duchess picking apart the words and fitting them into a pattern that would make sense to her. "I do believe you are right!"

Without warning, she was swept into the other woman's arms and hugged tightly. The tiny sigh of relief escaped before Gwendolyn could hold it back. It had been so very long since anyone had hugged her. The need to weep was nearly uncontrollable, but she dug deep not to do so, especially on her very first day caring for the Duke and Duchess of Wyndmere's babes. Knowing she would be able to hold it in until she was alone—as she had done all those years ago, helped her regain her equilibrium.

There was a soft knock on the partially closed door to the nursery before it opened slowly. Merry bore a tray containing an ornate silver tea service, while one of the footmen carried a large tray filled with scones, an assortment of tarts, and tiny sandwiches.

"What a lovely surprise!" she exclaimed. "Is there anything I can do to help?"

Merry waved her away while the duchess motioned for her to be seated. "You must keep your strength up," Persephone stated. "Neither Jared nor I would have you become overworked or overtired."

"I assure you, Your Grace—"

"Persephone," the duchess corrected.

"Er…yes, Persephone, as I was saying. I normally have a strong constitution. Today was an aberration. I would never do anything that would put your darling babes at risk."

"In light of the frightening missive that was delivered shortly before you arrived...that my husband has finally shared with me, there is more risk than you may have bargained for."

While the duchess poured, Merry filled exquisite bone china plates rimmed with tiny pale pink flowers with green leaves. Gwendolyn's eyes widened at the selection while Persephone laughed softly. "If you do not eat every crumb on your plate, I shall have no choice but to summon Patrick to remind you why it is imperative that you eat to keep up your strength."

Gwendolyn placed her teacup on its saucer. "The head of His Grace's guard?"

Persephone's eyes met hers over the rim of her cup. "As my darling duke is wont to say, indeed!"

"Is it part of his position here to hand out advice on the topic of how to take care of oneself while taking care of infants?"

Persephone set her cup down and nodded. "Yes, actually, ever since the man confided that he'd helped take care of his mother after the birth of each of his younger siblings—three brothers and three sisters!"

"I suppose that is not so out of the ordinary when one comes from a family of more modest means."

Persephone smiled knowingly. "By the by, he really hates to be called *Mr. O'Malley*. When he asks that you call him by his given name, please be sure to do so. It means that he's come to trust you...which is no small feat for the staunch head of my husband's guard."

Gwendolyn took the duchess' words to heart. "When and if the time comes, I shall not hesitate to do so."

"I must say that I admire your self-control," Persephone murmured.

Surprised by the duchess' interest and admiration, Gwendolyn asked, "You do?"

The duchess nodded. "I myself would have asked about the missive immediately." Waiting another moment, she seemed to be choosing her words carefully. "Aren't you the least bit curious?"

Gwendolyn paused before responding, "I did not think it was my place to request an explanation."

Persephone rolled her eyes. "There are times when I have found it best to cut through the jumbled morass surrounding a situation and get right to the heart of the matter."

"Ye have the knack for it, Yer Grace," a deep rumbling voice replied.

Persephone acknowledged the comment—and the man standing in the doorway, before asking, "Is something wrong, Patrick?"

He immediately replied, "Not a thing, Yer Grace. 'Tis another matter entirely. If I may have a word with ye."

"Of course."

The intensity and intimacy of the look O'Malley sent her way called to her on an elemental level she had not felt in years. Need swept up from her toes, driving the breath from her lungs. Deep green, the color of the forest at dusk, swirled with a potent mix of attraction and irritation in the depths of his eyes. Was he attracted to her, or was he irritated that he was attracted to her? She was not going to ask, nor did she intend to find out what the man was thinking.

"If ye'll excuse us, Mrs. Alexander."

The man's voice did not hint at what she'd seen in his gaze.

"Of course, Your Grace." She turned to Persephone and inquired, "Would you rather I leave, or stay here with the little ones?"

"Please stay and finish your tea. I shall return in a moment."

The duchess rose with a grace and poise Gwendolyn admired. She had been known to be a bit on the clumsy side for the first decade of her life and only managed to gain a modicum of control over her wayward limbs right around the time she'd met and fallen in love with Jonathan.

Attuned to O'Malley as she had not been to another since she'd lost her husband, Gwendolyn kept an ear out, not overly surprised to hear the depth of O'Malley's voice take on a hard edge. Was he upset with Her Grace? Was it something more?

What in the world could be so frightening that the duke and duchess thought she would resign her post after just accepting it? "I'll just have to demand that I be informed," she mumbled aloud.

"Will ye now?" O'Malley rumbled from where he stood in the doorway to the nursery once more.

The duchess slipped past him into the room, regaining her seat. "Patrick, please do not antagonize our nanny. The children and I are quite taken with her."

The man gave her one more frown before turning to reply. "As ye wish, Yer Grace."

A deep rumbling chuckle sounded behind the man. "Indeed."

Persephone was rising to her feet when her husband entered the room, motioning for her to remain seated as he strode to her side and gently lifted her hand to his lips. "I have the answers I required to a situation I never thought to face."

Gwendolyn watched as the duchess' eyes filled with tears, then blinked them away. "I've never encountered a situation such as this," the duchess began, "and confess I'm not certain my innate need to strike whoever would do such a thing is the right reaction."

O'Malley's smile spoke volumes. He apparently thought the duchess' reaction to be fitting.

The duke sighed. "I'm afraid that would not be wise, given the circumstances, my love." He turned his attention to Gwendolyn. "Mrs. Alexander, I have received news of a credible threat against my wife, our children, and me."

Horror was quickly squelched as an odd feeling of protectiveness swept up from Gwendolyn's toes. "I shall do whatever I can to protect the lives of both of you and your children, Your Graces." The vow came from her heart, and she knew without question she would follow it through to her dying breath.

"Ye'll have to get in line behind me and me cousins, Mrs. Alexander," O'Malley ordered. "'Tis our job to protect the lives of those we serve...not yers."

Gwendolyn recognized the signs of her temper kicking into high gear and fought the need to fire back at him. Her job depended on her ability to remain calm in all types of situations. "I trust how I handle my responsibilities in the nursery will be of no concern to you, *Mister* O'Malley."

A thrill of justified pleasure streaked through her as his jaw clenched and his eyes blazed with emerald fire. Lord help her, she wanted to fan those flames.

"I may not have the opportunity to *advise* when yer responsibilities collide with me own, Mrs. Alexander."

Before she could think of a comeback, the duke bowed over his wife's hand and inclined his head in Gwendolyn's direction. "O'Malley, a word." The two men strode from the room, leaving her to wonder if the duke would give the Irishman the setting down she felt he deserved...or if the duke would return to deliver hers.

She would have to keep her distance from the arrogant Irishman. He was a temptation she dare not indulge in while employed by the duke and duchess. Mayhap after she'd completed her assignment...good Lord! What was the matter with her? She hadn't had these thoughts—or urges, in the past decade!

O'Malley was the matter with her!

CHAPTER THREE

NEITHER THE DUKE nor O'Malley returned, leaving Gwendolyn to guess at what might have occurred and what the exact nature of the *credible threat* to the twins involved. The duchess seemed to be moving slower with each passing moment. She didn't feel right asking her now. Mayhap she would later after the poor woman had a chance to rest.

Gwendolyn tucked the twins in and shooed the duchess off to her room for what she decreed was a much-needed rest half an hour ago. The tired woman did not protest as Gwendolyn had feared. She was feeling a bit smug at having arranged things as they should be when her charges—infant and adult were resting. All was quiet as expected when she was in charge in the nursery.

Opening her journal and using the pencil she always carried with her, she jotted down pertinent information that would help her discern the twins' schedule. She planned to sit with Persephone and create one that would be amenable to all concerned. A routine was often the best way to approach the care and comfort of her tiny charges and had worked beautifully over the last few years.

Her information at the moment involved how often she'd changed them, and the duchess fed them. She noted the way they scooted around in their cradles until they were comfortable before falling asleep. Another notation was made pertaining to the positions they favored while sleeping—their angelic faces, with the sweetest smiles, turned to the side resting on their hands.

It was at moments such as these that she wished she had more of a talent with a paintbrush and watercolors. She could capture the moment of innocence and bliss. Tears came unbidden as she was thrust back in time remembering the still form of her son just moments after he'd been born—too early. Though she'd felt him tossing and turning before she'd gone into labor, his eyes never opened, nor his lungs filled with life-giving air.

The loud chirp of a bird just outside the window brought her back to the present. She reached into the pocket of the apron she'd designed for herself years ago and pulled out her handkerchief. Dabbing her eyes, resolving not to let her thoughts carry her away again, she rose from the rocking chair where she'd been sitting. Placing a hand to the glass, the bone-deep chill arrowed through her palm. She shivered. Was O'Malley still on the roof, or had he been assigned another spot?

She vaguely remembered O'Malley mentioning assigned posts. Though she could not recall the location of their positions, she knew they changed every four hours. A sense of dread filled her. Did she need to know where the guards' posts were? What of the number of men? Were the four men in the duke's guard sufficient enough...*proficient enough* to protect the babes from whatever the threat was? "So many questions for the duchess," she mused aloud. It would not do to ask the man in question, else he'd think she was plotting along with whomever had leveled that horrible threat.

"Mayhap I should ask Her Grace what the threat entailed."

"It would be best to leave the matter alone," a soft voice advised from behind her. She whirled around, hand to her breast.

"I'm sorry to have startled you, Mrs. Alexander." One of the maids approached quickly, quietly. "My name is Mollie. Francis and I are the upstairs maids. We take turns seeing to Her Grace's needs as well as the twins."

Gwendolyn swallowed the ball of fear lodged in her throat. "It's a pleasure to meet you, Mollie. Is there anything I can do for you?"

The young woman smiled. "That is the question I was about to put to you."

Gwendolyn echoed the younger woman's smile with one of her own. "I've urged Her Grace to have a lie down while I jotted some notations about her babes."

"Notations?" Mollie's look of confusion was one she'd experienced many times over the years once she'd started documenting the habits, likes, and dislikes of the infants entrusted into her care—and that of their parents.

"Aye," Gwendolyn acknowledged. "It's important to ascertain their habits as quickly as possible."

"I see," Mollie sounded a bit skeptical. "My mother just seemed to know instinctively what my younger brothers and sisters needed and when."

Gwendolyn nodded. "It seems to be inherent in most mothers that I've worked for, though some are not as interested in taking on the care of their babes as others. It is a bit more challenging when the babe is not your own."

If Mollie noted the change in the tone of Gwendolyn's voice, or her manner, she did not comment on it. For which, she was most appreciative. It was hard enough to have the constant reminders that she never had the opportunity to shower love on her son.

"Mrs. Alexander?"

They had never discovered who had taken Jonathan's life…

"Mrs. Alexander?" Mollie's voice increased in volume as she rushed over to tug on the bell pull.

Nor why they left his body in the alley with the refuse…

"Here now, Mollie," Flaherty rushed into the nursery. "You're making enough noise to wake the babes!"

"It's Mrs. Alexander, Rory. She started talking about notations for the little ones and her voice trailed off…"

As Mollie had hoped, O'Malley's cousin took matters in hand, as well as the new nanny. The auburn-haired giant scooped her into his arms and started to carry her out of the room.

Gwendolyn jolted. "What in the world? Put me down!" she demanded.

Flaherty smiled. "There now, Mollie," he proclaimed as he set Gwendolyn on her feet. "Ye see how it's done?"

The maid smiled up at the duke's guard, shaking her head. "I do, but the problem is I'd never be able to sweep anyone off their feet like you just did."

He inclined his head, spun on his heel, and left as silently as he'd appeared.

"Who was that man dressed in black?"

"Rory Flaherty, one of His Grace's guard here at Wyndmere Hall."

Hand to her throat, Gwendolyn willed herself to stop shaking. "Why in the world did he pick me up?"

Mollie's expression seemed pained as if she were about to confess something troubling. "You stopped speaking in the middle of a sentence and stared off into space." She wrung her hands together, adding, "You did not answer me when I called your name."

It happened again. Gwendolyn had no idea how to stop the episodes from occurring—other than ensuring she rested after arriving at her new posts. If she mentioned it to her new employers, would they sack her on the spot? What of dear little Richard and Abigail? They already had a special place in her heart.

"I do apologize. I fear I am more tired than I realized. My mind wanders when that happens. I am sorry for startling you, Mollie."

The maid seemed to accept her explanation, but Gwendolyn had a feeling she would be sharing what happened with the duchess as soon as she left the room. To ensure she would not be on her way back to London on the next mail coach, Gwendolyn added, "The journey up from London was more arduous than I'd imagined. So cold, and the roads were filled with obstructions due to the recent storm. I found myself quite out-of-sorts when I arrived."

"You could have rested longer. Their Graces would not have minded."

"I'll admit to wanting to jump right in, especially after hearing the littles ones crying a few hours ago."

"It is past time for your midday meal, Mrs. Alexander. Normally, Francis and I share duties watching over the children while whoever is attending the children eats. Allow me to bring something up to you. Forgive me for not paying attention to the time, what with the uproar downstairs—"

"Uproar?" Gwendolyn's heart started beating faster. "Concerning the children?"

Mollie nodded as she moved to the doorway to watch for one of the footmen to arrive in response to their summons. "His Grace is speaking to the new recruits from the village."

"Recruits?"

"His Grace is adding to the number of his personal guard outside the estate. We were surely blessed the day he hired on Patrick's kin."

How many did the duke require to handle the credible threat? "How many of O'Malley's kin did the duke hire?"

"Sixteen all together," Mollie answered. "Spread out between his four estates and two others belonging to his distant cousins, one of whom is married to the duke's sister."

"I see." There must have been some truth to the rumors of attacks upon the duke's person circulating around the *ton*.

"Is everything all right, Mollie? Mrs. Alexander?" Merry rushed into the nursery. "I just met Rory on the servants' staircase."

Gwendolyn sighed. "I should have followed the duke's and duchess' advice and rested longer but was so excited to begin caring for their precious babes, I ignored the signs that I was tired in the extreme."

"Such as?" Merry inquired.

"When travel catches up with me between assignments, I will stop speaking and stare off into space, while my body tries to get my attention."

Merry's eyes widened. "And how long does this condition last?"

"Not long," Gwendolyn assured her. "I should have mentioned it to Their Graces, but I thought it would not happen again this time."

"Does it happen whenever you travel?" Mollie wanted to know.

Gwendolyn's sigh was audible. "I am accustomed to the condition and the humors of my person that I have accepted it and learned to rest upon arrival."

Mollie glanced at the housekeeper and nodded. "I see."

"It won't happen again until I journey to my next position."

"I believe you should discuss it with His Grace as the duchess is still asleep," Merry admonished.

The tone of the older woman's voice put a hitch in the middle of Gwendolyn's chest. Would the duke send her packing as soon as she explained what happened? Dear Lord, she hoped not.

Merry had Mollie stay with the babes and accompanied Gwendolyn to the duke's study. A familiar dark-haired, mountain of a man clothed in black stood outside the closed door. The Duke's Guard must dress in black as she noted the footmen wearing a uniform of deep blue.

"Darby Garahan, may I introduce Mrs. Alexander, the new nanny."

He inclined his head. "We've met."

Before Gwendolyn could respond, Merry asked, "Can His Grace be interrupted? We have something of import to discuss with him."

Garahan's glance slid over the two women standing before him before answering. "Aye. Wait here."

Three sharp raps of his knuckles and the door was flung open to reveal O'Malley and the duke inside. O'Malley stared at Gwendolyn for long moments before his eyes narrowed and his gaze dipped to her mouth. Heat speared through her as his brilliant green eyes lifted, holding her captive. She'd overheard the name he'd earned as head of the duke's guard—*The Duke's Sword.* From the intensity she'd noted, she would do well to be wary of the man. He did not speak, though he stepped back to admit the two women.

The duke stopped pacing and glanced at his housekeeper. A silent exchange seemed to be happening, leaving Gwendolyn to wonder if something along these lines had been expected or had happened before. Was there more to the rumors that the previous nannies had been asked to leave for a far different reason than the babes did not care for them? *Why the subterfuge?* Was it the duke and duchess, or their staff, that did not get on with the nannies?

"How can I be of service, ladies?"

Merry quickly explained the situation she'd been summoned to, while Gwendolyn felt the heat of O'Malley's stare between her shoulder blades.

The duke's frown left nothing to the imagination. *He was incensed.* Truth be told, she would be too if their positions were reversed. "I cannot understand why you did not confide the extent of your exhaustion—or unusual condition, before my wife hired you."

Gwendolyn did not answer quickly enough to suit the duke. "I'm afraid that I have no choice but to let you—"

"Retire to your room for the rest of the day," Persephone announced, glaring at her husband. "My husband would wish you to have rested fully from your journey."

The duke's face flushed a deep red as he met his wife's glare with one of his own. "I believe we already asked that she do so. Apparently, she did not heed our advice, and took it upon herself to begin taking care of our twins before given leave to do so."

"I would have done the same," the duchess insisted. "Babes

crying can mean any number of things have occurred. Would you have had them screaming in hunger, or wet, uncomfortable, and cold?"

The duke scrubbed a hand over his face before raking it through his hair. "Bloody hell, Persephone!"

Gwendolyn watched in awe as the duchess marched right up to her husband and poked him in the chest. "You'll not use such language in front of Mrs. Alexander."

He grabbed hold of her finger, wrapped his other arm around her, and pulled her against his side. "I suppose I shall have to leave the common language to you, my darling."

Before the duchess could respond, the duke waved his hand at his housekeeper and Gwendolyn. "Merry, please see to it that Mrs. Alexander retires to her room, rests and recuperates. I understand Constance has prepared a delicious meal that will be served to our nanny in her room."

"Of course, Your Grace. At once."

Without another word, Gwendolyn was whisked from her employers' presence and back to the confines of her bedchamber. Relief speared through her as she was cossetted by Francis, who arrived to help her change into her nightrail and dressing gown. Merry arrived a few moments later with a tray and the luncheon Mollie had promised her earlier.

When assured she had everything she needed, Gwendolyn leaned back against the pile of pillows and closed her eyes. She had managed to avoid being sent back to London and the small, lifeless room she let in between positions. Coming to a decision, she opened her eyes and lifted the fork off the tray in her lap to eat. "Time to begin as you intend to go on—don't look back. Richard, Abigail, and the duchess need you."

Savoring the delicious and filling meat pie, Gwendolyn ate every bite before sipping from her cup of tea. The brew was strong, just the way she liked it. She felt her constitution level out and sighed. Adding an extra dollop of clotted cream and delectable berry preserves to her scones, she polished them off and drained the teapot.

"I shall have to thank the duke and duchess for not sending me home." She frowned, amending that last statement. "Mayhap I shall have to thank *the duchess* for not sending me home."

Content with her situation, now that things had been smoothed over, Gwendolyn leaned back against her pillow and closed her eyes.

She woke hours later to the swish of someone's skirts and a tray being jostled. Her eyes opened to find the duchess and Merry in her room. "Your Grace? Merry? Do you need me to see to the children?"

Persephone smiled at her. "You are to rest and regain your strength. Our son and daughter will have you on your feet all day tomorrow and through the night. Although we do allow you time to yourself—that is a subject we shall discuss on the morrow."

Gwendolyn looked at the duchess. "I cannot thank you enough, Your Grace."

"Persephone," she reminded her. "We've had a bit of a rough start, but I believe we shall overcome that slight obstacle and forge ahead." Surprising Gwendolyn by taking hold of her hands, the duchess squeezed them briefly before letting go. "I am so very happy to have you here. If there is anything you require, anything you need, please do not hesitate to let me know."

"Thank you, Persephone. What of His Grace?"

The duchess slowly smiled. "Leave His Grace to me. I shall see you in the morning."

"What about tonight's feeding?"

"My darling duke can handle one more night changing our twins while I feed them. Do not worry." She paused in the doorway. "Until tomorrow morning, then."

Relieved that her worries had been handled, Gwendolyn found her appetite was more than ready for the evening meal. Rising from her bed, she ate every bit of the flavorful stew, lingering over another cup of tea and two of their cook's delectable cream tarts for dessert.

"Tomorrow," she promised. "I shall not let you down!"

CHAPTER FOUR

L ORD RADLEIGH STOOD with his back to the library door, staring out the window at the snow-covered grounds surrounding his family's estate. No sign of the messenger he expected to return with news of retaliation, condemnation— something...he fumed. *Anything!*

Ignoring his threat was not the response he'd envisioned. He pictured himself high above his nemesis, waiting to drop the proverbial anvil atop the Duke of Wyndmere's head...crushing the undeserving prig like a bug.

His anger began to simmer, slowly increasing in temperature until it was a roiling, raging boil. His hands curled into fists at his sides. His jaw clenched as he fought against the need to scream a curse upon the duke's head. He would avenge his sister's honor and spread the *on dit* that it was the Duke of Wyndmere behind the lies concerning his sister's numerous liaisons. The truth held no value to Radleigh. Restoring his sister's good name was his first and only priority.

A knock on the library door had him spinning around. "Enter!"

The door opened to reveal his aging butler, the man's expression was haggard, and his uniform worn. "Begging your pardon, my lord."

Radleigh placed the blame for his butler's condition squarely where he felt it belonged...on someone else's shoulders—the duke's. "What is it?"

"You have a visitor."

He waited for the older man to hand him the visitor's card. When his servant did not move to do so, he asked, "His card? His name?"

The servant's eyes widened as he replied, "Thompson. He had no card, your lordship."

"Did he state his business?"

The butler shook his head, visibly trembling now as he confided, "He's wearing a red frockcoat."

A Bow Street Runner!

Radleigh had not anticipated that reaction.

Score one point to the duke.

CHAPTER FIVE

G WENDOLYN'S DAYS QUICKLY fell into a pattern, caring for the precious little ones, sharing her delight with the duchess each time Richard or Abigail rolled over, or waved their hands when she bent over their cradle to pick them up. She treasured every moment spent with the beautiful children in her care.

The one fly in the ointment was her overwhelming attraction to the stubborn head of the duke's private guard. His knowing glance, whenever their paths crossed, had her senses tingling and blood surging through her veins.

The man seemed to linger near the nursery for at least half of his day. *Was it one of his posts, guarding the twins?* Not wishing to attract any undue attention to herself by asking him, running the risk that the duke would hear of it and send her packing, her question went unasked.

Unaccustomed to having to handle an attraction to a man not her husband, her emotions shifted from incensed at his brazen approval of her form, to wantonly wishing he would take her in his arms and kiss her!

The wait was driving her to distraction, something she would not allow. She was well aware she had only retained her position in the duke's household because of the duchess' faith in her—that and the fact that their babes seemed to have become as taken with her as she was with them. She would not do anything to jeopardize her position.

As fate would have it, the choice was never hers to make.

PATRICK O'MALLEY CURSED beneath his breath. The woman he'd been trying to avoid was just rounding the corner of the house near the doorway to the rooftop, his station for the next few hours.

"Mr. O'Malley," she called out in greeting, setting his teeth on edge as she no doubt intended it to.

"O'Malley," he corrected for the umpteenth time.

She beamed at him. Did the woman know she tied him in knots every time she smiled in his direction? Was she trying to distract him on purpose? His temper started to percolate...not a good thing.

Deciding to confront the issue once and for all, he bit out, "Are ye tryin' to get me to toss ye over me shoulder?"

Shock leached the color from her face, but he did not feel remorse for startling the woman. When she did not immediately answer, he prompted, "Well? Are ye?"

Hand to her well-endowed breast, she rasped, "What on earth ever gave you that idea?"

"Ye're smilin' at me as if ye'd welcome me in yer arms."

Color bloomed across the curve of her cheeks. "I did not realize smiling at a man would cause him to think the way you do," she huffed.

Agitation deepened the color, adding an ethereal glow that captivated him. Her beauty tormented him, kept him awake nights. Her mouth held him in thrall when he should have been sleeping. Her generous curves had him fisting his hands in his hair in a bid to rip it out in frustration when he should be counting sheep. The woman was dangerous to his mind, his job, and his heart.

He was bloody well tired of suffering alone!

Before she had time to react, he hauled her into his arms and pressed his lips to hers in a searing kiss that demanded a response. Surrounded by her scent—sun-warmed honeysuckle, he was soon lost in the lushness of her mouth, the flavor that was uniquely Gwendolyn—a combination of tart cherries and sweet summer berries. The sound of her sigh as she wrapped her arms around his waist and raised up on her toes to capture his lips with soft, sweet kisses of her own packed a punch like a swig from his grandda's jug of *Poitín*.

He'd had his first sip of that potent illegal brew when he was but a lad of ten years. Ma had been incensed, but Da and Grandda had understood and deflected the worst of his mother's anger.

His body reacted swiftly, sharply. Before his hand slid to cup the curve of her backside, his wavering control snapped back into place. Ignoring her rose-tinged lips swollen from his kisses, and the glazed look in her whiskey-hued eyes, he rasped, "I beg yer pardon."

Before she could collect herself to reply, he'd increased the distance between them, yanked open the door to the rooftop and slammed it shut. Not trusting temptation—hers or his own, he bolted the door behind him.

A few chilly hours spent on top of the roof hadn't cooled the feeling rioting through him. How was he going to handle the situation? Now that he'd kissed her, he knew he would not soon forget her sumptuous flavor.

"What's got ye pacing and growling?" Eamon O'Malley demanded, shoving his cousin back against the door to their quarters. "Ye're acting like ye did the time that golden-eyed witch *Saoirse* handed yer heart back to ye."

The anger that had been simmering for the last four hours erupted. He never should have kissed the woman! It hadn't gotten her out of his system. It planted her firmly in his mind and his heart. Incensed that his plan had backfired, Patrick delivered a right cross that stunned his cousin, followed by the lightning-fast sucker punch that dropped him like a stone.

"Bloody hell!" Flaherty shouted, shoving Patrick out of the way to help their cousin to his feet. "What maggot's got yer brain on fire now?"

Garahan elbowed his way into the room. "Ye started without me?" Turning to Patrick, he asked, "What's the wager this time?"

Eamon ignored the sharp pain in his jaw, shifting it side to side, relieved that it wasn't broken. "Our illustrious cousin's got himself a woman."

Garahan stared at Patrick. "Cannot be Mollie. Ye'd never go behind yer brother, Finn's, back and court his woman."

Flaherty's eyes widened. "Francis, then?"

Eamon grunted. "She's a fair maid to be sure, but she's been hanging around the stables casting her lures at the farrier whenever he comes to check His Grace's horses."

Patrick raked a hand through his hair. "I didn't mean to punch ye, Eamon."

His cousin grinned at him. "Didn't ye now?"

Garahan cracked his knuckles.

A silent signal that had Flaherty slipping the rifle off his shoulder, placing it on the bench along the back wall of their quarters.

With a nod the others followed suit.

A heartbeat later they were paired off. "No hitting below the belt," Eamon warned. "We want to be sure and give our mothers grandsons and granddaughters to spoil."

Patrick's grin was quick and deadly. "No gouging of eyes."

Garahan shifted his weight from foot to foot. "Wagers?"

"Best two out of three falls?" Flaherty suggested.

Eamon tilted his head to one side as the howl of the wind roared past their quarters. He grinned. "Loser take's me midnight shift atop the roof."

The cousins stood with fists raised—ready to take on all comers...namely each other. Feet slightly apart, weight distributed evenly as they stood on the balls of their feet, ready to move in any direction.

Garahan slowly smiled. "I'll take that wager." His fist clipped the edge of Eamon's chin as his cousin leaned to the side.

"I'm guessing ye'll be taking me shift after all, Darby."

Garahan's eyes narrowed as he deflected the blow Eamon tried to land to his midsection.

"Ye want to watch?" Flaherty asked Patrick, "or do ye want to take a piece out of me?"

Patrick let his fists do the talking as the two men fought, evading blows, and delivering them.

"Bloody hell!"

Patrick froze as the duke's comment sluiced over him as if it were a bucket of snow.

Flaherty's shout of triumph filled the room as he landed a blow that had his cousin's nose gushing with blood.

"Enough!" the duke commanded. He pulled his handkerchief from his pocket and folded it before shoving it at Patrick.

Eamon used the sleeve of his coat to wipe the blood trickling from the corner of his mouth.

Garahan used his cuff to stanch the blood from the cut beneath his right eye.

"What in the bloody hell is going on here?"

The rumble of laughter coming from the O'Malleys had the duke straightening to his full height—a good four inches shy of Patrick, the tallest and the oldest of his personal guard, to glare at his men.

"I cannot countenance you shirking your duty to my family, my wife and our babes!"

Taken aback, immediately remorseful, Patrick apologized. "Forgive me, Yer Grace. I wasn't neglectin' me duties. As ye know, 'tis our way of practicin' while havin' a family discussion."

The anger radiating off the duke had Patrick wondering when their sessions beating on one another had become a problem for the duke. It hadn't been before today. They regularly set aside time to keep their bare knuckle skills sharp. *What changed? Had the duke received another threat?*

Searching for the words to express the extent of the remorse he felt for letting his employer down—though he knew not the why of it, he did feel the sharp arrow of the duke's disappointment. *He'd given his word.* Somehow, he had let the duke down. He needed to find out how and why. The man had taken O'Malley's brothers and cousins in to do a job that required the skills the O'Malleys, Garahans, and Flahertys had in spades. They were fighting men who came from a long line of men who'd fought to protect and preserve their families, their land, and their freedom for generations. Family discussions always included a bit of a dust-up...practicing their skills.

Blood dripped from the handkerchief he held to his nose, darkening the black of his coat. Patrick's gut clenched as he reeled with the knowledge that it did not matter what he thought, the man Patrick admired above all others felt he had let them down. It hadn't been more than twenty minutes that they'd spent pounding on one another, testing their skills, but the result was still the same...His Grace questioned *his* loyalty—*their* loyalty.

"It won't happen again, Yer Grace," Patrick vowed. "Ye have me word."

The duke didn't immediately respond and that, more than words, expressed the depth of his employer's anger. Had he completely lost the duke's trust? Would the duke's anger shift to his brothers and cousins? *He had to ask. Had to know!*

"I understand if ye think I've let ye down, Yer Grace," Patrick began, "What will it take for ye to let me win yer trust back?"

The men stood quietly with their hands at their sides, faces bruised, bleeding from the battering they'd taken and given— waiting for the duke to speak.

The duke's blue eyes glittered with unholy light a heartbeat before his fist delivered an uppercut that lifted Patrick O'Malley off his feet and into the wall. Without another word, the duke spun on his heel and strode from the building.

Garahan and Flaherty slipped through the door, watching the duke's angry strides increase the distance between the guard he'd placed his unswerving trust in toward the family they'd sworn on their lives to protect.

"He's coming around, lads." Eamon propped his cousin against the wall where he'd landed.

Patrick came to with a jerk, his eyes unable to focus, his head spinning. Eamon held up one finger—no wait…*was it two fingers?* Narrowing his eyes, his cousin's fingers shifted from one to two making his stomach flip over.

"How many fingers do ye see?"

Patrick groaned inwardly, no matter the injury or its severity, whatever number he told his cousin, Eamon's reply was always the same, *close enough.*

"One."

This time though, Eamon's eyes narrowed, and his jaw stiffened. *Not a good sign.* "Never thought His Grace had it in him."

"Didn't anticipate the blow," Patrick admitted. "Never saw it comin'." The ache in his jaw throbbed in time with the pain in his face. It had been some time since he'd suffered from such a blow. O'Malley had a job to do, even if he would no longer have that job a sennight from now.

He had to prove to the duke that his trust in him was not misplaced.

When the others walked back inside, he asked them, "Did His Grace say anything?"

Garahan and Flaherty exchanged a telling look before Flaherty replied, "Not a word."

"Do ye think he'll sack us?" Garahan wondered aloud.

Eamon seemed to be considering the ramifications. Rubbing his bruised jaw, he finally replied, "Not right away. He'll need time to assemble a new guard."

"We've men enough with the lads from the duke's staff and others from the village." Patrick struggled to get his feet under him and nearly went down. His cousins rushed to hold him up. "There's a stable lad and a footman on duty inside and two men from the village guarding the perimeter. How did I let His Grace down?"

Garahan spoke up. "Ye know he relies on ye to handle the rotation of his men, their shifts, and reporting to Coventry and King."

"Aye. Why then, isn't it enough that we had men performin' their duties in our stead?"

Flaherty frowned. "They aren't ye."

"He's never had an issue with me plans or the duty rotation before today…" his voice trailed off as the answer filled his aching head. "The kidnappin' threat."

"He's a man after our hearts, Patrick," Eamon stated. "He'd die to protect his family. The threat must have him losing sleep in a bid to watch over his precious babes."

"Aye," Patrick agreed. "I didn't think to ask if he needed me to personally stand guard by the nursery." Anguish slashed through his gut at the knowledge that he should have had the forethought to anticipate the duke's need. With what had occurred since the duke accepted his title, the attempts on his family, his wife, the family name…Patrick had anticipated the duke's every need and adjusted his men and their assignments to accommodate the duke.

As of late, he had been so wrapped up in the gut-wrenching beauty of Mrs. Alexander and his reaction to her that he had not been thinking clearly. He'd failed in his duty to the duke. His stomach roiled as the ache in his head and jaw trebled as he came to grips with the knowledge that he would have no choice but to resign.

Before he left, he would install his brother as his replacement. "I need to send a missive to Finn."

His cousins stared at him, as if they knew what Patrick had in mind. The intensity of their loyalty to family—and to the duke filled him with renewed purpose. They would stay on and see their duty through to the Duke of Wyndmere, no matter if Patrick was at the helm or Finn. Pride and loyalty ran deep in the O'Malley, Garahan, and Flaherty clans. Every one of them had bled protecting the duke and his family.

Resigned to do what his conscience and honor demanded, he announced, "Until Finn arrives to take on me duties, we need to prove to His Grace that it was a mistake—*mine,* and that it will never happen again—as I won't be here to make it. Whether or not His Grace sacks us...or forgives us, until then, we have a job to do."

The men readily agreed. "To yer posts then, and God help the man who shirks his duty. I'll be tossin' him from the roof meself."

"And if it's ye?" Eamon challenged.

Patrick's green eyes glittered with unholy light. "I'll jump."

CHAPTER SIX

PERSEPHONE BRUSHED THE tip of her finger along the curve of her son's brow. "Something's wrong."

Gwendolyn tucked Abigail in and hurried over to the duchess' side. She peered down at the little one. "He seems to be sleeping peacefully. Is there something amiss that isn't obvious?" She studied the little babe closely, hesitating before asking, because the answer could lead to a heart-breaking outcome. Ignoring the chill sprinting up her spine, she asked, "Mayhap a long pause in his breathing?"

Persephone lifted her head. "No, it's not that." The duchess pressed her lips to her son's forehead before laying him in his cradle and tucking his blankets around him so that he was warm and snug. "It has to do with Patrick."

Gwendolyn's heart beat wildly as she strove to keep her expression neutral. Even the man's name had an effect on her equilibrium. Patrick's green eyes reminded her of a sun-drenched meadow in spring while the memory of his kiss reignited the embers of passion inside of her to a conflagration.

Struggling to exert control over her traitorous emotions, she managed to tamp down on the need to be held in his arms again while he kissed every thought from her head. "O'Malley?"

The duchess placed a hand to Gwendolyn's elbow, steering her away from her sleeping babes. Once they were on the other side of the nursery, she confided, "Jared was visibly angry last night. When I asked him about it, he stared at me for long moments as if trying to discern my response to whatever lay heavy on his mind."

"What did he say?" Sensing there was more than a simple misunderstanding between the duke and his head guard, she waited for the duchess to confide in her.

"Not a word."

"Is that normal for His Grace to keep things from you?"

Persephone sighed, a long, drawn-out rush of air. "When we first met, yes. After we wed, he had been more open confiding his worries to me."

"Had been?"

"Er…yes. I've been so busy with the twins that I didn't notice right away. Thinking back, it seems he has not taken me into his confidence since our babes were born."

"Mayhap His Grace has been trying to protect you and not worry you with inconsequential matters."

"It started with the arrival of that missive from Gavin King."

"Who is Mr. King?"

"A trusted family friend who works for the Bow Street Runners. He has several men that have been on loan to my husband from time to time since that awful incident at our first ball."

Gwendolyn noticed the color had drained from the other woman's face. She needed to get to the bottom of her worry quickly. "Did the missive contain a warning or bad news?"

"A credible threat."

"I have not wanted to push you to explain the threat, but you're obviously distressed by it. Won't you confide in me? I may be of help to you."

"King informed my husband of a kidnapping threat."

The bottom dropped out of Gwendolyn's stomach, but she hid her distress from the duchess. She marveled at the woman's strength, carrying such a worry. She owed it to Her Grace to do all in her power to devise a plan to guard her charges.

"This horrible threat, the duke's anger, and possibly involving the head of your husband's personal guard have led you to believe that something even more dire is very wrong?"

"I would not be so concerned if my husband would share his worries with me. Not knowing if there has been another threat, or if something terrible has happened that he has yet to share with me is intolerable!"

Choosing her words with care, Gwendolyn asked, "Have you questioned His Grace again this morning?"

The duchess paced in front of the window looking out over the rear gardens. "He was up before me and nowhere to be found."

"Well," Gwendolyn considered, "your home is quite large. Mayhap whoever went looking for His Grace just missed him."

Persephone stopped pacing only to wring her hands.

Immediately concerned, Gwendolyn placed her hand on the other woman's forearm. The duchess stopped the telling motion and let her hands drop to her sides. "Dr. McIntyre advised that I was not to be distressed in any way as it could directly affect my feeding our precious babes."

"Then let me ask His Grace for you. Surely if I lead with that directive from your physician, he will no doubt rush to explain the situation to you."

Persephone's relief was palpable. "Thank you, Gwendolyn. That may be the way to force Jared to confide in me."

The twins whimpered. She and Gwendolyn returned to the babes, placing soothing hands on the little ones' backs, gently coaxing them back to sleep with circular motions and whispered words.

Relieved the babes went to sleep without too much persuasion, she motioned for the duchess to sit in one of the rocking chairs, while she walked over to the bell pull. "Why don't I ring for your mid-morning tea? You should relax while the babes are sleeping, while I go in search of His Grace."

Persephone smiled. "That would be lovely."

Gwendolyn's summons was answered quickly by one of the upstairs maids, Mollie. "What can I do for Your Grace?"

"I'd love a cup of tea."

The maid smiled. "Cream tarts or lavender scones?"

Persephone laughed softly. "You do know my favorites."

Mollie tilted her head to one side. "Constance and Merry are concerned that you have enough to drink and eat…" She blushed as if embarrassed that she'd nearly mentioned the personal topic of the duchess eating enough while nursing her babes.

Gwendolyn interjected, "Isn't it wonderful that your staff is aware of what you need in order to care for your babes without a wet nurse? Not many mothers in your societal position would spend as much time as you do with their babes. The ones I have worked for relied heavily on a wet nurse. They were more concerned with recovering their figures so they could go out and about in the society they craved."

The duchess sighed. "Jared and I discussed it at length. He was insistent we hire one at the physician's urging. Once I held our babes, I just couldn't bring myself to agree—they are our babes and my responsibility to feed as long as I am able to."

Mollie nodded. "Back home, mothers cared for their babes unless their health was too precarious after the birthing." She blushed a deeper shade of red, "Begging your pardon, Your Grace. I did not mean to discuss such with you."

Persephone rose from her seat and walked over to her maid. Placing her arm around the younger woman's shoulders, she hugged her. "You and Francis are like sisters to me. I've always wanted sisters to confide in but was an only child. That you have experience from helping to care for your mother during her confinement, and after, is comforting."

Shifting her gaze to meet Gwendolyn's, she added, "Now that our babes are in the excellent care of Mrs. Alexander, my husband and I are catching up on the much-needed sleep we've been missing in between feedings."

Gwendolyn's heart filled with gratitude that she'd been given the opportunity to work for the Duke and Duchess of Wyndmere. Between the couple, their staff, and the duke's personal guard, she felt secure in her ability to care for the twins without being constantly questioned by the duke's personal physician every other day. She shuddered visibly. Her last assignment caring for the viscount's heir had been exhausting...vexing.

Mollie paused in the doorway. "Are you chilled, Mrs. Alexander? Do you need me to fetch your shawl?"

Gwendolyn shook her head. "Just remembering something that's best forgotten."

"Oh?" Persephone prompted. "With a former infant in your care? Was the babe ill?"

She hesitated before confiding her thoughts. It was her policy to be direct and upfront with her employers whenever possible, though not to discuss other assignments in depth. "For every three positions that seem Heaven-sent, there are one or two that are vexing in the extreme." Smiling, she added, "But the babes of those difficult employers are usually angels."

"In comparison to our two darlings?"

Gwendolyn's smile broadened. "Richard and Abigail are angelic in temperament as well as looks."

Persephone nodded. "'Tis good of you to acknowledge what everyone here knows."

She smiled in response. "If you'll excuse me, I'll just see to that errand for you."

The duchess' trust humbled Gwendolyn. "Will Mollie be staying with you until I return?"

"Of course. I'll just ask one of the footmen to relay your request for tea," the maid stated as she rang the bell pull. "And advise I shall be attending you until Mrs. Alexander returns."

"Thank you, Mollie." Gwendolyn turned to the duchess. "I shall return shortly, Your Grace."

The duchess inclined her head. Gwendolyn swept from the room determined to find the duke and plead with him to understand the precarious emotional state that Her Grace was in worrying about what information or secrets he was keeping from her.

CHAPTER SEVEN

"AND YOU'RE CERTAIN no one knows of your connection to his lordship?"

The stable lad looked over his shoulder toward the entrance to the alley and shrugged. "Never spoken to him or of him."

The big man grumbled and cuffed the younger man on the back of the head. "Best keep your ears and eyes open. The duke's staff may tell us something we need to know so you can nab the prizes and hand them off to me."

The stable lad rubbed the back of his head before responding, "At the stroke of midnight, behind the church—near the oldest gravestones."

"Remember not to let the duke's guard get the jump on you."

The lad drew himself up to his full height and lifted his chin in challenge. "I'd like to see them try."

"Don't let your guard down, mind?" After a pause, the man threatened, "I'll break your hands if you do."

The lad promised. "The head of the duke's guard is on the outs with the duke. I'll outsmart them—you have my word. The twins will be in your possession by tomorrow night!"

The two parted company, heading in opposite directions.

AN HOUR LATER, the stable lad was leading the duke's stallion out of his stall.

"Where have you been, Guy?"

He buried the panic deep. It wasn't like the stable master to question his whereabouts. "Cook sent me on an errand," he lied.

"You do not report to Constance," the stable master reminded him. "You report to me. Understood?"

Guy tightened his grip on the stallion's bridle. Would the man question the cook and discover his lie? The horse shook his head in protest, lifting him off his feet.

"Easy now," a deep voice warned from behind him. "Ye can let go of his bridle now, lad. He'll not hurt ye."

Mortified that he'd been caught unaware by the head of the duke's guard, he groaned. Mayhap it would be harder than he thought to sneak inside and up to the nursery. He'd have to come up with a better story than the one he'd fed the stable master—one that would allow him to go back to the village before the evening meal.

Not waiting for a response, the guard turned to continue on his rounds. "O'Malley!"

The stable master's call had O'Malley stopping in his tracks. "Aye?"

"I need to speak with Constance." He turned to stare at Guy before adding, "On an urgent matter."

"Do ye not trust the lad to lead His Grace's Thoroughbred out of the paddock?"

The other man frowned. "After what just happened, I wonder."

"I can handle the horse," the lad assured them.

O'Malley chuckled. "There's a right way to handle a horse of this temperament and a wrong way."

"Would you mind turning the stallion out in the corral while the lad and I speak with Constance?"

Guy froze, searching his mind for an excuse to stop the man—or the game was over, the job in shambles, the bag of coins out of reach. His hands broken…the price for failure.

O'Malley had a hold of the stallion's bridle once more. "What is it, lad?"

Icy fingers of fear slashed through the young man at the thought of the pain he'd suffer, of the life he'd no longer be able to lead, of being reduced to begging for his daily bread.

"Best fess up." The stable master placed a hand on Guy's shoulder.

Guy hung his head and blurted out the first thing that came to mind. "It's my ma, she's awful sick. If I don't bring her something to eat before dark, she'll succumb to the fever again."

"Why didn't you say so in the first place?"

"And have you think my ma's health is more important than working for the duke?"

"Yer ma's health is of equal importance, lad. Best ye see to her." With a nod to the stable master, he stated, "I'll let this one loose to graze in the pasture and speak to His Grace meself."

The stable master patted Guy on the back. "Stop in the kitchen and ask Constance for some broth and bread to take to your ma."

Surprise overtook the fear. The men believed his tale! He nearly felt sorry for having to dupe them. The theft would likely cause the duke and duchess pain beyond what his fourteen years could comprehend. But the lure of a bag filled with coins when he handed the infants over to the man from London was his driving thought.

Rushing along the path leading to the kitchen, Guy fought against the urge to laugh aloud.

Chapter Eight

TRUST DIDN'T COME easy to O'Malley. The lad was newly hired, on a recommendation from a friend of a friend of the stable master. He latched the gate behind the horse and watched the lad rush off down the path. If he hadn't been watching so closely, he would have missed the unholy look of glee on the young man's face.

The hairs on the back of his neck stood on end and his gut iced over. He needed to alert the duke—but would the duke heed his warning or ignore it? *Wouldn't matter.* The duke needed to know what O'Malley had seen and his gut reaction to it.

Deciding to act as if the incident yesterday had not occurred, he knocked on the door to the duke's study.

"Enter!"

O'Malley opened the door and waited on the threshold. "Yer Grace." Waiting for the duke to look up from the papers spread across his desk, he wasn't surprised to see the dark look leveled at him.

"Please advise Humphries and Merry that I am not to be disturbed."

The duke's disinterest hurt his pride, but more, the friendship they had formed while working together. "I've urgent news."

The duke sighed and leaned back in his chair. "Get to the point, O'Malley."

He shoved emotions that had nothing to do with his job, and everything to do with the fractured issue of trust between them, deep. "'Tis about the new stable lad."

The duke listened intently to what O'Malley had to say before speaking. "I shall speak with Humphries and Merry who will alert the senior staff."

Before O'Malley could offer, the duke cut him off. "Have Eamon speak to the rest of the guard. Send Garahan and Flaherty to speak to the men from the village."

His gut curdled as the acid of truth washed through it. The duke would never forgive his breach of trust. With a brief nod, he spun on his heel and quit the room. His stride increased as the magnitude of his blunder threatened to overwhelm him. Blinded by a truth he had to accept, he didn't see Mrs. Alexander until he knocked into her. Splaying a hand to her spine to keep her from falling, heat from her back seared his palm.

The lush curves plastered against him had shock waves of need sprinting through his blood. His iron-clad control crushed those needs and brought him to his senses. "Beggin' yer pardon. I didn't see ye."

Her sharply indrawn breath had him wondering if he'd injured the woman. "Are ye all right?"

Instead of answering, she squirmed until he let go of the hold he had on her. "Steady now, I would not want ye to fall."

Her whiskey-colored gaze locked on his. Lifting her chin, she challenged, "Then you should have taken better care to take note of your surroundings."

The words on the tip of his tongue slid back down his throat. "Ye have the right of it. If ye'll excuse me."

HURT FLASHED IN his emerald bright eyes before he blinked, and it was replaced with resignation as he turned to leave. "O'Malley!

Wait!"

He looked over his shoulder. "Aye?"

She moved to his side so as not to be overheard. "The duchess has asked me to speak with His Grace. Something happened yesterday that has the duke acting strangely—something he has yet to confide in Her Grace. Do you know what it might be?"

Pain leached the color from his eyes until they were a lifeless yellow. "Ye'd best be askin' His Grace." Without another word, he stalked down the hall to the servants' staircase.

Gwendolyn watched the jerky motions of the man as he wrenched the door open and then closed it behind him. The thundering of his footsteps descending to the kitchen indicated that O'Malley knew exactly what was wrong with the duke. She suspected O'Malley was at the heart of the issue.

Steeling herself to face the man who had been ready to send her home, she squared her shoulders and strode down the hall to the duke's study and raised her hand to knock. The door swung open, surprising a squeak out of her.

The duke lifted one brow in silent question, waiting for her to speak.

"I do beg your pardon, Your Grace. I've come on behalf of Her Grace."

His jaw clenched as he inclined his head and stepped aside so she could enter his domain. She hesitated, noting the man had not moved from the doorway. "It will only take a moment of your time, Your Grace."

He sighed. "My wife is like a dog with a bone," he murmured.

"Your Grace?" Had he really just mumbled that? Should she leave and tell the duchess the duke was not available?

"I must have a word with O'Malley before I speak with my wife."

"Oh," she remarked, "I just ran into him a moment ago. He took the servants' staircase to the kitchen."

The duke frowned. "I need to speak with *Eamon*."

The duke's words added to the supposition that Patrick was at the heart of the problem. "I see. I shall let Her Grace know you will attend her shortly."

He inclined his head in silent dismissal. He was gone before she could thank him. Not wanting to risk the duke returning to speak to the duchess before she did, she rushed to the nursery.

Relief spread up from her toes. The duchess was sipping a cup of tea, sitting in the rocking chair as she had been when Gwendolyn left to speak with the duke.

The duchess smiled when she entered. "Well, that did not take long." Setting the cup on its saucer, she asked, "What did he say?"

Gwendolyn quickly explained what had occurred—including nearly being run over by Patrick.

Surprise filled the duchess' gaze before one of disbelief took its place. "I do not believe for a moment that Patrick would ever shirk his duties!" Rising to her feet, she put her hands to her hips. "The O'Malleys are bare knuckle champions in Ireland."

"I see." Although she really had no idea where the conversation was headed, she did have a rudimentary knowledge of the art of bare knuckle fighting. One of her O'Toole cousins back home had been the toast of the seaside town he'd grown up in.

Persephone sighed. "It is part of the reason my husband hired the lot of them, sight unseen, before we wed…" her voice trailed off as she amended that last statement. "Mayhap it was just after we wed." Waving her hand in the air as if to dismiss what she'd just said, she continued, "They are sharpshooters and can handle a pistol as well as a rifle, a sword as well as a blade…"

Sensing there was more, Gwendolyn urged, "But?"

"They are always honing their bare knuckle skills on one another."

"I see." At least she thought she did until the duchess added, "They never spar with any of the staff or the guards we have had to hire on from the village."

"They fight amongst themselves?"

"Practice," Persephone corrected. "They must keep their skills sharp. I cannot tell you the number of times that skill has come in handy before the duke and I were married—and after."

"What does that have to do with the rift between His Grace and Patrick?"

"Their bond of trust goes deep," Persephone whispered. "If something were to test that bond, shake that trust…that would explain the way the two of them are acting."

"Nothing at all like when I arrived," Gwendolyn remarked. "They sought one another out numerous times during the day."

Tears welled up, but Persephone blinked them away. "We must find out what is behind this. I will not let Patrick resign his position."

"Do you think it will come to that?"

The duchess turned toward her, and the crippling sorrow in the woman's gaze arrowed through Gwendolyn. Resolved to keep the duchess' spirits up, along with her ability to take care of her twins, she offered, "Tell me what I can do to help."

Persephone drew in a deep breath and slowly let it out. "You need to seek Merry's assistance. Find out if a missive has been sent to Penwith Tower, London, or Lippincott Manor."

"Of course. Is there anything else?"

The duchess reached for Gwendolyn's hand and squeezed it before letting go. "Do not let anyone overhear your conversation with Merry. We have additional staff that His Grace hired a few weeks ago. It would be best not to trust any one of them."

With a glance at the sleeping infants, she nodded. "I shall use the servants' staircase and return as quickly as possible."

A quarter of an hour later, Gwendolyn returned. Persephone was feeding Richard while she hummed a soothing lullaby. "Your Grace?"

She shifted her son to rest against her shoulder, gently rubbing her hand up and down his back. "What did you find out?"

The little one belched loudly causing the duchess to smile. "Now you'll have room for more." Settling him to her other breast, she leaned back in the rocking chair.

A sharp shaft of envy speared Gwendolyn's heart. She would never know what it was like to suckle her son. At eight and twenty, she'd been on the shelf for nearly a decade and would likely remain there.

"Is something wrong?"

The quiet question snapped her back to the present. "Merry said a missive was sent to Penwith Tower."

Persephone frowned. "Finn."

"Who is Finn?"

"One of Patrick's brothers."

"I know you mentioned it, but I cannot remember. How many brothers does he have?"

"Three."

Gwendolyn sighed. "I was an only child."

Persephone smiled. "As was I. It would be my guess that Patrick has asked his brother to return to Wyndmere Hall for one reason only. To assume Patrick's role as head of my husband's guard."

"What if Finn's employer will not release him from his position?"

The duchess' eyes filled with mirth. "Thank goodness, that is not a possibility."

"Are you quite certain?"

"Penwith Tower is one of my husband's estates on the coast of Cornwall. It is currently under restoration."

"I see. Where do the rest of Patrick's brothers work?"

"His brother, Dermott, is stationed at Lippincott Manor where my good friend Aurelia and brother-in-law Edward, Earl Lippincott, live. Patrick's other brother, Emmett, is currently stationed at our London town house."

"Mollie mentioned O'Malley having more cousins working for His Grace."

"His other cousins are spread out between my husband's three estates as well as Chattsworth Manor, the home of my good friend Calliope and her husband Viscount Chattsworth, and Summerfield Chase, the home of my sister-in-law Phoebe and her husband Baron Summerfield. Both gentlemen are distant cousins of my husband."

"Does His Grace feel responsible for his cousins by ensuring he has guards stationed at their estates as well as his own?"

"Indeed," the man himself rumbled from where he stood on the threshold to the nursery. "I would do all in my power to protect my entire family."

"Your family is no doubt grateful for your magnanimous gesture."

His smile barely reached his eyes as he watched his wife nursing their son. A familiar lightness seemed to envelope the duke. Gwendolyn remembered that look from the day she'd arrived. "At times, they are," he finally replied. "If you would excuse us. I need to speak with my wife."

Gwendolyn nodded. "Shall I stay here with the twins?"

Persephone shook her head. "Abigail will no doubt wake, wanting to be fed, the moment I put Richard back to bed."

"I shall be in my bedchamber."

"I'll have Mollie fetch you back shortly."

With a curtsey, she left the duke and duchess and slowly walked to her room.

Engrossed with adding tidbits of information to her journal, she was surprised to find Mollie standing in the open doorway. Setting the journal aside, she put down her pencil and stood. Brushing her skirts, she was a bit dismayed at the wrinkles there.

"I must look a sight. Does Her Grace need me right away?"

Mollie shook her head. "I'm to ask if you'd like to have a bite to eat in the conservatory before taking a healthful stroll outside."

She tilted her head to one side, considering the suggestion. "I take it Their Graces are still in the nursery and do not wish to be disturbed."

Mollie smiled. "Her Grace does not want you to feel as if you are a prisoner, kept indoors all day, every day."

She laughed softly. "I am grateful to Her Grace. I'd love nothing more than to clear my head with a bit of the brisk, bright day that awaits me before I eat. Let me grab my cloak."

Mollie shook her head. "I'll fetch it for you, Mrs. Alexander."

"Thank you. I'm looking forward to walking outside. Do you have a suggestion as to which path to take? I noticed several when I arrived the other day."

The maid nodded. "Take the one to the left, it'll take you through the gardens and around to the front of Wyndmere Hall."

"I imagine it would be something to see come spring."

"Oh, it's just lovely! The perfect spot to watch for faeries at daybreak."

"Do you believe in faeries?"

Mollie nodded. "And the little people, sprites, dryads, and the like."

She wished she still believed in a bit of magic, but that had been torn from her when the midwife solemnly told her that her son wasn't breathing. Clearing her throat, she accepted her cloak and thanked the maid.

For the first time since she'd accepted that first position as nanny, she wished she were able to spend more than a few months in one spot. What would it be like to see a babe learn to crawl, to walk, to run?

She sighed. *That door was closed to her—she'd bolted it herself.*

Passing by the entrance to the conservatory—and the meal waiting for her, she let herself outside and followed the path to the right—no need to wonder what the gardens would be like come spring, she wouldn't be here. She'd visit the stables instead, knowing she'd find comfort in the familiar surroundings—the scents and sounds of horses like those she'd grown up with.

She heard the argument as she approached the stables. Worry filled her recognizing Patrick's voice. Shielding herself behind a tree, she paused to listen.

"And I say ye've *shite* for brains!"

"I don't give a rat's arse what ye think."

The duchess did not need another round of bare knuckle fighting to come between her husband and the man responsible for their protection. She needed calm in her life. And by all that was holy, Gwendolyn was going to see to it that Persephone had it!

Going with her gut, she rushed into the stables and was shoved from behind. She landed hard on her hands and knees.

"Gwendolyn!" The deep rasp of concern wrapped around her, warming her, easing the worst of the shock from her bones. "Are ye hurt? Can ye stand?"

She took stock of her injuries as feeling slowly returned.

A black-clad knee settled alongside of her as the large hands beneath her arms lent a much-needed warmth as the cold of the day had already seeped into her bones.

"Forgive me," Patrick's voice cracked. "Let me help ye." He slid his hand around her waist and slowly helped her to her feet. When she wobbled, he shifted his hold, sweeping her into his arms.

The heat of the man radiated through her, warming her, as fire raced through her veins. *Had she rattled her brainbox when she'd landed on the cold-packed dirt? She hadn't felt like this in more years than she could recall. Desire, sharp and painfully sweet.*

"GRAB THAT BLANKET, Darby!" Patrick ordered as he walked toward the tack room. Since there were no windows in the room, it would be warmer. The need to protect the woman sluiced over him like a bitter wind off St. George's Channel, where it flowed into the Irish Sea.

Castigating himself, wondering how he'd ended up injuring a woman who came under his protection, he strode into the tack room. Loath to let go of her, he sat on the cot still cradling her in his arms.

Garahan handed him the horse blanket. "Do ye need me to

inform His Grace?"

"Please do not," Gwendolyn spoke from her toasty cocoon. "I actually came to speak with you on behalf of Her Grace."

O'Malley sighed. If Her Grace was involved, things would become entangled with her wishes versus her husband's. There would be a backlash that would only upset the duchess and enrage the duke. He had to refuse whatever the request was.

"She's worried you plan to relinquish your duties to Finn."

He stiffened in response. The duchess had come to understand him far better than he'd anticipated. He needed to deflect her supposition. "When Darby and I are satisfied ye've not been injured, please let Her Grace know she has no reason to worry."

"And how long will that take?" she demanded. The woman was getting her grit back.

He chuckled despite his worry Gwendolyn had been injured. He hadn't meant to knock her to the ground—he'd been aiming to shove his cousin against the wall. "If ye're warm enough, let me see yer hands and wrists."

"I'm warm and feel much better."

"Nevertheless, Lass, let me see yer hands." His voice brooked no argument.

She lifted her chin high. "No, thank you."

Surprise had him snorting to cover his laughter. "When ye get yer grit back, it's with a vengeance."

"I believe I'll take that as a compliment."

"I can't have ye thinking it is," Garahan advised. "He is well used to being obeyed."

Patrick cleared his throat. "'Tis the truth of it. Now, show me yer hands—if ye don't mind."

The woman had the temerity to glare at him. Why in God's name would she? He was trying to help her! "Ye're acting like a horse's—"

"Backside," Garahan interjected. "Ye'll want to mind yer words and watch yer tone."

The reminder had him rounding on his cousin. Garahan

silently challenged him to refute his words. Patrick capitulated. "I beg yer pardon, Mrs. Alexander. I'm not normally short of temper—"

The deep rumbling laughter echoed through the tiny room. When Garahan caught his breath, he agreed. "He is only short of temper when his authority is called into question, he's crossed, or challenged by a slip of a lass."

Patrick shot to his feet before he realized he still held Gwendolyn protectively in his arms. Gently setting her down on the cot, he closed the distance between himself and his cousin. They stood toe-to-toe and eye-to-eye...well almost, since he had an inch on the man.

The hard yank on the back of his greatcoat had him looking over his shoulder. "What do ye think ye're doin'?"

"Getting your attention, *Mr.* O'Malley! Now that I have it, I will remind you that Her Grace is trying to prevent another situation like this one seems to be headed toward. If you have a care at all for Her Grace, then please calm yourself."

Anger was replaced with guilt. "Beggin' yer pardon, Mrs. Alexander." He'd never been so close to losing his temper in front of a lady before and vowed to do all in his power to see that he didn't in the foreseeable future. Too much was at stake. Not his livelihood...his position with the Duke of Wyndmere would end as soon as he could turn over his duties to his brother. 'Twas his honor and that of his family name.

"Finn," he rasped. The last conversation he'd had with his brother finally made sense. Finn had asked the duke to transfer him to Penwith Tower for more than one reason...the one Patrick had not understood at the time hit him between the eyes. *His brother left because of Mollie Malloy! He'd seen the way she cared for him after the duke's home had been attacked and Finn was knocked unconscious. The two had been inseparable after that...until Finn had requested the transfer to Cornwall.*

Taking a step back, he shook his head at the realization. "I'm an *eedjit!*"

"I won't be disagreeing with ye."

"*Eedjit?*" Gwendolyn asked. "What exactly does that mean?"

Garahan grinned. "What does it sound like?"

She frowned. "Obviously it is not a compliment."

"'Tisn't," the dark-haired guard agreed.

"Leave off, Darby." Turning around, O'Malley asked one more time, "Would ye please show me yer hands? I need to see if they're bruised and need tending."

Gwendolyn held them up for his inspection. He took them in his own, carefully brushing the dirt from her palms. "They may pain ye for a day or so, but there's no visible cuts or bruisin'."

"What about her knees?" Garahan prodded.

She shot to her feet, drew in a breath, her spine as stiff as a rod. "I will not show my knees to either of you!" She picked up her skirts, spun around, and yanked open the door.

"Faith, she's got fire to go with her grit!"

O'Malley sighed. "'Tis what has me mind turnin' to mush whenever she slips into it."

"Finn left for the same reason." Garahan stated what was now obvious to O'Malley.

"I hadn't known, would not have understood. But now…"

"Are ye thinking to interfere in yer brother's personal affairs?" Garahan wanted to know.

O'Malley stared at his cousin. "Last I heard from James, ye're still after devilin' him any time he looks twice at a woman."

Garahan grinned. "Can't help it if I'm wanting to know if I should steer clear of a fair face because me brother is interested in pursuing her, or if I've a clear path to woo the lass."

O'Malley grumbled, "I can see why James is wantin' to punch ye most of the time."

Garahan sighed. "'Tis his right as the oldest to keep the rest of us in line." He paused before adding, "Ye're avoiding answering me question. Do ye intend to interfere with Finn and Mollie?"

"I'm thinkin' it over."

He turned to walk away, but Garahan got in his way. When

O'Malley tried to shove past him, the bull of a man didn't budge. "Faith, ye're a pain in me arse!"

"Do ye have feelings for Gwendolyn?"

O'Malley didn't want to admit it, least of all to his younger cousin. He shoved his shoulder into Garahan's to move him out of the way.

This time, Garahan grinned. "Ye've only an inch on me in height, but I outweigh ye. If ye answer me question, I'll let ye pass."

"Oh, will ye now?" O'Malley imagined the satisfying feeling of his fist connecting with Garahan's big mouth…but that would have to wait until later.

"Aye."

"Whatever I feel for Gwendolyn will not interfere with me duties. 'Tis best left alone."

Garahan stared at him.

O'Malley could all but see the wheels turning in his cousin's brain. But O'Malley had far more on his mind than he would admit. He'd been relieved of his position as head of the duke's guard and would no doubt be dismissed. Entangled with that was a woman with curves that drove him mad and eyes the color of the finest Irish whiskey…

"Do ye plan to speak to His Grace again?"

"Nay."

"But—"

O'Malley's hand shot out and grabbed hold of Garahan's coat, surprising his cousin with the unexpected move. "'Tis done, and past time for me to write me last report for His Grace." He shoved Garahan backward and strode to the door.

"Patrick, wait!"

He paused in the doorway, shoulders slumped, heart heavy. "Tell the others we'll be havin' a meetin' this evenin'."

He walked past the stalls, acknowledging the snorts and snuffles as if His Grace's horses were bidding him goodbye. Mind weary, he trudged along the path leading to the rooftop rather than their quarters to pen his report.

The chill in the air would clear the troubles from his head—though nothing would clear the woman from his heart.

CHAPTER NINE

T HE DUKE STOOD with his hands behind his back, facing Patrick's second in command. "Do you have anything further to report regarding the stable lad?"

Eamon's stance matched that of the duke's. "Nay."

The duke frowned. "Patrick relayed information that called the youth's intentions into question."

Eamon had already answered the duke. What more did the man want? What did he expect?

The Duke of Wyndmere frowned. "There has been sufficient time for you to have had the young man followed. Whom did he meet with in the village? Is his mother truly ill? I require facts."

"Begging yer pardon, Yer Grace. If me cousin received word from the village about Guy's whereabouts—or the condition of the lad's mother, he'd have relayed the information to me. I would report it to ye immediately."

Eamon hadn't a clue what the man was thinking, or why he wasn't speaking to Patrick directly. The duke's guard relied on their leader to supply them with any vital information pertaining to their duties as well as their rotation schedule. Without Patrick as the head of the guard, the men were ill at ease. In truth, he was bloody well furious with his cousin. If he could lay blame, it would be squarely at the feet of the man standing in front of him.

"Something on your mind, O'Malley?"

"Aye," he readily agreed. "Though I cannot think ye'd care to hear what it is."

The duke stood at attention, his hands curling into fists at his sides.

Finally! Eamon had gotten through and had the man's anger focused on himself instead of his cousin.

"If you wish to continue in my employ," the duke stated, "you will not hold anything back."

Eamon grinned. "If ye insist, Yer Grace."

"I do."

"Patrick is the eldest of our clan. Having worked for the fifth duke, he's the most experienced in organization, ferreting out information from those whose lips are sealed, and hauling yer brother from his carriage to his bedchamber."

The duke's face lost all expression. "Indeed."

"Meaning no disrespect, Yer Grace, but ye asked."

The duke inclined his head regally. "None taken. Do you plan to continue in Patrick's stead as head of my guard?"

Eamon had been raised like the rest of his cousins—always speak the truth. O'Malleys, Garahans, and Flahertys were men of honor. They swore to protect their families to their last breaths. Once they gave their word, they would die to defend it.

"If it be Yer Grace's wish. I will. Though in truth, I cannot say I look forward to it."

The duke sounded as if he were strangling before clearing his throat and adjusting his cravat. "It appears I am as yet unused to those in my employ speaking their minds, although I did ask Patrick to always do so."

"'Tisn't easy for him to do so. As a rule, we O'Malleys keep our thoughts close to the vest."

The duke seemed to be considering his next words carefully. "Does that apply to your Garahan and Flaherty cousins as well?"

"Aye, Yer Grace."

"And if I were to demand that you keep nothing from me?"

Eamon was quick to respond. "If that be yer instruction, then of course we would follow it to the letter."

The duke relaxed his stance, and Eamon followed suit. He hoped the duke would end this meeting quickly. He needed to change his shirt before resuming his patrol. He'd sweated through to his skin having to face the duke and answer his questions. With the frigid weather, he'd succumb to fever or lung infection within half an hour.

"Is there anything else ye need me to tell Patrick and the men?"

"What is the current frame of mind of the men, given they now report to you instead of Patrick?"

Eamon shrugged.

"A shrug is an inappropriate response, O'Malley."

He was not cowed by the duke, still he hesitated to speak.

"Out with it!"

"Not one of us is in favor of yer decree, Yer Grace."

The man did not seem surprised by his declaration. His words confirmed Eamon's thoughts. "I did not expect the change to be accepted readily."

"Then ye'll let me tell me cousin he is to return to his duty as head of yer guard?"

"My dictate remains. My mind is unchanged. You are the head of my guard and will continue to report directly to me—not Patrick. Understood?"

"Aye. Will there be anything else?"

"Report back to me within the hour. You should have news by then."

"Aye, Yer Grace." Dismissed, Eamon kept his expression neutral until he'd reached the side door that led to the gardens. The chill sliced through his bones to the marrow.

Walking quickly, he reached their quarters, changed, and was halfway to the stables when the stable master intercepted him. "Have ye news then?"

The older man hesitated. "You understand Guy was recommended by a friend of a friend of mine?"

Eamon had his answer. "Do you have any particulars I can relay to His Grace?"

The stable master looked away, then back. "Rumor is, young Guy has been hanging around with a chap from London."

"And?" Eamon prompted.

"He's been wagering at cards."

He nodded. "So, the lad's come into some blunt then."

"There's more."

Eamon braced for news that the lad was working for the bloody bastard that threatened the duke's family.

"He was overheard planning to snatch the duke's babes."

Immediately on alert, O'Malley turned to leave.

"Wait!"

He glanced over his shoulder. "When?"

"Tonight."

"How many?"

"Four."

Eamon grabbed the man by the arm and rasped, "Patrick's on the roof. Tell him everything ye've told me. I've got to speak to the duke!"

He took off at a run and nearly ran into the man as he opened the door by the gardens. "Yer Grace!"

The duke's eyes glittered, then hardened. "When?"

Eamon relayed what he'd been told while the rigidity in the duke's stance intensified. "Shall I warn Mrs. Alexander?"

"Leave that to me. I shall inform her after I speak with Her Grace. I trust you will alert the men and then relay your plan for protection."

"I've sent word to Patrick."

"I thought I told you—"

Time was of the essence, and O'Malley didn't have the time to debate with the duke. "Begging yer pardon, Yer Grace, but ye said I was to report to ye, not Patrick."

"And you sent word—"

O'Malley interrupted the duke a second time. "Aye, that I did.

He already has a number of plans in mind to defend yer home and yer babes. Ye can trust him...ye can trust us."

He spun on his heel and strode off to meet with his men.

"O'Malley!"

He glanced over his shoulder. The duke's anger washed over him. He inclined his head and kept walking. The babes' protection was more important than any bloody protocol.

"I did not dismiss you!"

Knowing it would mean the end of the lucrative position he'd held working for the duke, he made the decision to put the twins' welfare above all else. Patrick had plans in place. It was time to speak to him to see which plan to initiate.

PATRICK OPENED THE door as Eamon reached for it. "Has the duke told Mrs. Alexander yet?"

"Nay, said he'd tell her after he spoke with Her Grace."

"What else did he say?"

"Nothing important, he was too busy spouting off about not dismissing me."

He stared at Eamon and shook his head. "His Grace is deservin' of our respect, Eamon."

"Once the threat's been taken care of and the babes are safe, I'll be apologizing to His Grace."

"And if he decides to replace ye as head of his guard?" Patrick demanded.

"'Twill be me bloody pleasure to let Garahan or Flaherty take me place."

Patrick knew Eamon spoke the truth. "We'll deal with that later. I need to speak to Mollie while ye fill Garahan and Flaherty in."

"Are ye certain she's up to the task?"

"She and Francis will be ready," Patrick assured him. "They've been takin' turns carin' for the babes during the night— when the kidnappers mean to strike."

Eamon went over the plan aloud. "Mollie and Francis will

wait until the babes are fed, then take the babes to their rooms on the third floor and bolt the door."

Patrick's smile was lethal. "The kidnappers won't find the cradles empty. I've seen the decoys the lasses have swaddled to look like the twins."

"Will they have time to place them in the cradles?"

"Aye," Patrick assured him. "Then they'll slip out the rear door to the nursery and up the servants' staircase to their quarters."

Eamon nodded. "I told His Grace ye'd have more than one plan in place." He turned to go and paused to ask, "What happens if the kidnappers arrive before Mollie and Francis spirit the babes away?"

"They'll have had to somehow get past ye, Garahan, and Flaherty."

"And if they do?"

Patrick smiled. "They'll have to kill me to get to them."

"Ye'll be standing guard outside the nursery?"

"Aye."

"What if Mrs. Alexander hears something and investigates?"

"She won't. Her Grace has said the woman sleeps like a stone."

Eamon didn't hesitate. As always, he accepted Patrick's word without question. "Anything else I need to tell our cousins?"

"Everyone knows the plan."

"Including the duke and duchess?"

Patrick hesitated and Eamon swore. "Ye haven't told them yet?"

"'Tis better if they don't know." He planned to have handled the threat before the bloody bastards crossed the perimeter onto the duke's estate.

"I'll speak to the others."

"Alert them that there is a strong possibility of an attempt tonight."

"I will."

"Do not take them into yer confidence about our plans."

Eamon paused before nodding. "Watch yer back," he warned.

"Watch yers."

The men parted, intent on executing the beginning of Patrick's plans to protect the duke's family. Eamon strode to the door to the servants' staircase leading to the kitchen, while Patrick headed in the opposite direction.

A quarter of an hour later, those involved knew what was expected of them.

Waiting for the kidnappers to strike was part of their intricate plan and, in Patrick's mind, no challenge. Extracting the name or names of those behind the plot would be.

Praying no one would be injured, he checked in with the men at their stations off and on throughout the afternoon and early evening. By six o'clock, everyone involved knew what was expected. Seven o'clock had the men from the village ready to intercept any intruders.

If they got past the first band of protection—around the perimeter, then one of the men the duke hired from the village was in on the kidnapping plot. If they got past the next band of protection—onto the immediate grounds, the footmen, groundkeepers, and stable lads would be ready to intercept them.

If there was someone else in on the plot—a footman or another member of the duke's household staff, it would be up to the four of them: Patrick, Eamon, Darby, and Rory to neutralize the intruder or intruders.

God help the kidnappers if they somehow made it through to face down the Irishmen sworn to protect the duke and his family with their lives. Patrick's jaw clenched as he sent up a prayer that the Lord would see to it that did not happen.

As he was patrolling the darkened hallway leading to and from the nursery, he paused to add, "If it be Yer will, take me life to protect the babes."

Drawing in a deep breath, he continued down the length of

the hall, passing the door to the servants' staircase leading to their sleeping quarters, and the next one leading to the kitchen. He glanced out the window overlooking the north side of the duke's home and froze.

"They're early."

Patrick's contingency plans included this possibility. He opened the door leading down, alerting the footman stationed there. Moving swiftly, silently, he extinguished the flames inside the sconces along the way as he alerted the others stationed in the circle of protection around the nursery.

As he extinguished the last two flames—on either side of the nursery door, he heard heavy footfalls...two men—not the rumored four...and then silence.

O'Malley knew their last line of defense had been breached— just as he'd planned.

He braced for attack.

CHAPTER TEN

INTIMATE KNOWLEDGE OF the layout of the duke's home was to Patrick's advantage. He pressed himself against the wall in the darkness and waited for the footsteps to draw closer. There was a muffled sound of a scuffle on the back staircase. Only one set of footsteps continued. He paused to wait for the third step from the top to groan under the weight of a man. When he heard the faint squeak, he knew the intruder was smaller and lighter than his men.

Relief was short lived when the door opened. Eyes like a cat, O'Malley noted the outline of the stable lad he'd been expecting. He slipped out from where he'd been leaning against the wall and clapped a hand to the lad's mouth, dragging him back toward the staircase.

The lad struggled but was no match for O'Malley's strength. He'd been expecting the lad to fight dirty, but was surprised when the bloody bastard bit the palm of his hand. He sucked in a breath, increasing the hold he had on the young man. "Ye've made yer second mistake, Guy."

The lad stiffened and stopped struggling. "Ye'll be answerin' to His Grace while we wait for the constable to arrive."

"Patrick?"

He answered his cousin's raspy call. "Threat contained." When his captive started to struggle again, he shook him hard.

"Ye'll not want to try me patience. I've a need to pummel some sense into ye."

Garahan walked toward him with a lantern held high. "His Grace has been informed of the situation, but not—"

"O'Malley?"

"Bloody hell," he mumbled as he turned around to face the woman standing in the open door to the nursery. "What are ye doin' in the nursery?"

"My job," she huffed. "Who is that and why are there no sconces lit?"

"None of yer concern—" he growled, only to be interrupted by the nanny.

"These babes are my concern as is everything that happens in and around their nursery. I demand you tell me what is going on!"

Garahan finished lighting the sconces along both sides of the nursery door, shedding much-needed light on the situation. "He has the right of it, 'tisn't yer concern."

A TINY CRY had everyone falling silent. Gwendolyn placed her hands to her hips. "Now you've done it! You've woken Richard and Abigail!" Furious with the men and His Grace for not alerting her to the severity of the situation tonight, she spun around and closed the door behind her.

Soothing the babes was her priority. She picked Richard up and put him beside his sister, so she could rock the two of them together. Unused to being beside his sister, he fell silent and stared at her.

Pleased she would not have to summon help while she walked the floor with an unhappy infant, she brushed the tips of her fingers along the gentle curves of their cheeks and then the arches of their brows. Humming quietly, she let the lullaby her mother and grandmother had sung to her as a child lull them to sleep.

She straightened and bumped into someone standing directly

behind her. The scream strangled in her throat as she fought to swallow it. She did not want to wake the babes after they'd just settled back to sleep. With a prayer to her Maker and faith in her heart, she slowly turned around. "Your Grace?"

"Mrs. Alexander," he rasped. "I can see now why Persephone is dead set against having me send you packing." He eased around her and traced the shell of Richard's tiny ear with the tip of his finger, then did the same with Abigail. "They are accustomed to being cossetted, comforted…loved by me, my wife and our staff."

She nodded, not quite knowing what he expected her to say. Did he understand that she loved these babes already?

Motioning for her to follow him, he led her away from the cradles. "I am indebted to you, Mrs. Alexander. I had hoped the threat was not imminent. I was wrong."

"I gather Patrick handled the situation?"

He frowned but did not disagree.

"Was it part of his plan to let the intruder get this far so that he would be cocky and get caught?"

The duke stared at her. "An interesting point and one to take under consideration."

"Why else would Patrick and your guard allow anyone this close to your babes?"

"Why else indeed?" The duke inclined his head. "I shall send someone up with a tea tray."

Before she could do more than thank the man, he was gone. "Probably to intercept Her Grace. Poor woman, he should have confided in her—or at least warned me!"

Pulling her journal and pencil from the deep pocket of her apron, she sat in the smaller of the two mahogany rocking chairs, amazed at how perfectly it fit her short stature. Her feet touched the ground, instead of dangling over the edge of the seat as they had in a number of the other nurseries where she had been employed.

Comfortable, she made a few notations regarding the thwarted kidnapping attempt first and then how she calmed the twins by placing a fussing Richard in his sister's cradle alongside of her. She smiled remembering how quickly he calmed and made a notation that it was something of import to consider with twins. After all, they had shared a womb for months. It only made sense being close after they were born would soothe them. With a sigh, she closed the journal returning it to her apron.

"I'll need to arm myself—or at least leave some sort of weapon in the nursery that will not appear to be a weapon," she mused aloud.

Not wanting it to be too obvious, she finally settled on something that would surprise both the staff—and an intruder. Her reticule…she could fill it with rocks! "I'll have to add a special lining of coarse, strong material. It wouldn't do to have the seams split and the rocks go flying every which way."

She was more than ready for a spot of tea when the tray arrived along with Mollie and Her Grace.

"Gwendolyn! Are they all right? Are you?" she asked, rushing over to their cradles, surprised to note that they were sharing one. "No wonder they are so quiet. Why haven't I thought to put them together before?"

"I haven't had the care of twins before. It was something I hoped would be soothing to them before placing Richard in Abigail's cradle."

She picked up her son and brushed a tender kiss across his brow and settled him back in his cradle. Bending over Abigail's, she pressed her lips to her daughter's brow and sighed. "They act as if nothing disturbed them."

"I was here during the attempt, Your Grace, and can assure you it wasn't until I heard the sound of a scuffle and opened the door to see what was going on that I discovered what had nearly occurred."

"Then you did not know about the imminent attempt to steal our babes?"

"I wish we had been alerted. I would have been better prepared to defend them."

The high color on the duchess' cheekbones was an indication she was incensed. "I have informed *His Grace* I will not tolerate being kept in the dark about these heinous attempts!"

Mollie served the tea and then stood with her hands at her waist, tears glistening in her eyes. The duchess was still in high dudgeon and didn't notice at first, but Gwendolyn had. "What's wrong, Mollie?"

The maid sniffed back her tears and whispered, "I wanted to tell Your Grace...but I was sworn to secrecy."

"Why don't we sit down and have a restorative cup," Gwendolyn suggested. "I find it helps with digestion as well as having a calming effect."

The duchess inhaled one deep breath and then another. A glance at her maid had her asking, "Mollie, won't you join us?"

The maid hesitated, but the duchess would not be denied. "Why don't you have a few sips first...then tell me the whole of it—don't leave anything out."

The maid did as she was bid. While the women sipped the flavorful brew, the extent of Patrick O'Malley's brilliant plan unfolded. "He is a genius," the duchess proclaimed. "I would never have thought to spirit our babes up to your bedchamber, Mollie. Francis knows of this, too?"

"Aye, Your Grace. Patrick laid out his plans the moment the twins were born."

The duchess slowly smiled. "The lengths he has gone to, and continues to, in a bid to protect our family humbles me."

Gwendolyn had to agree. "I put the question to him earlier when I heard a commotion and opened the door only to find the hallway was dark and a scuffle taking place."

"What did you ask him?"

"If it was his intention to let the intruder get past the first two lines of defense in order to give him a false sense of security."

Persephone set her teacup on its saucer. "I had not thought of that. How would that have aided the intruder's attempt to steal our babes?"

"He would be cocky—and that would lead to his apprehension...not to the success of his illegal endeavors."

Mollie's eyes rounded listening to their conversation. "I never would have thought of that, Mrs. Alexander."

"Please, call me Gwendolyn."

Mollie nodded. "I heard from Garahan that you intend to arm yourself...do you think to carry a weapon?"

Gwendolyn slowly smiled. "No. I intend to have more than one on hand here in the nursery."

The duchess frowned. "I'll not have a pistol or knife near my children!"

She immediately sought to correct that assumption. "Not a pistol, nor a knife, Your Grace."

"What then?" she demanded, pushing to her feet.

Gwendolyn rose as well, but not to challenge the woman, to soothe her. Extending her hand to the duchess, she confided. "I plan to have a handful of sizeable rocks sewn into a special pouch."

"A pouch?" Mollie inquired before the duchess could speak.

"In my reticule. It would not seem unusual to have one on hand. If I happened to leave my apron with its pockets in my room, but had my reticule, I would have a place to store my journal and pencil that I keep with me at all times."

"To make notes of the babes' habits and care," Mollie added.

Gwendolyn was relieved when the duchess squeezed her hand before slipping her arm through hers. "A wonderful notion. I wish I had thought of it myself."

"New mothers have their hands full with a new babe—and you were blessed with two of them!"

Persephone smiled as she motioned for Gwendolyn to take her seat. Once she had, the duchess did the same. "That we have been," she confided. "I do believe your idea of rocks in a reticule is inspired. My sister-in-law, Phoebe, used something similar when she set out to rescue Baron Summerfield."

"Her husband?"

"She'd received a ransom note and was told to come alone. Along with the small bag of coins she hoped to distract the kidnappers with, she grabbed a brass paperweight."

"Did she intend to throw it?" Gwendolyn asked.

Persephone smiled. "Apparently, my darling husband told her it would add power to the uppercut and right cross he had been instructing her to use in order to defend herself."

"Good heavens! Did he feel there had been a need?"

"There was at the time."

Gwendolyn shook her head at the realization that hers was not the only life filled with darkness. "What happened to your sister-in-law?"

"She added the brass paperweight to her reticule. At the last minute, she decided to arm herself with another weapon—one she would have at the ready...a handful of ribbon-wrapped hatpins!"

"And here I thought I had a unique idea," Gwendolyn mused. "His Grace's sister sounds like a woman to be reckoned with."

"I'm so very proud of the woman Phoebe has become— especially after all she has been through."

Though the duchess did not speak of the horror that circulated the *ton*, Gwendolyn sensed there was more than a bit of truth to the rumors. "Then I have your blessing to leave two or three weapons here?"

"Absolutely. If I should be alone in the nursery, if and when someone else dares to sneak into our home, I shall feel confident I can hold them off with one of your rock-filled reticules."

"A woman alone must learn to take care of herself."

"How long have you been alone, if you do not mind my asking?"

Gwendolyn set down her teacup and folded her hands in her lap.

"You do not have to answer that question if you do not wish to," the duchess assured her.

"I was married to the love of my life for two years before they were taken from me eight years ago."

"They?"

Gwendolyn realized her blunder after the words were said. She steeled herself to answer without letting her emotions take hold of her. "I was seven months along when the Watch found my husband—murdered in the alley behind his bookshop."

Persephone sat forward in her chair. "Dear God! Did they capture the bastard?"

Gwendolyn did not flinch at the harsh word and answered, "No. They never did."

Tears filled the duchess' eyes as she asked, "And your babe?"

Gwendolyn felt her throat tighten, but she refused to give in to the tears that would follow. "He never took that first breath," she whispered. "The midwife tried everything she knew, but he was born too early."

Overwhelmed with the memory of the loss of her beloved and their son, she didn't realize the tears had started to fall until she felt herself wrapped in a cocoon of feminine warmth and solidarity—Mollie and the duchess had sandwiched Gwendolyn between them.

Encouraged not to hold back her tears, she wept until she felt weak from letting go of the horror and hatred she'd been harboring toward whoever had taken her husband's life—it had been a double murder. The shock of her husband's death had brought on her early labor...the murderer had taken the life of their babe as well.

"Mollie, be a dear and step outside and ask one of the footmen to come in."

She eased her hold on Gwendolyn and rushed to the door, but instead of a footman standing guard, it was Patrick.

He strode into the room and demanded, "What happened to Mrs. Alexander?" When the duchess did not answer quickly enough, he asked, "Where are ye hurt, Lass?"

The sound of his voice cut through her anguish long enough for her to stop crying and place a hand to her heart.

"I'll have the bloody bastard's guts for breakfast!"

Her eyes rounded in shock as she shook her head at him.

"WAS IT ONE of the men from the village?" he demanded. "Did he force himself on ye?"

Persephone was watching Patrick closely and did not miss the fire in his eyes or the flare of anguish entwined with the anger. She placed a hand to his arm, directing his attention to her.

"Beggin' yer pardon, Yer Grace, but I need to know who hurt Gwendolyn."

Her brow rose in silent question, but he ignored it, asking again, "Who hurt ye, Lass?"

The duchess took it upon herself to respond. "It was a long time ago, Patrick, we were encouraging Gwendolyn to let the hurt go. She's been holding on to it for too long."

He straightened and took a step back from the woman who had yet to look away from him. "Yer pardon, Mrs. Alexander. Mollie, what were ye after when ye opened the door?"

The maid glanced at the duchess, waiting for her nod before answering, "I was going to ask one of the footmen to send up a bottle of brandy."

When Gwendolyn shuddered, Persephone smiled. "Mayhap a bottle of Irish whiskey instead?"

At the other woman's nod, the duchess asked Patrick, "Would you mind sending for it and then letting us know when it arrives?"

"I'll send one of the lads for it now." With one last glance at Gwendolyn, he asked, "Are ye certain sure, it wasn't anythin' one of the men from the village did?"

"I'm sure," she rasped. "Thank you for asking."

"Ye'd let me know?"

In a voice just above a whisper, she answered, "Yes."

"I'll have yer word before I go."

Persephone's sigh was audible. "Best answer the man. O'Malley is as stubborn as a goat."

His rusty chuckle echoed in the room. Finally, Gwendolyn gave her word. "I promise."

"I'll send for the whiskey."

Mollie closed the door behind O'Malley, but the duchess didn't notice, she was staring at her nanny. "I think I know the reason why Jared has been so angry."

Startled, Gwendolyn asked, "You do?"

"I have never seen Patrick focused on anything but his duties. I highly doubt he has shirked in any one of the many duties my husband has assigned to him. Mayhap the fact he is not totally focused on our protection every moment of every day will have been noted by my husband. With the lives of our children in the balance, it would be unacceptable to him."

"Why are you not beside yourself with worry and anguish by what nearly occurred?"

Persephone was quick to respond. "I have complete faith in Patrick and his guard to protect our babes. He has put himself in harm's way—with or without a weapon—more times than I can count."

"I…er…heard it whispered he has earned a moniker." Gwendolyn's eyes met the duchess'. "Is it true he nearly cleaved a man in two with one slash of his broadsword? Does he still carry a broadsword?"

The duchess shook her head. "All of my husband's men have been known to wield a sword, but Patrick's favorite blade is his dagger."

"Tales of derring-do have a way of becoming embellished," she noted. "But Patrick's courage and skill with whatever weapon is at hand is not one of them. He has never failed in his promise to protect us with his life—his brothers and cousins have sworn the same oath and are equally skilled with all manner of weapons."

Gwendolyn seemed to be considering Persephone's words. She asked, "Do you believe he has not performed his duties as he vowed?"

"I am quite sure he has not failed in that regard," the duchess was quick to respond. "The man is a workhorse and demands perfection from his men—even though they be brothers and cousins, he would not allow anything to interfere with his duties."

"Then what reason could the duke have for this change of heart where Patrick is concerned?"

"His trust in him has been shaken," Persephone told Gwendolyn. "My husband is a man of conviction. Once his mind is made up, it would take a miracle to change it."

"I see."

"Moreover, I am not sure the trust Jared feels has been broken can be rebuilt."

"This is all my fault," Gwendolyn rasped.

"How could you possibly take responsibility for any of this?"

"Everything changed when I arrived, did it not?"

Persephone agreed. "That doesn't mean—"

"If I've somehow distracted the man, it is my fault. Although I did not knowingly distract him. I would never do that. I haven't even looked at another man since my darling Jonathan."

Persephone slowly smiled. "You've looked at our Patrick."

Gwendolyn hung her head. "It happened so fast…when I was stepping down from His Grace's carriage."

"While we wait for our beverage, why don't I tell you how Jared and I first met? It was the night of the Hollisters' ball. I was wearing a divine gown in a bilious shade of yellow—"

"Bilious yellow?"

"Actually," the duchess remarked, "more of a putrid shade of yellow-green."

"I am quite sure you looked lovely," Gwendolyn stated.

The duchess smiled. "My very good friend remarked that it looked like the contents of a cow's stomach."

"How on earth would she know? Was she the daughter of a farmer?"

Persephone shook her head as her laugh filled the room, easing a bit more of the tension, allowing Gwendolyn to listen in rapt silence as the duchess regaled her with the tale of falling in love with the Duke of Wyndmere at first glance—albeit hers had been a bit skewed given the fact she was wearing someone else's spectacles. The three women were smiling when O'Malley returned, crystal decanter and a tray of glasses in hand.

"I see ye've stopped caterwauling."

"I beg your pardon?" Gwendolyn asked.

The duchess snorted with laughter. "As you can plainly see, O'Malley. Thank you. You'd best return to your post before my husband returns and starts firing ridiculous questions at you."

He inclined his head, and sent one last heated glance Gwendolyn's way, before closing the door behind him.

"Such a handsome man," the duchess said as she poured a splash of whiskey into a short glass and handed it to her nanny. "Don't you agree, Gwendolyn?"

When she didn't answer, Persephone urged, "Drink up. It'll clear your head. You'll need one if we are to put our plans into place."

"Plans?" Gwendolyn and Mollie asked at the same time.

"We have to get that stubborn husband of mine to rescind his removal of Patrick as the head of his guard...and then we have to get Patrick to admit how he feels about you."

Gwendolyn shook her head. "I have never let anything distract me from my duties to my charges. I do not intend to let that happen now."

"I admire your conviction, Gwendolyn, but must say it already has happened. He's captured your interest. Has he captured your heart yet?"

Gwendolyn tossed back her glass of whiskey and set it on the table. "I do believe Richard and Abigail's nappies are in need of changing."

Persephone acquiesced but was not deterred or distracted from her new goal. She would keep at Patrick and Gwendolyn until they admitted they'd fallen head over heels for one another.

She sighed. Love at first sight had changed her life for the better. How could she not help one of the men who had come to be like a brother to her and the woman who'd opened her heart to her babes so quickly and completely?

The duchess would not be swayed. She intended to see Patrick and Gwendolyn wed before the daffodils bloomed.

CHAPTER ELEVEN

P ATRICK CONTINUED TO pace outside the nursery long after
Mollie and the duchess had retired to their rooms. He'd
never questioned his decisions before the duke relieved him of his
position. Had he made the right decision allowing the stable lad
to enter the house? His confidence in himself and his abilities
churned in his gut, but reason quickly returned and, with it, the
knowledge that he would make the same decision in a heartbeat.

"Ye're going to wear a hole in the blasted carpet," Flaherty
grumbled as he paused to speak to his cousin.

O'Malley glanced down and noted the rug was a bit flattened
in a definite line that ranged from one side of the nursery door to
the other. "It's part of me job to keep a weather eye on both ends
of the hallway." His eyes narrowed as he stared at his cousin. "No
one is going to get past me."

"We all know that for a fact. 'Tis His Grace that needs con-
vincing."

"I've already told ye, 'tis done. There is no goin' back."

Flaherty looked as if he were about to say something. Instead,
he shook his head. "Ma was right. No one has a harder head than
an O'Malley."

Patrick glared at his cousin though, in truth, he wanted to
laugh. "Sure and she'd be right now."

"Ma's always right—at least that's what she's been telling Da all these years."

"Anything to report?"

"All's quiet," Flaherty replied. "I'll be sending Garahan to patrol the front of the house while I take his position at the back."

"From the inside," O'Malley reminded him.

"We're not daft or hard of hearing," Flaherty mumbled as he shoved Patrick with his shoulder to move him out of his way.

O'Malley scrubbed a hand over his face. "I'll not be easin' up on anyone until King's reinforcements arrive."

"When will they be arriving?"

"I overheard His Grace alerting Humphries that they could be arrivin' as early as midday."

"Why didn't he speak to ye himself?" Flaherty demanded. "'Tis a woman's trick to ignore someone…not a man's. How do ye put up with this *shite*?"

O'Malley shook his head. "'Tisn't me place to question His Grace. It never was, though I have a time or two in the past."

"What about now? Shouldn't ye be questioning why he's not keeping ye in the know?"

"Nay." When Flaherty opened his mouth, O'Malley ordered, "Let it be, Rory."

His cousin mumbled about thick-headed Irishmen and blind-eyed Englishmen as he walked away.

Patrick continued down the length of the hallway, silent as ever. It wouldn't do to wake either the duke or the duchess at this late hour. He'd be leaving that to their—his thoughts were interrupted by the insistent cry from the nursery.

He retraced his steps and opened the door to find Abigail in Gwendolyn's arms. "What are ye doin' in here?" he demanded.

She shushed him as she jiggled the babe while she whispered nonsense words to the little one. When the babe settled down, she turned to glare at him. "My job."

"Even I know it's not yer job to be feedin'—"

"*Mr.* O'Malley, do not finish that statement!" she huffed as her face flamed a bright red. "How could you even think to mention such an intimate topic to me?"

He scratched his head. "I'd have to be blind not to know how a mother feeds her babes. I've six younger siblings of me own."

"I refuse to continue this conversation," she hissed.

The door to the nursery swung open behind them. The duchess paused on the threshold before shaking her head at the two of them. "If I take my daughter, do you intend to clobber the man?"

Gwendolyn's shocked gasp woke Richard. She handed Abigail off to the duchess and rounded on O'Malley. "Now see what you've done!" Aggravated in the extreme, she mumbled to herself as she scooped the babe out of his cradle and proceeded to jiggle and repeat the same nonsense words she'd been soothing his sister with.

"Thank you, Patrick," the duchess said as she settled into one of the rocking chairs. "I am quite sure you and Mrs. Alexander can continue your discussion after breakfast if you two are of a mind to."

Summarily dismissed—although without the dressing down Gwendolyn felt the man deserved, she watched him incline his head to the duchess before he turned to glare at her as he shut the door.

Following a circuitous path from the cradles, around the rocking chairs, and over to the window, she finally calmed Richard while Persephone was burping his sister. "Thank goodness Jared did not wake up. I'd hate to think what he might have said. He does not do well on little or no sleep."

"I'm sorry to have upset you, Persephone, but that man…" she fell silent, mortified at their conversation and O'Malley's reaction to something she was too embarrassed to think about.

"Why don't we switch?"

Complying, she placed her hand to the little one's back and began to rub in circles from the base of her spine to between her shoulders. She'd discovered years before that the motion soothed the little ones while at the same time encouraged them to release any bubbles.

"Oh my," the duchess laughed softly. "That was a big one, wasn't it?"

Gwendolyn smiled. "I'm surprised you are able to sleep. I beg your pardon, I did not mean to speak of it."

Persephone shrugged as she shifted Richard to her shoulder and rubbed his back. "It cannot be ignored. It's best to talk about it. Until we know for certain that the threat has been contained once and for all, we need to be on guard."

"Did you get any sleep at all?" Gwendolyn asked.

The duchess smiled. "I managed a few hours. Did you?"

Gwendolyn was settling the babe in her cradle before answering. "A bit."

"We'll have to ensure that you have a few hours in a row, else you won't be able to take care of our darlings." Placing her son in his cradle, she sighed. "They should sleep now for a few hours. Why don't you get some rest?"

"I'm not tired," Gwendolyn replied. "I have a few notations to make. I'll sit with them."

"Patrick is right outside," the duchess reminded her. "Are you certain it won't bother you to have him in such close proximity?"

Gwendolyn frowned. "I'm sorry if I've added to your worry."

"Not at all. With him guarding the nursery and you inside ready to soothe our babes, I have nothing to worry about." She paused with her hand on the doorknob. "I'll ask Humphries to have one of the fainting couches brought up later in the morning. That way, I know you'll be able to rest while the babes are sleeping."

"Thank you, Persephone."

"You are most welcome. Goodnight."

The quiet of the nursery wrapped itself around Gwendolyn, contenting her. She may never have babes of her own, but there had been many that had been entrusted to her care over the years. It would never have been her first choice, but it was a decision she had made long ago. Out of the ashes of her despair, a faint ray of hope and light led her to where she was today…at Wyndmere Hall taking care of the duke's and duchess' darling twins.

She sighed as she rocked, humming to herself. Her journal slipped from her lap though it did not wake her.

THE DOOR OPENED swiftly as O'Malley entered the chamber. He glanced from side to side, ensuring nothing was amiss. He steeled himself, anticipating his body's reaction to the woman who'd taken hold of his mind and his heart. The leather-bound book at her feet must have been the sound he'd heard as he walked past the door.

He picked it up and placed it on the table between the rocking chairs. Unable to stop himself, he traced the tip of his finger along the curve of her cheek, the line of her jaw. She sighed in her sleep.

"Ah, Gwendolyn," he whispered, pressing a kiss to her brow. "What have ye done to me, Lass?"

Not expecting a reply, he walked over to check on the twins. Satisfied they were asleep, he paused once more by her side, picked up the shawl from the back of the other rocker and draped it over her.

"Sleep well, Lass."

Gwendolyn stirred but did not wake as the door quietly closed.

CHAPTER TWELVE

"W HEN DO YE plan on sleeping then?" Garahan barked.

Patrick shrugged. "Ye'll have to be askin' Eamon as he is the one who's reportin' to the duke."

"The man's hired on enough extra hands from the village. Not one of us should be denied a few paltry hours of sleep," Flaherty added.

Patrick didn't look up from where he sat, sharpening the blade he kept in his boot. Finally satisfied, he slid it back into the sheath in his boot. He stood and scanned the room. "Have ye checked yer powder, then?"

His cousins frowned at him.

"We've not been dropped on our heads since the last time ye asked," Flaherty reminded him.

"Why don't ye ask if we remember how to fire the blasted rifles?" Garahan demanded.

Eamon opened the door to their quarters and sighed. "Ye're arguing again? About what?"

Patrick shook his head. "Nothin' and everythin'. I'm off to speak with Humphries."

"Does the duke know the man confides in ye still?" Eamon asked.

Patrick shrugged. "Wouldn't matter if he did, would it? His Grace has yet to seek me out to speak to me."

"He's wrong," Flaherty grumbled.

"And well he knows it," Garahan added.

"What in the bloody hell can we do about it?" Eamon demanded. "Something's got to be done. Me temper cannot take answering directly to the man who hands out orders as if he's God Himself."

Patrick paused in the doorway. "Ye know he's fightin' against the fear that has the man by the throat. Listen to him, respect him."

"Don't ye deserve respect in return?" Garahan rasped.

Patrick shrugged. "I'll let ye know when King's men arrive…unless Eamon finds out before I do."

The men did not say a word until their cousin closed the door behind him.

FLAHERTY SHOT TO his feet. "How can we just stand by and watch him shoulder the blame for something out of his control?"

Garahan watched him pace back and forth a few times before answering. "'Tis what he expects us to do. How can we not oblige him when he is the reason each one of us has been working at a job more suited to our skills than anything we've done since leaving Ireland?"

Eamon raked a hand through his hair until it stood on end. "What in the bloody hell am I supposed to do?"

Flaherty shook his head, while Garahan stared at his cousins for long moments before answering. "Ye'll continue to report to the duke until we either see the whites of Finn's eyes or receive word he isn't coming."

"Do ye think he'd refuse?" Flaherty wanted to know.

Eamon's sharp bark of laughter had his cousins glaring at him. "I would have if I'd known what the blasted job entails."

Garahan's stomach growled. He rubbed a hand over it before asking, "Have ye eaten yet, Eamon?"

"Nay. Constance bid me to tell ye lads she's keeping breakfast warm for us."

"With the duke's new orders, when are we supposed to eat, let alone sleep?" Flaherty's anger was a palpable thing.

"Patrick wouldn't want us arguing or speaking ill of the duke," Eamon reminded them. "We'll eat in shifts as we normally do. If the duke has a complaint, he'll bring it to me first. I'd be only too happy to tell him what's on me mind as he's been asking me to."

"That's fine then," Garahan's stomach growled louder this time.

Flaherty grinned. "Ye'd best let Darby take the first shift eating."

The men gathered their weapons and filed out of their quarters. Garahan headed to the kitchen. Flaherty continued to his station on the roof, while Eamon went in search of the duke to give his overnight report.

⋙⋘

"I'VE NEVER SEEN anything like the way those babes react to Mrs. Alexander," Mollie told Constance as they had a quick cup of tea before continuing with their duties.

"They certainly did not take to Mrs. Abbott," Constance remarked. "Her Grace discovered that the woman's first—and only day, on the job. The babes screamed from the time the woman came into the nursery to change the little ones until she left."

"They knew that woman had a sour disposition," Mollie agreed.

"At least she was not as bad as the second nanny they hired."

Mollie set her cup on the table and sighed. "Her Grace was loath to leave the twins alone even though she and His Grace seemed pleased with their choice."

"Thank the Lord Her Grace has an excellent sense of smell." Constance got up to stir the simmering pot.

"Speaking of smell," Mollie said as she shuddered. "It is hard to believe something that smells awful has such restorative powers."

Constance laughed. "Calf's foot jelly may not smell appetizing, but it'll set you to rights."

Mollie smiled at the older woman. "How awful for Their Graces that their second and third choice of nannies hid such nasty habits from them. Their references were excellent."

"Probably paid someone to forge them," Constance remarked. "Mrs. Terrance had the bottle of blue ruin stashed beneath her pillow, and Mrs. Packard had an entire case of laudanum!"

"The duke was right to send for the constable with those two, leveling charges against them."

"Back to Mrs. Alexander," Constance began, "she's got a big heart. How sad that her husband was murdered, and she lost the babe she carried."

"Her Grace is convinced she and Patrick belong together," Mollie confided.

"Is she?" The cook moved the pot to the back of the cook stove and wiped her hands on her apron. Going to the sideboard, she selected the largest of her bowls and proceeded to measure out flour.

"Can I help with the breadmaking?"

Constance nodded to the sideboard. "I've bread rising already and am making a large batch of cream scones."

"Oh, are we expecting company? I can't imagine why Merry didn't mention it. I'll have to make up the beds in the guest chambers."

"Not company exactly," Constance advised. "I overheard Humphries speaking with His Grace earlier. Apparently, Mr. King is sending four of his trusted men to add to His Grace's guard."

"Will they be staying with the guard in their quarters or on the third floor in the servants' quarters?"

"Merry hasn't said a word, so I wonder if she hasn't heard."

"Heard what?" the housekeeper asked, walking into the kitchen.

Mollie and Constance stared at Merry, until she said, "Out with it!"

Constance told her what she'd heard and Merry sighed. "It isn't like the duke and duchess not to confide in us. When are the men supposed to arrive?"

"Sometime this afternoon. I will have plenty of fresh scones on hand for when they arrive. Mollie was going to ask whether or not to set out fresh linens."

"Are we having unexpected guests?" the duchess asked, entering the kitchen.

"Your Grace!" Constance wrung her hands. "Forgive me for speaking out of turn, but you see—"

"She overheard Humphries," Mollie interrupted.

"I am going to ring a peal over that man's head!" The duchess whirled around, but before she took two steps, Mollie was in front of her. "Please don't, Your Grace. It isn't Humphries' fault."

The duchess' eyes narrowed. "I was referring to my husband."

Mollie's eyes widened. "His Grace?"

"Aren't you afraid he'll become angry?" the maid asked.

"Oh, I am counting on it." The duchess marched off in search of her duke.

"Do you think there will be any backlash?" Mollie asked, still standing in the hallway.

"No telling what His Grace will say or do. He's been unpredictable ever since he received word of the threat to those darling babes," Merry replied.

"We shall all do our part and be ready for anything," Constance agreed. "Once I finish with the scones, I'll start on the meat pies for the men."

"Why don't you start upstairs in the spare rooms in the servants' quarters as well as the guest chambers, Mollie?" Merry suggested. "I'll send one of the footmen out to the guards' quarters with the extra linens."

Mollie hurried off to do Merry's bidding.

Merry sighed. "Things will smooth out here again, Constance. Just as soon as the duke has taken care of this horrible threat."

"You're right, of course. It's the waiting and worrying that has everyone on edge."

"Well, between the two of us, we shall see that Humphries confides what he knows. That way we can keep a level head and see that our staff does as well."

Constance fixed a fresh pot of tea and set it to steep on the table. "Your tea will be ready and waiting for you."

"Thank you. I'll be back in a trice."

CHAPTER THIRTEEN

"HUMPHRIES, YE KNOW I'd lay down me life for His Grace and his family," Patrick stated.

"That's why I've decided to confide in you."

"And no other missives from King or Coventry have arrived since the message that King is sending Thompson, Franklin, Greeves, and Jackson to add to the duke's protection?"

"No missives, however, there is a rumor from the village that was just reported to me."

"By a trusted source?"

"I cannot vouch for the source," Humphries replied, lowering his voice. "Can we ignore even the slightest chance that a rumor could be, in fact, close to the truth?"

O'Malley agreed. "I wouldn't take that chance with His Grace and his family. What have ye heard? Are the men arrivin' by mail coach or on horseback?"

The butler related what he knew. "Two men will be arriving by mail coach, one in a private coach, and one on horseback."

"King's idea no doubt. It'll keep anyone from suspectin' that reinforcements are arrivin' from London." His gut ached as another knot of tension pulled taut. "Ye're a good man, Humphries. I'm relieved ye haven't lost faith in me."

"On the contrary, O'Malley. Given all that has occurred, I have even more faith in you." The older retainer shook his head and sighed. "You'll have to excuse His Grace. He's had to shoulder the responsibilities and financial situation thrust upon him while grieving over the loss of his father and brother and hasn't had a moment to collect himself."

"He's proven himself to be a man others can look up to and trust," O'Malley acknowledged. "I'm afraid his lettin' his need to pull back the ranks and dig in to keep his family safe are what's keepin' him from seein' the full extent of the threat or threats coming from more than one source."

Humphries shifted his stance from confiding in O'Malley to full attention. "Your Grace, is something wrong?"

"Yes, as a matter of fact there is, Humphries." The duchess smiled at Patrick before continuing. "I must speak with His Grace immediately. Do you know where he is?"

"His Grace was in his downstairs study not a quarter of an hour ago."

"Thank you."

The men watched her rush off. O'Malley was the first to speak. "She's vexed."

"Quite," the butler agreed. "I believe she may have been to the kitchen and discovered we are about to add to the household protection."

"The kitchen? Did you confide in Constance?"

Humphries' shoulders slumped. "Not yet, but the walls have ears. I intended to speak with Merry and Constance after I'd apprised you of the change in the situation. They need to know to be prepared."

O'Malley's look was grim. "They were invaluable when they stood beside ye and the rest of the staff when Hollingford and his men attacked."

Humphries' face looked bleak. "The night lightning struck the tree by the stables."

"Ye're to be credited for ensuring every member of the staff was on hand to band together to protect the duke and his family. More than one of the staff and me men were injured."

"Your brother, Finn," Humphries remembered. "He had us worried for a time with the blow to his head."

Patrick agreed. "Aye, but Mollie sat by his side until he regained consciousness and got him through the worst of the wound fever."

Humphries sighed. "It was a black night."

O'Malley added, "Merry and ye have made certain the staff rises to the occasion and the ever-changin' needs."

"Thank you. We do our best."

"And yer best includes keepin' me abreast of rumors and news. Me cousins are all fine fighting men, with their fists as well as skilled with rifle, pistol, sword, or blade. As the oldest, they've looked to me for years. Eamon isn't as yet accustomed to the job His Grace has thrust upon him...moreover, he is not certain he wants the job."

Humphries frowned. "But he'll do it just the same?"

"Aye," O'Malley was quick to agree. "Eamon'll do the job."

"Without complaint?" Humphries asked.

O'Malley grinned. "Well now, I didn't say that, now did I?" He opened the front door, intent on relieving his cousin on the roof.

The crack of a rifle shot echoed in the cold, clear air. "Alert His Grace and the men inside!"

O'Malley pulled the door closed behind him and ran around the front of the house to the door to the roof. Taking the steps two at a time, he paused, opened the door, and looked out. Flaherty lifted his Kentucky long rifle, took aim, and fired.

"Rory!"

His cousin looked over his shoulder, then reloaded. His motions were smooth as he poured in the measure of powder, placed the bit of fabric over the end of the barrel and then the lead ball. O'Malley waited while his cousin shoved the ramrod into the long barrel. Rory added a bit of powder to the pan and lifted the rifle, used the sight, took aim, and fired again.

"How many?"

"Five."

O'Malley repeated the same steps as his cousin, loading his long rifle. "Where are they?" He waited for Flaherty to point them out before picking the first intruder to fire at.

"Have ye hit yer target?"

Rory snorted. "I never miss, ye know that."

Patrick paused before firing. "Ye're shootin' to wound—not kill."

"Aye, His Grace needs to know who in the bloody hell is behind this latest attack on his family."

O'Malley found his target and fired. Satisfaction filled him as he heard the man scream. "He won't be holding a rifle again anytime soon."

"One left, ye want him?" Flaherty asked.

O'Malley grunted and his cousin put the butt end of his rifle on the rooftop and watched him load, take aim, and fire. Smooth movements, no sign of emotion until the job was done.

"By now, Humphries will have alerted the men and the staff. I was on me way to relieve ye, but I'll ask ye to stay and keep an eye out for stragglers stationed where ye couldn't see them."

Flaherty inclined his head. They reloaded and took positions on opposite ends of the roof facing the woods just beyond where the open land surrounded the front of Wyndmere Hall. They'd be ready if there were any others hiding in or behind the trees.

The sound of carriage wheels and horses announced the arrival of reinforcements, while the crack of a rifle firing and answering report from atop the carriage reassured them King's men were already on the job.

"Who's yer man riding on top of the carriage?" Flaherty wanted to know.

"Could be any one of King's men. They are all proficient with a pistol or rifle. Though Thompson is the one handy with a blade."

"Ah, that's all right then. Good to a group of well-rounded men at yer back," Flaherty commented. "I wonder now, if they'd be up for a bit of practice—man to man."

O'Malley shook his head. "'Tis how I ended up in this situation. No bare knuckle fighting unless His Grace agrees." He raised his hand in the air and the man atop the coach nodded. "I wonder when the others will be arriving."

As if on cue, a man on horseback came into view, cantering up the drive in front of a smaller carriage. "Why don't ye go down an introduce yerself? Eamon will fill the men in on what they need to know."

"And if they be wanting to speak to ye?"

"I'll be here manning me post as instructed."

O'Malley watched his cousin slip his rifle over his shoulder and walk away. It was only right that Eamon assume the responsibility the duke tasked him with. "I'm not the only man who can organize and plan," he scoffed. "Faith, though I'm the only one of us willin' to do the job."

He was more than ready for news a few hours later when Garahan joined him on the rooftop to take over his position. His cousin filled him in on how quickly the attackers had spilled their guts. "Hired through a connection they had on the docks," his cousin remarked. "No name, just a description. King'll get to the bottom of it."

"'Tis what he does best," O'Malley agreed.

"Do ye think there'll be another attempt?" Garahan wanted to know.

O'Malley sighed. "Aye. Until King or Coventry uncovers who is behind the threats."

Garahan swept the perimeter before turning toward his cousin. "Ye had the right of it, patrolling the rooftop earlier in the day—'tis warmer."

O'Malley agreed. "But that only means I'll be back at midnight."

"That's not what I've heard," his cousin remarked.

O'Malley paused with his hand on the door. When his cousin hesitated, he sighed, accepting the fact the duke had finally made his decision to dismiss him. "I'd best be packin' me bag, then."

"Wait!" Garahan grabbed hold of his cousin's arm. "'Tisn't that at all. Her Grace is demanding that she'll have ye as the overnight guard stationed outside the nursery and no other."

O'Malley had no idea why, so he asked, "What else did she say?"

"Plenty. Ye could hear her voice raised in anger toward him."

"The duke?"

"Oh, aye. She's got a fierce temper when it concerns her babes."

"What did the duke have to say to her request?"

"Wasn't a request, 'twas a demand."

"That won't sit well with His Grace," O'Malley predicted.

Garahan chuckled. "Nay, it did not. But the staff are all in favor of it."

"Well then, I'd best see if I can beg Constance for a bite to eat."

"She's keeping a plate warm for ye—meat pies with crust so flaky, it'll melt in yer mouth."

O'Malley's stomach rumbled in reply. "I'd best collect me dinner before one of King's men sweet talks Constance into giving it to them."

"The kitchen was a bit crowded," Garahan warned. "His Grace was in his element handing out orders."

"I thought he was leaving that to Eamon."

"It appears Eamon has refused to continue in yer position as head of the guard."

Patrick's blood chilled in his veins. "The duke did not dismiss him—did he?"

"Nay, Her Grace wouldn't let him."

"I'll have to thank Her Grace meself—for requestin' me as guard to the nursery and for not lettin' His Grace sack Eamon."

"I'm thinking Eamon won't be thanking her anytime soon. He was looking forward to striking out on his own, looking for work at one of the nearby estates."

"Shoveling *shite*, no doubt," O'Malley quipped, leaving his cousin with a smile on his face and a promise to make sure his relief brought a few scones...Garahan was mad for scones.

CHAPTER FOURTEEN

G WENDOLYN LISTENED AS Francis related word-for-word the *contretemps* between the duke and the duchess as she changed the twins and settled them down for the night.

"Has Her Grace always spoken her mind?"

Francis smiled. "Yes, though she was more hesitant to do so when she first married His Grace."

Gwendolyn marveled that the duchess was a force to be reckoned with. She'd worked for more than one titled family and had witnessed more than one argument that had ended with hurt feelings, yet another that ended with an ultimatum. "She's not afraid to confront the duke, is she?"

"Her Grace has a big heart. She loves His Grace—we've heard her tell him so quite often."

Gwendolyn sensed there was more the maid wanted to say. She prompted, "But?"

Francis sighed. "We've also heard her tell His Grace he's a horse's…er…behind."

Gwendolyn pulled her journal and pencil from her apron pocket, but before she could jot down her morning observations, Francis stopped her. "Please do not write down anything I've told you about the duke and duchess!"

Gwendolyn blinked. "Of course not. I would never break my promise not to repeat anything you've told me."

The maid had a hand to her breast as the color returned to her face. "Thank you. What are you writing? If you don't mind me asking."

"I've been keeping track of how long the babes are sleeping in between feedings. Her Grace has been able to sleep a bit longer each night, as their little bellies are able to handle more milk."

"You take your job seriously."

Gwendolyn smiled at the maid as she sat down to make her notations. "Without question. It's my life's calling."

Francis remarked, "It's a bit of a scientific study."

Gwendolyn laughed softly. "I suppose you could put it that way. I prefer to think of it as being more of a steward, if you will, keeping track of everything and anything pertaining to my precious charges."

"They are precious," the duchess stated from where she stood in the doorway.

Gwendolyn stood and walked over to Her Grace with her journal open. Pointing to the new entry, she confided, "If this trend in their feedings and sleeping continues, I predict you shall be enjoying a full night's sleep very soon."

The duchess surprised Gwendolyn by wrapping her arms around her and dancing about the room.

"I had no idea there was to be a celebration this evening."

The two stopped dancing. The duchess flew across the room into the duke's arms. "Gwendolyn has given me such wonderful news, Jared!"

His smile softened the stern set of his jaw and slowly reached his brilliant blue eyes. "Indeed." Shifting his wife so she stood anchored to his side, he commented, "I gather this has to do with Richard and Abigail?"

"Do share the good news, Gwendolyn," the duchess urged.

A bit unsure of doing so, as she'd only ever shared her journal notations with her charges' mothers, she hesitated.

The smile left the duke's face. "Is there something wrong?"

Gwendolyn immediately rushed to assure him, "No, not at

all, Your Grace. I merely hesitated to share my observations because this is the first time one of the fathers has asked to hear them."

The tension left his face as he nodded. "Duly noted. Please continue."

As Gwendolyn shared what she'd recorded and her reasoning behind it, the duke's entire demeanor shifted from on guard to relaxed and at ease. "I daresay a full night's sleep is cause for celebration—once it occurs."

The duchess scoffed. "Leave it to you to put a damper on things, Jared."

The duke surprised everyone by hugging the duchess close and pressing a kiss to the top of her head. "It was not my intention, my darling. I fully intend to celebrate—privately, when the time comes."

With that, he nodded to the women and strode from the nursery.

The duchess stared at the open doorway, not speaking. Finally, she dragged in a breath and placed a hand to her hair as if to push any errant pins back into place. "That man drives me to distraction."

Francis sighed. "His Grace is a man of many moods."

Gwendolyn's heart ached, witnessing the love between the duke and his duchess. Though she'd lost her family, it was wrong to hold on to it all these years. It was past time she accepted those responsible for her husband's murder would never be brought to justice.

It was time to let it go.

"I never realized how many until we were wed," the duchess admitted. Sighing, she confided, "Truth be told, I even love his difficult moods."

Her words arrowed through Gwendolyn, hitting their mark. She had felt the same about her Jonathan. Now was not the time to dig up those feelings she'd buried. "You must be the envy of all of your friends."

Persephone smiled. "I doubt that, as my closest friends are as happily married as I am."

"To difficult men?" The question popped out before Gwendolyn could stop it. "I beg your pardon, it is not my place to ask such intimate questions."

The duchess' eyes were as round as saucers as her mouth closed. "Yes!" she gasped, as if catching her breath. "They married men just as difficult as my darling, Jared."

Waving a hand in front of her face, she plopped down onto the fainting couch. "I could do with something sweet." Turning to Francis, she asked, "Would you mind asking Constance to have a tray sent up?"

"Right away, Your Grace. Do you have a preference?"

The duchess shook her head. "Not really, just something sweet to go with a cup of tea. I'm not ready to retire and the tea will help me stay awake until our darlings wake for their next feeding."

"It is wise to keep up your strength," Gwendolyn advised as she returned to her seat and her journal. "It shouldn't be a surprise that a mother of twins requires more rest and sustenance in order to care for her babes." Her hand flew over the pages as she recorded yet another interesting fact.

"You are so wonderful with Richard and Abigail," the duchess remarked. "Have you ever given a thought to marrying again? Having children of your own to care for?"

That last question sliced through Gwendolyn's middle. She placed a hand to the icy cold spot, surprised there was no visible wound, no blood flowing from it. *Words could leave a deeper cut…one that would never heal.*

Needing to answer her employer, she acknowledged aloud what she'd vowed silently, "I'll never marry again."

The duchess rose from her seat and crossed to where Gwendolyn sat, journal clutched in one hand, her other pressing against her belly. "Forgive me, Gwendolyn. I did not mean to cause you pain."

She shook her head, but her throat was still too taut to speak. "Please?" The duchess held out her hand.

Gwendolyn stared at it for long moments until her brain began to work again. She set the journal down on the table between the rocking chairs and clasped the duchess' outstretched hand. The strength and warmth surprised her. She glanced down at their joined hands and felt her throat loosen enough to respond, "There is nothing to forgive, Persephone."

With a brief tug, she was in the duchess' arms. "It is all right to cry."

She shook her head and eased back. "Not when I am on duty."

"I have never been one to bow to the restrictions of the *ton*," the duchess advised. "With regard to our nanny or out and about in society."

Francis returned with a footman in tow, hefting the tray containing the tea service and requested dessert.

The duchess directed the footman to place the tray on the mahogany side table and thanked him. After he left, she asked Francis to join them and to pour.

Gwendolyn felt drained, but that was her reaction whenever the past returned to torment her. The duchess' innocent question had been the catalyst this time. What would be the trigger the next time? Because as sure as the sun rises every morning, someone would ask the question that would threaten to tear her heart apart.

She went through the motions, accepting the proffered tea, declining a frosted teacake or scone. Sweets at night would keep her awake for hours when she should be sleeping.

Francis was called away with the promise to return at her appointed time to watch over the babes.

"You are far too quiet," Persephone stated. "I promise not to ask you again but cannot help but think you are throwing your chance at happiness away because of the trauma from your past."

Gwendolyn's breath snagged in her lungs and, for a moment,

she feared she would not be able to let it out or draw air back in, until the need for air had her doing just that. Hands trembling, she set her teacup and saucer aside. "Forgive me if I do not share your belief. I have yet to meet anyone who has suffered as I have."

Persephone frowned, then squared her shoulders. "I'd like to share a bit of my past with you, if you do not mind."

Gwendolyn nodded.

The duchess told a tale of friendship, a bond between a young maid and her new mistress, and the dark and tragic ending.

Gwendolyn felt the sadness the duchess still carried. "You blame yourself?"

When Persephone inclined her head, she rushed to reassure her. "It was not your fault. You could not have known what would happen to your maid that day."

"I feel responsible." She paused, then inquired, "Have you heard the rumors of what occurred at the first ball we hosted as the new Duke and Duchess of Wyndmere? It was also to launch Jared's sister, Phoebe, who had missed her debut a few months earlier."

"Er…yes, I was in London at the time, but did not truly believe what I'd heard."

"A madman held a knife to dear Phoebe's throat while he proclaimed that Jared had been murdered."

Gwendolyn reacted to Persephone's words and the anguish behind them. "I thought it a Banbury tale."

The duchess clasped her hands in her lap. "I will never forget that night, nor the courage Phoebe showed in the split second it took for their brother, Edward, to leap into the fray to disarm the viscount and free his sister."

She swallowed audibly. "The earl was injured, was he not?"

Persephone looked away for a moment, as if to gather herself, then replied, "He required a number of stitches to close the knife wound."

"What of your injury?"

"A wrenched shoulder, nothing more." The duchess got to her feet and paced from the door to the fainting couch and back again.

Gwendolyn rose to her feet and intercepted the woman, slipping her arm through Persephone's. "I cannot even begin to imagine what you witnessed, or what you and your new family suffered at the hands of that madman."

Guiding the duchess over to the couch, she urged her to sit and quickly sat beside her, reaching for her hand. She patted it gently before slipping her arm through the duchess' once more. "I have been selfish in my grief, not believing anyone other than me ever suffered what I had. Refusing to believe anyone would carry their grief so close to their heart that it would threaten their sanity."

"I had to learn that particular lesson quickly," Persephone rasped. "Poor Phoebe was out of her mind with fear and grief, plagued by nightmares. She needed me…needed her brothers. Without the excellent care of Dr. McIntyre and the staunch support of our London staff and the staff here at Wyndmere Hall, she may not have fully recovered."

Gwendolyn felt one of the walls she'd erected around her heart crack. "You are far braver than I'd thought, Persephone. You've given so much of yourself to your family and fought alongside them to save your sister-in-law. From the other *on dits* I had heard at the time, you helped defend this very home from that same evil man who thought to destroy your husband and his family." Drawing in a deep cleansing breath, she let it out slowly and whispered, "I have been a coward, afraid to do as Jonathan would have wanted…grieve for his death and that of our babe, and then go on with my life. Grasping happiness with both hands."

"Why haven't you?" Persephone asked.

"I have made a life for myself, but until I arrived here, I did not acknowledge I shut off my heart, wrapping it in cotton batting to keep it safe from ever having to risk losing someone I love."

They sat, arms linked, sharing bits and pieces of their lives that had brought them to this moment, sitting side by side on the pale green velvet fainting couch. "I will forever be grateful to you, Persephone."

The duchess smiled. "For demanding my husband not send you packing?"

Gwendolyn nodded. "And for putting yourself in the middle of whatever occurred between His Grace and O'Malley, insisting if he was letting the man go that you wanted him as your overnight guard in the nursery."

Persephone's soft laugh felt like a hug. "And here I thought you'd thank me for bringing Patrick's handsome face and form to your notice…along with his many attributes."

Gwendolyn could not hold in her laughter. "You are as determined as His Grace to have your way, aren't you?"

The duchess was smiling as she rose to her feet. "Without question. Mayhap I should start a journal of my own, listing all of my friends and acquaintances that I've successfully brought together." She paused, lost in thought, before adding, "They are all quite happily married."

Gwendolyn rose to stand beside the duchess and thanked her again. "Although I do not plan on marrying, I do thank you for helping me see how holding tight to my grief was as crippling as the events that caused it."

The little ones began to whimper in their sleep. "Let me see if I can soothe them back to sleep while you rest until it's time to feed them again." Gwendolyn rushed over to the cradles and began her nightly routine of soothing the twins. When they were once again sleeping, the duchess remarked, "You are a godsend, Gwendolyn. Thank you."

"My pleasure, Persephone. See if you can sleep for a bit. I'll send Francis or Mollie for you if the babes don't rouse you from your sleep wanting to be fed."

"I think I will. You should rest for a bit yourself."

"I'm not tired but promise to lay down for a little while if it will ease your conscience and help you fall asleep."

"It would."

"Then I shall."

When the duchess continued to stand in the open doorway, Gwendolyn shook her head and walked over to the fainting couch and sat down. "Satisfied?"

"As soon as you are laying down, I will be."

With a groan, she did as the duchess bid her.

Persephone was smiling as she closed the door behind her.

Gwendolyn sighed as her eyes closed of their own volition. Breathing deeply, contentedly, she let her mind wander until it led her straight to the waiting arms of the heartbreakingly handsome Irishman who'd stolen her heart.

CHAPTER FIFTEEN

"Ye wanted to see me, Yer Grace?" Flaherty waited until the duke bid him enter.

"I am quite sure you know why I've asked to speak with you."

Flaherty winced and muffled a groan with a cough. "Aye."

The duke's gaze riveted on the third member of his guard that he would be promoting to head guard. "Why is this so bloody difficult?" he mumbled.

Flaherty fought to hold on to his laughter. It would not do to have the duke think he did not respect the man. His entire guard held him in great esteem…well except for the man's recent error in judgment relieving Patrick of his duties.

Instead of the irritation he expected to have to soothe, Flaherty was surprised to see a look of total bafflement cross the duke's face before he threw his hands up in the air.

"I have been doing my damndest to ensure my family is continually protected from threats that seem to be a part of our lives." Raking a hand through his hair, he lifted his gaze to meet Flaherty's. "Where have I gone wrong? O'Malley gave me his word that he and his family would protect mine to their last breath."

The duke's gaze never wavered. In fact, the intensity darkened it to the point where Flaherty was waiting for the explosion of temper. After a few moments of silence, he shifted from foot to foot.

"Out with it!" the duke demanded.

"Yer Grace?"

"You obviously have something to say." He motioned with his hands. "Out with it!"

"I'd be happy to tell ye. Though, I don't know as ye'll want to hear what I have to say, Yer Grace."

Sinking into the chair behind the scarred, ancient oak desk where the last five dukes had handled the affairs of the title and estates, he replied, "I'm sitting down. Enlighten me."

Flaherty would rather chew on rusty nails, but the man had ordered him to speak. He couldn't remain silent. "'Tis yer decision to remove Patrick from head of yer guard that we question."

"We?"

"Aye, the lot of us. Even if ye had me brother, Seamus, or cousin, James Garahan, who are currently stationed elsewhere, standing beside me, they'd be telling ye the same."

"What of the rest of the O'Malleys?"

Flaherty grinned. "They would have told ye the day ye laid down yer decree."

The duke tapped the tips of his fingers together three times. Flaherty had seen him do it more than once and knew it to be a sign the man was thinking over what he'd been told.

"Is that why Eamon asked to be relieved of the duty, because he didn't agree with my decision?"

"Not at all, Yer Grace. Eamon's not one for making up duty rosters or schedules. He'd rather be in the thick of things, following orders."

"I see."

"The sixteen of us stood before ye and yer man Coventry that first day and vowed to guard ye and yer kin with our lives. We've each one of us bled for ye—and yer family. We Flahertys, Garahans, and O'Malleys are men of our words. Once given, we'd die to keep it."

The duke put his head in his hands.

Flaherty sensed the man was grappling with something and had a feeling it began with the missive regarding the kidnapping threats and escalated the day he planted a facer on Patrick. Taking a chance, going with his gut, he stated, "Our respect for ye trebled the day ye knocked Patrick unconscious with one perfectly placed blow."

"May I ask why? It was not my best moment," the duke admitted.

"It only happened once before. The last time Patrick was leveled by such a blow was when the golden-eyed witch, *Saoirse*, distracted him in the middle of a bout."

"*Saoirse*?"

"Aye, the woman he'd pledged his heart to."

"What happened?"

"He looked away for a split second. It was long enough for Ian O'Mara to land a blow that knocked him senseless."

The duke rubbed a hand over his chin. "I take it he lost the bout."

"Aye, and the woman."

"Does this have anything to do with Mrs. Alexander?"

"It may," Flaherty hedged, not wanting to speak out of turn as it wasn't his heart or head that had been muddled by the lovely nanny.

"I see. She's here to watch over our children. I cannot have her distracted."

"Patrick understands that and even though we'd had many discussions in our quarters in the past—"

"By discussions, I assume you are referring to beating the bloody pulp out of one another."

"Nay, Yer Grace. We were practicing and honing our bare knuckle skills, nothing more. There's times when carrying a rifle or sword is too large a weapon, if ye ken my meaning."

"Indeed."

Jared paused before asking, "What about the patrols while the four of you were *practicing*?"

Flaherty's irritation spiked. He'd been trying to keep it under control, but when the duke questioned them not performing their duties, the simmering shot straight to boil. "We have the men from the village ye hired taking our shifts for the half an hour we take every day to meet."

"And hone your skills," the duke added.

"Aye. Will that be all, Yer Grace?"

The duke slowly stood. That he was beyond irritated wasn't lost on Flaherty. "Find O'Malley and tell him I need to speak with him."

"Eamon will be patrolling by the outbuildings. I'll send him at once."

"Not Eamon—Patrick."

Flaherty's anger dissipated and relief filled him. "Thank ye, Yer Grace. Ye'll not regret putting him back in charge."

"How do you know I'm not sending him packing?" the duke demanded.

"Because ye're an intelligent man, Yer Grace. One to be respected and revered."

The duke raised one eyebrow in silent question.

Flaherty grinned. "Faith, we all know ye miss yer late night meetings with him. He's a good man to have at yer back, and as a friend."

The duke waited until the man closed the door behind him before shaking his head in wonder. *Was it as easy as that?* Did every one of his private guard believe he would reinstate Patrick and things would go back to normal? Wanting to observe O'Malley's reaction firsthand, he got up and opened the door.

Ten minutes later, he had his answer. O'Malley's face was devoid of expression, but the light of hope in his eyes was all he needed to see.

The duke admitted to himself the real problem was that Patrick was not personally guarding his babes twenty-four hours a day. The man had never been derelict in his duties, he had the patrols covered.

"Ye wanted to see me, Yer Grace?"

"Indeed." He met the man halfway to the door, hand extended.

Patrick's eyes widened, but he did not hesitate to grasp the man's hand and give it a hearty shake. "I'm sorry I wasn't personally guarding the twins for ye, Yer Grace, or on the patrols meself."

The men parted and the duke motioned for O'Malley to have a seat. The former head of his guard stood in front of the chair but did not sit until the duke had.

The duke nodded. "You have a number of other duties. I should not have expected you to handle every patrol, schedule meetings between your men, the men from the village, and my staff," he paused before adding, "let alone *practicing* during your family discussions."

He was pleased to see the light of hope burning in O'Malley's gaze. "I'd like to offer my apology for doubting your word, and for questioning your loyalty and your trust."

Patrick cleared his throat to speak. "Beggin' yer pardon, Yer Grace, but 'tis me fault for not assurin' ye that there were others capable of takin' me place in the shifts and patrols. I've already told the lads no more practicin' our skills."

"You'll have to tell them I've asked you to continue to do so. I won't have it said my personal guard has rusty bare knuckle skills."

"They'll be pleased to hear it, Yer Grace." He rose to his feet. "Will that be all?"

The duke waved at him to sit back down. When he complied, the duke nodded. "Her Grace has advised me in no uncertain terms that she would not see you dismissed and expects you to take the overnight shift guarding the nursery."

"Garahan told me."

"I see. What else did he tell you?"

"That Eamon asked to be relieved of his new position as head of yer guard."

"Indeed. I had been about to ask Flaherty if he wanted the job. After our meeting, I realized the perfect man for the job was still in my employ. Wasting a man's skills isn't something I normally do."

"Wastin'?"

"You've already proven you are more than capable of handling the job as head of my guard. I would be foolish not to ask you to return to your duties."

"I thought ye'd be lettin' me go."

The duke shook his head, anguish flashing in his gaze. "At first, I thought that was the answer to the problem. Then I realized *I* was the problem."

"How could ye be?"

"I let my fear of our babes being kidnapped take root in my soul. Nothing and no one but you would be able to protect them—every hour of every day. Nothing and no one but you could man each and every patrol—every hour of the day."

"Were I in yer place, I'd have felt the same. Family is me heart, I'd die to protect mine. Me brothers, me cousins, and I gave our vow to protect yer family with our lives. We would die to uphold that vow."

The duke rose from his seat, walked around his desk, and held out his hand a second time. When Patrick took it, the duke vowed, "I promise to discuss any and all fears that may hold me back in the future—or have me acting like an *eedjit*."

O'Malley grinned as their hands fell back to their sides. "I promise not to let me head be turned by any female."

"Ah, there's the rub. Persephone reminded me of the night we met at Hollisters' ball and how unnerved she was because she sensed she'd lost her heart to a man she could never marry." He smiled. "It wasn't until Coventry brought the way I'd been acting to my attention that I realized the same thing."

"But ye came to yer senses and look at what ye have, Yer

Grace. A lovely wife and beautiful family."

"Who are under constant threat. I've lost so much sleep since the twins were born, but not just because of their penchant for wanting to be fed at two o'clock in the morning. The kidnapping threats scare the bloody hell out of me."

"Ye've nothin' to fear if me and mine are watchin' over yer family, Yer Grace."

"Then you'll return to your duties?"

"Aye."

The duke hesitated before asking, "And to our late night discussions?"

"'Twould be me pleasure, Yer Grace. I've missed them."

"Excellent. I'll expect you to return to your duties within the hour, and see you in my upstairs study half an hour before your midnight shift at the nursery."

"Thank ye, Yer Grace. Ye won't be sorry."

"I know I won't. Thank you, Patrick."

CHAPTER SIXTEEN

"WHAT IN THE bloody hell happened?" Lord Radleigh demanded.

The big man standing before him shrugged.

"If you do not want to end up at the bottom of the Thames, you'd best speak up!"

"The lad came highly recommended. How was I to know he was all talk?"

"I expect you and your cronies to do the job you agreed to. I want those brats in my hands in a fortnight. No later!"

The man wrung his cap in his hands. "What do you plan to do with them?"

Radleigh ground out, "That is not your concern."

"I've spent my prime working the docks picking pockets and mayhap a mugging or two...not snatching babes out of their cradles."

"Which was why you assured me the youth you'd hired would do the job." Radleigh paused for a moment, studying the man's face. "Your connections were the reason I hired you. However, I am quite sure I will be able to find someone else with adequate connections to do my bidding should you fail me."

"I will not fail."

"See that you do not—your life depends on it."

CHAPTER SEVENTEEN

"JARED! THERE YOU are." Persephone nearly collided with her husband as she rushed to his side.

Steadying her, he looked down into her upturned face and saw the mix of emotions that had haunted his sleep. "As you can see." He dug deep to act as if nothing were the matter. Her peace of mind was everything to him.

She leaned into him for a moment before easing out of his arms. "Where have you been?"

He raised one eyebrow and she blew out a frustrated breath. "Do not use that ducal expression on me. I demand to know where you have been and what you have been up to."

"I do not react well to demands, my love."

"Neither do I," she retorted. "However, you have no problem issuing them through our staff and your personal guard."

He slowly smiled, admiring her fiery spirit. "I shall endeavor to cease making unnecessary demands upon you, Persephone."

She sighed. "Excellent. Now as to why I was searching for you...I dem—er...am curious, when do you plan to come to your senses and let Patrick return to his duties as head of your guard?"

Brushing a lock of blue-black hair out of her eyes, he let his fingertips linger, tracing the curve of her cheek, following the line of her jaw.

"Jared?"

The husky sound of her voice was that of a siren's. Unable to look away, he watched for the signs that she was as captivated by him as he was deeply under her spell. Her brown eyes deepened to the color of warmed chocolate. The pulse at the base of her neck fluttered and she leaned toward him. He was not a man to deny himself the pleasure of kissing his wife.

He bent his head until their lips were a breath apart. Watching her eyes widen, he pulled her flush against him and plundered. The taste of her ignited his blood. He was on fire for her.

When she sagged against him, he lifted his head, supremely satisfied she knew where his frustrations lie. "I do not know how much longer I can hold out, waiting for you to be healed from the birth of our babes."

The sound of her muffled laughter against his waistcoat irritated him.

She looked into his eyes. "You are not the only one suffering. I am not immune to your frustrated passion every time we are in the same room together."

He groaned, confiding, "I cannot lay beside you without being driven mad by the sweet scent of lilacs. How much longer?"

"Dr. McIntyre cautioned against continuing our…er…marital relations until at the very least five weeks. It takes longer to recover after birthing twins."

He laid his forehead against hers and fought to slow down the beat of his heart. He would not beg…but God help him, he would if it came down to that.

"You have yet to answer my question. When are you going to rescind your decree and reinstate Patrick to his duties?"

He laughed aloud. "God, you are frustrating, Wife."

Her eyes blazed with anger. "Oh, am I?"

The duke chuckled, lifting her hand to his lips and pressing a kiss to the back of it.

"I have just dealt with one of the frustrations that have been affecting my mind, my sleep…and my heart."

"Have you? And?" she urged.

"I have met with Patrick and apologized."

Persephone's eyes widened. "Thank God!" Tears filled her eyes as she cupped his face in her hand. "He accepted?"

"Aye, Wife."

"What are your other frustrations?"

He would not tell her all of them. He needed to protect her from the latest threats to their family. "There is a frustration," he rasped. "One that only you can assuage."

Struggling to catch her breath, she whispered, "We do not have to wait until the week's end to—" her cheeks flushed a delightful shade of rose. "That is, we could…" her voice trailed off and he chuckled.

"God how I love you, Persephone. I promise we shall go slowly." He brushed the tips of his fingers along the line of her jaw, vowing, "I would never willingly hurt you."

"I know you wouldn't, and I trust you, Jared."

Breathing deeply, he inhaled the sweet scent of lilacs and Persephone, then kissed her passionately before he eased his hold on her. "Tonight then."

"Tonight. As to the other frustrations you refuse to discuss with me, is there nothing you can do to ease them until the situation changes?"

His hands curled into fists. Realizing what he'd done, he relaxed them again. "Pounding the bloody hell out of something…" Fighting to control the anger just below the surface of his calm, he added, "or someone."

Instead of the shocked expression he expected, she slowly smiled. "I may have a solution to your problem."

"Indeed. What might that be?"

"I must seek permission before I share my idea with you. Hopefully, I can tell you tonight."

"Tonight," he rasped, leaning down to capture her lips one last time before returning to his duties.

"Tonight," she promised.

>>><<<

Taking the servants' staircase to the kitchen, the duchess went in search of O'Malley. Constance was rolling out dough when she entered the kitchen. "Cream tarts?"

"And berry tarts," the cook replied. "Is there anything in particular you'd like me to prepare for your afternoon tea?"

"Do you have any more dried lavender buds?"

The cook smiled. "Lavender scones, it is, Your Grace."

"What would we do without you, Constance?"

"Muddle through I imagine." The cook placed her rolling pin to the side and asked, "You look like you have something on your mind. Is there anything else I can do for you?"

"Yes, as a matter of fact. Do you happen to know where Patrick is patrolling at the moment?"

Constance smiled. "We're all so glad His Grace came to his senses."

Persephone sighed. "I was beginning to worry that he wouldn't."

"You should have more faith in His Grace," Constance told her. "He always does the right thing. If there is something troubling him, he'll work through it and straighten out whatever the issue is."

"I do have faith in Jared," she remarked. "What had me worried is his stubborn nature."

The cook sighed. "It's a family trait." Nodding to the back door, she added, "I believe Patrick is over by the stables."

"Thank you." Her hand was on the door before Constance's voice rang out. "You'll catch your death if you don't at least put on a shawl."

Persephone frowned. "I do not have time to go fetch mine."

"Take mine. It's on the hook with the aprons in the butler's pantry."

"Thank you." She snatched the woolen shawl and hurried

outside, instantly grateful for the added warmth when the cold breeze took her breath away.

Pulling the shawl over her head, she followed the path to the stables intending to ask the stable master if he had seen O'Malley. Opening the door to the stables, she sighed in relief as the lack of breeze and relative warmth of the building surrounded her.

"Your Grace, what brings you here today?" the burly stable master asked as he walked toward her.

"I'm on an errand," she explained. "For the duke." She'd get the answers she sought more quickly if she invoked her husband's name.

Winters smiled at her. "I cannot imagine His Grace would send you on an errand in this cold without a proper coat." He slipped out of his and held it out to her. "Please," he asked, "won't you slip this on? I wouldn't want you to catch your death of cold."

From the set of the man's jaw, she sensed arguing would not be prudent. She let him place the coat around her shoulders and was immediately surrounded by the soft warmth of his worn coat. "Thank you, Winters. You are so kind. Promise me you'll stay inside until I can return it to you."

Without missing a beat, he replied, "Of course, Your Grace."

She noted he did not look her in the eyes when he agreed. She'd used that tactic many times herself and had a feeling he would go about his business with or without his coat. She decided to see to her errand as quickly as possible and return the man's coat. "Have you seen Patrick? I need to relay a message from His Grace." Persephone mentally crossed her fingers as she uttered that fib.

The stable master grinned. "I'm seeing him now."

"Thank you, Winters."

"Yer Grace? Shouldn't ye be tucked into the nursery or yer sittin' room out of this bitter cold?"

She smiled at O'Malley. "I need to ask a favor."

"Whatever ye need, consider it done."

Gratitude filled her knowing he meant it. The man would do whatever she asked without question because of his vow to the duke to do all in his power to protect, defend, and aid his family. "Thank you, Patrick."

When she paused, he motioned for her to follow him to the other end of the stables where they would not be overheard. "What can I do for ye?"

"First, I must tell you how happy I am that Jared reinstated you. We will all feel much safer knowing you are once again in charge of his guard."

"'Twas a surprise to me as I was thinkin' he'd be helpin' me pack me bags and showin' me to the door."

"I would never have let that happen."

He smiled. "Though I cannot be sure His Grace would agree, it warms me heart to hear ye say it. By the by, does this favor involve His Grace?"

"Er…yes. How did you know?'

"I overheard ye mention that it was an errand for His Grace and could not help but wonder if he knows where ye are and what ye're goin' to be askin' of me."

She sighed. "Well, I did tell Jared that I had an idea that would help him with his current problem with frustration."

His eyes widened.

"He confessed he had many things frustrating him," she rushed to explain. "Although he did not tell me what or who frustrated him, he did say his frustration could only be eased by pounding the bloody hell out of something…" she paused to add, "…or someone."

O'Malley's eyes glittered with interest. "Did he now?"

"Aye."

"And ye thought of me?"

She laughed. "Everyone knows you practice weekly—if not daily, to keep your fighting skills honed."

"We also sharpen the blades we carry, keep our powder dry, and rifles and pistols well oiled. I cannot help but wonder why that would interest ye."

She put her hands on her hips, not an easy thing to do wearing Winters' bulky coat. "And here I'd given you credit for being able to read a person's mind." Blowing out a breath of frustration, she told him, "I would like your permission to suggest Jared take part in your next family *discussion*."

Patrick's green eyes gleamed as if he were imagining sparring with the duke. "What if he were injured? What would happen then?"

Persephone grinned. "Rumor has it, he knocked you clean off your feet and left you unconscious. I don't believe you have to worry on his account."

Patrick frowned at her. "'Tis a crime to assault a member of the *ton*, especially a duke."

"It wouldn't be assault if you and your men were *practicing* your moves."

"Again, I ask ye, what if he were injured? Would ye have us pull our punches?"

She studied his face, noting his concern. "I would, but Jared would be appalled if I even suggested such a thing. His pride would be in question."

O'Malley nodded. "There are times when a man's pride is all that he has left."

Before she could ask him if he'd ever experienced such, he continued. "After I speak to me cousins…and if they agree to include him in our sparrin', we'll need someone standin' at the ready with supplies."

"Supplies?"

"Aye. A bucket of snow outside our quarters."

"Whatever for?"

"To treat bruisin'."

"Anything else?"

"Bandages, boiled threads, salve, short planks of wood—with the edges smoothed—no splinters mind, to immobilize any badly injured joints."

Persephone's ire began to build. "You obviously do not believe that my husband is up to the task of bare knuckle fighting with you and your family. Do you?"

Patrick grinned. "'Tis the truth he got in a lucky blow the other day. And no, I do not believe he is up to the poundin' we'd be givin' him."

The need to defend her husband had her promising, "He'll wipe the floor with you."

O'Malley's eyes narrowed. "If ye were not the duchess, and mayhap a lass from the inn in the village, I'd be askin' ye to place a wager on that."

"Done!" she held out her hand, spit in the palm, and waited for Patrick to do the same.

"Are ye daft?"

She took a step closer, spit-slickened palm up. "Nay. Confident in my husband's ability to knock you off your feet for a second time."

O'Malley tilted his head back, staring at the posts and beams running the length and breadth of the stables.

Shock mixed with her anger. "Are you counting?"

"Aye," he replied.

"I demand you look at me!"

He did as she bid while slipping the linen square from his pocket and handing it to her. "I'll not ever wager with ye, Yer Grace. I have deep respect for ye and yer title. 'Twouldn't be proper, and ye know it."

She wiped the spit off her hand. "I'll just have this laundered for you."

He sighed. "'Tisn't that I don't believe I'd best yer husband. I know I will."

She snorted out a laugh and shook her head. "Has anyone ever told you that you are maddening?"

"Nay, but many have told me I drive them to drink."

"If I agree to have someone standing by, mayhap one of the footmen, with the supplies requested, would you agree?"

"Aye, though I'm thinkin' mayhap His Grace should start with a feedbag. I can hang one on that beam over there." He pointed to a dark corner. "If he still needs to let go of his frustrations after that mayhap we can include him in our next *discussion* and see what happens. I'll be speakin' to the lads first."

"Of course. Thank you, Patrick." Slipping out of Winters' coat, she handed it to him. "Please see that Winters gets his coat back."

He held his hands out in front of him. "I'll not be responsible for ye catchin' yer death out here, Yer Grace. I'll follow ye to the kitchen, ye can hand it to me then."

"But I don't think—"

"'Tis obvious. If ye cannot think of yer own health, then think of yer babes and what they'd do if ye were in bed with a lung ailment. Who would feed them, then?"

Guilt washed over her embarrassment that he would bring up such a topic to her. She'd only just become accustomed to discussing the topic with her husband. Without question, though, Patrick was right. "Thank you for caring enough to remind me of the error in my thinking." She put the coat back on and reached for the door.

His reach was longer than hers. He opened it for her. "'Tis a cold one today." Looking up at the thick gray clouds, he predicted, "We'll be havin' snow by midnight."

"Will we?"

"Aye, me da taught me to watch the sky and gauge the weather by the wind shifts, the clouds, and the animals we kept on the farm."

"You are a man of many talents." She tried to match her steps to his. When she couldn't quite manage it, she asked, "Would you mind slowing your steps—just a bit."

He immediately shortened his steps. "Beggin' yer pardon, Yer Grace."

She smiled up at him. "Thank you. Gwendolyn has free time in the afternoons. I think I'll suggest she take a healthful walk to clear the cobwebs from spending all day and half the night with our darlings."

"Ye're not as wily as ye think, Yer Grace."

Feigning shock, she watched his face for a sign that she'd fooled him. His brimmed with laughter.

She shrugged off his comment. She'd succeeded in planting the thought of Gwendolyn in the stubborn guard's head as she'd planned to do all along. "Oh, I don't know about that, Patrick."

He opened the door to the kitchen and waited for her to remove the coat and hand it to him. "I'll return this to Winters and continue on me patrol."

"Thank you. I'll be speaking to His Grace about what we discussed shortly."

"See that ye remember my suggestion of the feedbag first. After I speak to the lads, ye can mention the rest of it."

Knowing she would have to acquiesce in order for the man to get on with his duties, she grumbled, "Very well."

His smile told her he was well aware of her thoughts. She would have to work on keeping her face devoid of expression in the future. Not an easy task, but she would succeed if she set her mind to it.

Patrick was whistling softly as he took the path back to the stables.

Relief filled her. Her babes, her husband, and their staff were once more under the man's leadership and the protection of the duke's guard.

There was no safer place to be.

CHAPTER EIGHTEEN

"Precious," Gwendolyn whispered as she pressed her lips to the little one's forehead. As she rocked Richard, she began to hum. Instead of closing his eyes, he was watching her. "You're going to be a charmer," she told him, wondering yet again how someone so tiny could grab hold of her heart so quickly.

Tracing the tip of her finger along the arch of one eyebrow and then the other, she crooned, "You are supposed to fall asleep when I hum to you, dear one. It's going to be your sister's turn to rock, but I know you'll fuss if I put you in your cradle unless you are ready to fall asleep."

Her mother's trick to get her to fall asleep when she was a babe seemed to be working on Richard. Continuing the soothing motion of tracing one eyebrow and then the other as she hummed, he finally closed his eyes.

"That's it, find your sleep, Richard. I hear your sister beginning to fuss. She knows it's her turn."

When the little one in her arms settled into the rhythmic pattern of slumber she had been waiting for, she sighed in satisfaction. Without missing a beat—or missing a note, she continued to hum the lullaby as she rose to her feet and slowly walked over to his cradle. "There now, sweet babe," she whispered. "Sleep."

"No need to fuss," she soothed his sister. "I'm here until your mamma comes back. You know I'll take good care of you for her." Lifting Abigail into her arms, she walked back over to the rocking chair, sat, and began to hum the lullaby that lulled her brother to sleep.

As Abigail quieted, and snuggled closer, another piece of the wall surrounding Gwendolyn's heart cracked. Although she knew it was beyond time to move on with her life and open her heart and truly begin to live again, it was times like these when she knew she had to do all in her power to protect her heart. If she opened her heart and loved with all her being again, only to lose the ones she loved a second time, she would not survive.

Humming softly, she watched with wonder as the tiny babe in her arms fought to stay awake. Tracing the arch of one brow and then the other, she marveled that something so simple could soothe one so little.

By the time she'd managed to lull both babes to sleep, she was more than ready to spend a part of her afternoon break outside before returning to share her latest observations about the twins with Persephone over a cup of tea and hopefully a scone or two. She'd grown quite fond of Constance's lavender scones.

"Are they still asleep?" Mollie asked, entering the nursery.

"Richard's been asleep for half an hour. I just this moment settled Abigail in her cradle. They should sleep for a while longer. Is Her Grace resting?"

Mollie sighed. "She was rushing about earlier looking for His Grace. Then I heard she was outside speaking with O'Malley."

"Patrick or Eamon."

"Patrick."

"I wonder what that could be about," Gwendolyn mused aloud.

Mollie slipped her arm through Gwendolyn's. "I heard from Merry that the duke rescinded his decree."

"About demoting Patrick?"

Mollie's smile said it all.

"That's wonderful news! I'm sure His Grace will be happier now that things are going to be working smoothly again."

Mollie sighed. "If only Finn were here."

"Ah, Patrick's brother who is in Sussex," Gwendolyn acknowledged.

"That would be his brother, Dermott," Mollie corrected.

"Hmm...then he's in London?"

Mollie laughed softly. "Nay, he's stationed at Penwith Tower, His Grace's crumbling tower on the coast of Cornwall."

"So many O'Malleys," Gwendolyn muttered.

"That's only half of them," she stated. "Don't forget he has four O'Malley cousins—Eamon is one of them."

"And Flaherty and Garahan cousins, too."

"You may be meeting some of them when the guard rotates."

"Oh? Does that happen often?"

Mollie smiled. "Every four months or so. At times it's hard to keep up with who is stationed where."

Gwendolyn's heart stuttered in her breast at the thought of Patrick leaving Wyndmere Hall before she did. "Will the men be given orders to move while I am here?"

Mollie smiled as if she knew what Gwendolyn did not ask. "Patrick has always been stationed wherever the duke and duchess are. If they travel to London, he accompanies them. From what I've observed, Patrick will not be assigned else-where...even if the worst happens—and it already has, when he was relieved as head of the guard. He remains with the duke."

Relief washed over her. Forcing herself to think of some-thing—anything else, to clear her head and thoughts of the devastatingly handsome guard, she remarked, "I'll leave you to your quiet time with the babes."

"Are you going for a walk?"

"After I fetch my cloak. I understand it's too chilly for just a shawl."

"Aye, that's for certain. Enjoy the fresh air."

"Thank you, I plan to." Gwendolyn closed the door behind her and returned to her bedchamber to collect her cloak. Remembering how chilly it had been yesterday, she grabbed her scarf and gloves. Although they were not as fashionable as her other footwear, she had grown accustomed to wearing serviceable boots with low heels. They were made of sturdy leather and had enough room inside them to accommodate a warm pair of socks over her stockings. Over the years, she had learned the best way to dress for the cold was in warm layers.

At the last minute, she grabbed one of her rock-lined reticules. "Now I'm prepared for anything." Happy to be heading outside for a breath of fresh, chilly air, she descended the back staircase and swept through the kitchen. Greeting both Merry and Constance, she promised not to stay outside for too long and replied yes, she would be taking tea with Her Grace when she returned.

Alone, she turned to the left intending to walk through the sleeping gardens. It would be diverting to imagine what plants would be blooming there come spring. Head down, intent on studying the larger snow-covered mounds—hiding what she assumed would be shrubs, and the much smaller ones—which were no doubt herbs or perennials, she didn't realize she wasn't alone until she plowed into an immovable object.

She stumbled backward and would have fallen on her backside if not for O'Malley reaching out to steady her. "Steady, Lass."

She looked up into eyes the color of dew-laden grass and, for a moment, her mind went blank. Staring at the strong line of his jaw—noting the blond stubble there, she wondered if it would be soft or prickly. Jonathan's dark beard had been rough to the touch. Her fingers itched to find out.

"Lass?"

She blinked. "Yes?"

"Are ye all right?"

"I beg your pardon, O'Malley. I did not see you standing there." She hoped the apology would ease his frown, but it didn't.

"Is something wrong? May I help you with something?"

"Ye can pay attention to where ye're walkin' in the future."

"I already apologized for bumping into you."

"'Tisn't the issue, 'tis the fact that ye didn't answer me. I thought ye'd knocked the senses right out of yer head."

She glared at the man currently trying his best to intimidate her. Well, she wasn't having it for one minute. "Hardly," she retorted. "I'll just get out of your way then, shall I?" Stepping back, giving him plenty of room to walk past her. Instead, the man surprised her by moving to stand close enough that she could feel the heat radiating off him.

The heady feeling of standing so close to the man who had been haunting her thoughts—and her dreams, threatened to overwhelm her. She took a step back.

He scowled at her, then mumbled something she could not quite hear—something about hard heads and stubborn women. Not wishing to hear what the difficult man thought, she turned around and marched back the way she'd come. Yanking the kitchen door open, she rushed inside, closing the door behind her.

"Is anything the matter, Mrs. Alexander?"

Tamping down on her irritation, she answered, "Not a thing, Constance. Why do you ask?"

"You seem a bit rattled."

She *was* rattled. If she hadn't been, she would have thought to use her rock-filled reticule and whack O'Malley in the chin with it. "It's nothing I cannot handle but thank you for your concern."

When the cook turned back to peeling vegetables, Gwendolyn noticed the woman was smiling. Needing to pull herself together before she sat down with the duchess, she hurried through the room to the servants' staircase. Once she was in her bedchamber, she hung up her cloak, put her gloves, scarf, and reticule away, and began to pace.

"What is wrong with that man?" she wondered aloud. "He has a reputation for knowing—and seeing everything. How did *he* not see me?" The more she tried to reason out what had occurred, the hotter her temper burned. He had to have watched her until she bumped into him.

She stopped mid-pace and castigated herself for letting the man get under her skin. Needing to collect herself she walked to the washstand, lifted the pitcher, and poured the now-cold water into the bowl. After washing her hands and face, she felt a bit better. Not as angry. Drying her hands, she glanced at her reflection in the looking glass and decided to re-pin her hair. The task settled her fractious nerves. In control once more, she left to join the duchess.

"There you are, Gwendolyn!" the duchess beamed. "I was about to send someone to fetch you."

Gwendolyn noticed the accoutrements for their tea had already been laid out on the side table. "I'm so sorry to be late. I ran into—er...my walk took a bit longer than I anticipated. I hope that it isn't a problem."

The duchess tilted her head to one side before replying, "Not at all. I'm glad you're here." Motioning for her to sit, she poured a cup of tea and handed it to Gwendolyn. "I do enjoy our chats over tea. What observations about Richard and Abigail have you made today?"

Gwendolyn smiled and felt her world right itself. Putting Patrick O'Malley out of her mind, she shared bits and pieces of her discovery earlier. The duchess was very interested and planned to try the fingertip to the eyebrow method of soothing her babes.

Gwendolyn cautioned her, "It has worked for me with every babe I've had the honor of caring for. However, it doesn't seem to work all of the time for their mothers—or wet nurses. One of the wet nurses suggested it was because the little ones had a keen sense of smell and knew when it was their mother—or the one feeding them, that held them." She shook her head and added, "Isn't it a marvel that babes so small instinctively recognize their mothers?"

"Fathers, too," Persephone remarked. "They know it is Jared

as soon as he has them in his arms. I believe it's the depth of his voice resonating against them."

"Only half of those I've cared for had a father interested in holding their little ones." She sighed before confiding, "It is a refreshing to find that both His Grace, and you, are so involved in the care of your babes."

Persephone smiled. "We agreed if we were blessed with children that we would take an active part in their upbringing and their lives. We believe it is an extension of the vows we pledged the day we were wed."

Gwendolyn braced herself and was ready when the duchess' words sliced through to her very soul. The memory of Jonathan pledging to do the same filled her. He often placed his hands upon her swollen belly marveling at the active thumps and kicks she endured all the while wondering if it would be a boy or a girl. If it was a boy, they would name Jonathan after his father. If they had a girl, they would name Melinda after her mother.

Knowing her limitations, she cleared her throat and asked after Persephone's mother.

The duchess advised that her mother was planning another visit in another month or so. "She so hates to travel in the cold weather."

Gwendolyn shivered. "A wise woman to wait. I heartily agree with her. Traveling in the winter is most definitely not pleasurable."

After enjoying a second cup of tea, and although she shouldn't have—since she'd already eaten a cream tart, she added a dollop of jam to the clotted cream on her lavender scone and took a healthy bite. "Mmmm…delicious. Constance is a master with pastries, among other things."

"As are all of Jared's staff."

When Gwendolyn took another bite, and her mouth was full, Persephone drawled, "I heard you had a run in with Patrick in the gardens a little while ago."

She nearly choked on the scone but managed to finish chewing and swallowed. Taking a sip from her teacup, she blotted her mouth with her napkin and proceeded to twist it into a knot. "I was quite intent studying the snowy mounds in your gardens, trying to imagine what was hiding beneath them when I inadvertently walked into him."

"How odd."

"In what way?"

"Patrick normally doesn't miss anything in his surroundings, it's what enables him to do his job. Were you hurt? I can only imagine bumping into the man would be like walking into a brick wall."

She covered her mouth with her hand but couldn't keep the snort from escaping.

Persephone's eyes lit with humor. "I have it on good authority every one of my husband's guards are quite fit and…er…heavily muscled. If you'd have seen them without a shirt on—"

Gwendolyn's gasp had Persephone immediately adding, "It is not what you think. When Jared and I first came to Wyndmere Hall with his sister, Phoebe, the same madman who attacked his brother and sister in London tried to launch an attack on Wyndmere Hall. Most of the men, and our staff, suffered injuries—not all of them serious. The ladies Aurelia and Calliope were on hand to help Phoebe and me patch them up. Their shirts were in tatters covered with ash, dirt, and blood from fighting the blaze—after lightning struck the old oak tree by the stables, and from defending our home from various positions in and around the grounds surrounding Wyndmere Hall."

"I cannot imagine how you managed to fend off the attack, let alone set up an infirmary to take care of the injured."

Persephone shrugged. "One does what is necessary to protect one's family, staff—and in my husband's case, his personal guard. We used the kitchen, the pantry, and the room just beyond it."

"Do you realize how fortunate you are, Persephone?"

Tears glistened in her eyes. "I was blessed the night I stumbled backward into Jared's arms and say a prayer of thanks daily."

Gwendolyn's eyes widened. "I thought he reached out to straighten your spectacles."

Persephone sighed. "That was after I'd stumbled, and he caught me. By the by, my husband is every bit as broad through the chest and shoulders as our guard. But I must confess, I find him far more handsome than any of his guard with his dark hair and brilliant blue eyes."

"'Tis good of you to admit, my love."

Persephone rattled her teacup against its saucer. "Jared!"

His knowing smile had Gwendolyn setting her cup and saucer on the table and gaining her feet. "I believe I shall return this tray to the kitchen."

No one answered. The duke and duchess were too busy gazing into one another's eyes. Quietly closing the door behind her, she met Mollie in the hallway and passed off the tray and the information the duke and duchess were in the nursery and not to be disturbed.

Mollie was smiling as she descended the stairs to the kitchen. Gwendolyn followed in her wake. Her mind filled with images of the broad-shouldered, broad-chested head of the duke's guard.

How had the man managed to set himself front and center in her thoughts again? With a sigh, she entered the kitchen, pleased when asked to lend a hand setting out the plates and flatware to feed the extra men who had arrived the day before.

"Will Mr. King's men continue to patrol outside, or will they be taking a shift inside as well."

Constance answered without looking away from the roast she was taking out of the oven. "No one has mentioned it, though I'm sure we'll find out soon enough."

"I noticed Patrick is still handling the late night shift outside the nursery. Do you think he'll continue to do so now that's he's returned to his former position?"

The cook nodded. "Knowing our Patrick, he will. He knows how important it is to the duke and duchess."

"What about me?" Gwendolyn could not help but ask. "I sit with them through the night in between feedings."

"The babes have become quite attached to you, which gives Mollie and Francis a few moments to catch their breaths. It wasn't so with the previous nannies."

"They are such sweet babes. They've already got me wrapped around their tiny little fingers. But I was referring to me protecting the babes."

"If not for the threats, there would be no need for extra precautions. But in light of the past, and the heinous kidnapping threats, do you blame the duke and duchess for asking Patrick to stand guard while the babes sleep?"

She shook her head. "In all good conscience, I cannot fault them. I've never been in a situation like this before. It'll take some getting used to."

"You are more than up to the task, Mrs. Alexander."

"Thank you. Would you mind calling me Gwendolyn? Mrs. Alexander sounds so very formal."

"It would be my pleasure."

"I've tried asking Mollie and Francis to do so as well, but they haven't yet."

"They are young, and so eager to please. They started as scullery maids and were given the opportunity to serve as upstairs maids when we had to hire on more help what with Their Graces settling here as their main residence and receiving visitors. Shall I instruct them to do so?"

"Not at all. Whenever they are comfortable doing so is fine with me."

"Merry and I were talking earlier and agree that you are a godsend, Gwendolyn. Those babes, and the duke and the duchess, are lucky to have you caring for them."

Gwendolyn's eyes filled at Constance's words of praise. "It is I who is lucky to have the privilege of taking care of Richard and Abigail. I love taking care of them."

Later when Gwendolyn was resting before her late night

shift, she marveled at how fortunate she'd been to secure her position in the duke's household. The only problem she'd encountered was a certain Irishman. She'd have to be careful not to let his lilting brogue, face and form distract her from her duties.

She had a feeling it would not be an easy a task.

CHAPTER NINETEEN

"AH, PATRICK," THE duke greeted him as O'Malley was about to knock. "I have a few things to discuss with you before your shift guarding the nursery."

"Aye, Yer Grace."

The duke indicated the chair across the desk from him. Patrick sat and waited for his employer to speak first, then he would relate his earlier conversation with the duchess and the meeting he'd had with his men.

"I'd like you to use one or two of King's men inside with the next shift if possible."

"Of course, Yer Grace. Would ye be wantin' me to add them or move me men around?"

"Add them. Strength in numbers. They more than proved themselves the last time they were here protecting Wyndmere Hall."

"They helped turn the tide, adding to the patrols of the perimeter and the road to the village."

"Indeed." The duke looked down at his appointment book and then met Patrick's gaze. "Where do you think their skills would be best suited?"

"Thompson's skill with a blade is lethal. I know for a fact his brawn is equal to his skill with his fists."

"If I remember correctly, King's other men are equally proficient with a rifle or pistol."

"They handle themselves well enough, though only Thompson is more apt to go with his fists first."

"Why don't we start with Thompson and Greeves inside tomorrow evening. The rest of the day is, of course, up to you. Late evening is my biggest fear."

The duke had admitted his fears twice now and O'Malley's admiration for the man deepened. "Da often mentioned it takes a strong man to acknowledge his weaknesses, and a brave man to admit to his fears and pushes forward anyway."

"I'd like to meet your father. He sounds like a wise man, having raised four strong and intelligent sons."

O'Malley looked away for a moment, cleared his throat and replied, "He's been gone for a decade, but if he were still alive, he'd be pleased to meet ye, Yer Grace."

"I'm sorry, Patrick. I know how hard it is to lose one's father and mother."

"Ye've had to shoulder responsibility ye didn't expect all the while doing yer best to protect yer brother and sister. Yer parents would be proud, Yer Grace."

"Thank you, Patrick."

"Another thing Da always said, trust yer gut. It'll tell ye what ye know to be fact. A man's household is most vulnerable at night when everyone is sleeping—unless ye're fortunate enough to have those ye've designated as yer personal guard, and the protection of a handful of Bow Street Runners, as yer overnight protection."

The duke grinned. "I could not have said it better. Now, what have you been waiting to tell me?"

"Yer Grace?"

"I'm not the only one who carries the weight of responsibility. Has something occurred today that I need to know about?"

O'Malley shook his head. "I'm not sure where to begin."

"Let's start with the who, then move on to when and where. Short, sweet, and to the point," the duke advised.

"Her Grace. Tomorrow. In our quarters."

The duke's face lost all color. "I beg your pardon!"

The way it must have sounded to the duke hit O'Malley between the eyes. "Bloody hell! Ye asked to keep it simple. I gave ye the who, when, and the where."

Scrubbing his hand over his face, the duke bit out, "Now tell me the what."

"Her Grace asked if I'd speak to the men about includin' ye in our weekly family *discussions*."

The duke threw back his head and laughed. "Dear God, I love that woman! What did they say?"

"I'd best tell ye what I told Her Grace."

"You dared to deny her?" The irritation in his employer's voice was hard to miss.

"Not exactly. I suggested that ye may wish to start with the feedbag I've hung from one of the beams in the stables. If ye'd rather, I can hang one in our quarters. If we wrap yer hands, ye'll have less bruisin' and cuts."

"What else did you suggest to my wife?"

"That if ye were set on poundin' the bloody hell out of someone...then ye'd best have one of yer staff standin' at the ready with supplies."

"What kind of supplies?"

"A bucket of snow for the bruisin', bandages, boiled threads, salve, short planks of wood with the edges smoothed and no splinters to immobilize any badly injured joints."

The duke glared at O'Malley. "I'll have you know I was the man to beat growing up in our village."

O'Malley grinned. "Yer brother mentioned yer tendency to cheat."

"The devil you say!"

"Tossin' dirt in yer opponent's eyes is not exactly fair play, although I've been known to do the same meself."

"Why hasn't Persephone mentioned this to me yet?"

"I needed to get the lads to agree. While they all are willin' to test their mettle against Yer Grace, not one of us wishes to cause ye any injury."

"Because of the consequences you'd face having assaulted a duke?"

"There is that," O'Malley admitted. "But we've all taken quite a likin' to ye, Yer Grace. And to be honest, not one of us wishes to face the wrath of the duchess."

"Ah, there's the rub." The duke leaned back in his chair. "I think I can convince Her Grace not to hold it against any one of you should you happen to best me sparring. Although I highly doubt any of you will."

"I've already asked the lads how they feel about pullin' their punches, so ye won't feel the full force of them."

The duke shot to his feet. "Bloody hell, O'Malley!"

"Would ye have the lads worryin' that they'll be spendin' time with yer village constable if they didn't?"

The duke started to pace. O'Malley knew he would have to wait for the duke to finish before they could continue their conversation. When the duke resumed his seat, he asked, "Do I need to put it in writing that I will not hold anyone responsible if I am injured?"

"Can I tell ye the truth?" O'Malley rasped.

"Please."

"'Tis Her Grace that I'm more worried about. I learned early on that a woman's anger may be slow to boil, but once it's reached that point, ye'd best be prayin' to yer Maker that yer death is quick."

The duke's snort of laughter was echoed by O'Malley's. "I love a feisty woman," the duke admitted.

"Her Grace is a woman beyond compare. Ye're a lucky man, Yer Grace."

"Indeed. Now back to our problem."

"'Tisn't a problem if ye can convince Her Grace not to have us hauled before the magistrate if we bruise ye."

"I shall speak to my wife this evening."

C.H. ADMIRAND

"Our next family discussion is set for tomorrow after the midday change of the watch."

"I am looking forward to it."

"As are we." Patrick turned to leave and remembered one more point. Turning back, he asked, "Would ye agree that whoever ye have standin' at the ready should promise not to speak about our *meetin'*?"

The duke's brow furrowed. "Excellent suggestion. Why not ask one of King's men? Their silence regarding their assignments is an intrinsic part of their job."

O'Malley nodded. "Thompson?"

"Send him to me first thing in the morning."

"Aye, Yer Grace."

Patrick was smiling as he headed to the nursery. He'd enjoyed the last few nights standing guard, listening to Gwendolyn quietly humming or singing the babes to sleep.

Lord willing it would be quiet again tonight.

⟶⟫⟩⟨⟪⟵

"THEY REALLY ARE inept," King's man, Thompson, rasped, pitching his voice low. Sound carried quickly on cold, clear nights like this.

"Why don't we end it now and subdue them?" one of the duke's footmen asked.

"'Tisn't our job to attack," Garahan advised the men. "Our job is to defend."

"What if attacking is the best way?" Thompson asked.

"It has been in the past, but I'm thinking to let those two fumble their way closer. Flaherty's on the roof with his Kentucky long rifle. Me cousin is dead accurate."

"Long rifle, you say?" Thompson nudged Garahan. "I've been wanting to get my hands on one of those American rifles for a while now. I missed my opportunity to fire one the last time I was here. Think he'll let me fire off a few rounds?"

154

Garahan snorted. "I doubt it, but ye can ask."

"Are those two in range yet?"

Garahan squinted at the men skulking toward the front of Wyndmere Hall, then up at his cousin's position behind one of the gargoyles on the roof. "Another foot or two and—"

His words were cut off by the echo of a rifle shot. They watched in silence as one of the intruders dropped his weapon and grabbed hold of his arm, screaming. In the time it took Flaherty to reload, the other man had moved closer. This time, his cousin shot the pistol out of the man's hand.

"Think he got a piece of that one's hand," one of the duke's footmen whispered.

"Or grazed it," Thompson mused.

Garahan shrugged. "Either way, they aren't getting past us this night." With a nod to the moaning would-be kidnappers, he grumbled, "Let's take care of this rabble and send for the constable."

⤜⤜⤜⤜

THE DOOR TO the nursery swung open. Patrick stood in the doorway, face grim, jaw tight. "Fetch Mollie and Francis!"

"I cannot leave the babes!"

He strode into the room. "I'll be standin' guard until ye return. Fetch them quickly, shots have been fired from the roof. We need to hide the babes upstairs!"

"Of course," she whispered.

He used the tip of his finger to prod her toward the door. Without looking back, she rushed down the hallway and opened the door to the staircase leading to the servants' sleeping quarters. Stumbling up the steps, she ignored the ache in her shin and rattled up the steps.

The door swung open before she could turn the knob.

"Mrs. Alexander! What are you doing here?" Mollie asked.

"Who's watching the babes?" Francis demanded.

"Patrick. Shots were fired. He needs you two to come and get the babes."

"We heard the shots, sounded as if Flaherty was standing right next to our heads," Mollie added.

"Hurry," Francis urged.

The women remembered to muffle their steps as they descended, but when they reached the hallway leading to the nursey, they ran full out. Time was of the essence!

O'Malley was waiting for them, rifle still over his shoulder and pistol tucked into the front of his trousers.

"How do you intend to defend those darling babes?" Gwendolyn demanded while Francis and Mollie fashioned bundled blankets exchanging them for the babes they now held to their hearts.

Ignoring her question, he stepped outside of the room and surveyed the area before motioning to the young women, and their precious bundles, that the coast was clear. "Lock yer door and prop a chair beneath the doorknob."

When the maids nodded, he added, "Do not let anyone inside but me!"

"Yes, Patrick," Mollie whispered.

"We won't," Francis promised.

Watching until the door to the staircase leading to the upper floor quietly closed behind the women, he turned back to Gwendolyn. "Just how willin' are ye to protect those babes?"

"I'd do anything in my power to protect them," she declared.

"Go inside and make sure those bundled blankets look like yer charges sleepin' in their cradles. Then do what ye'd normally do while they sleep."

Hands to her hips, fire in her eyes, she hissed, "You want me to sit while the kidnappers could be on their way inside?"

"Ye said ye'd do anythin' within yer power. I'm thinkin' sittin' in that rocker would be it."

"Why—"

"Ye said ye trust me. I'm askin' ye to shut yer *gob* until this is finished!"

Gwendolyn gasped, outrage pouring through her veins, heating her blood. She opened her mouth to speak, but O'Malley's glare had her closing it. She walked over to the rocking chair, sat, and pulled her journal from her apron pocket.

Satisfied he'd gotten her to do as he'd ordered, he slipped outside and closed the door behind him.

Hands shaking, she dropped her pencil twice before she could settle the adrenalin coursing through her. She opened the journal, turned to the next page, and began to write. "The second kidnapping attempt began with shots being fired from the roof..."

Dear God in Heaven! How was she to protect those darling babes from harm? A pouch of rocks was no match for a pistol or rifle! Tears welled in her eyes. Though she tried to stop them from falling, one escaped, trickling from the corner of her eye along the edge of her cheek. She wiped it with the back of her hand, but another took its place.

"I can cry later," she whispered into the darkened room. The candle on the table beside her was her only light. O'Malley had extinguished the others, while giving her orders.

With him standing guard outside the nursery door, unknown intruders trying to break into the duke's and duchess' home, and the babes secreted upstairs with the upstairs maids, Gwendolyn accepted that she had no control over the situation.

But there was one thing left that she could do...she prayed!

CHAPTER TWENTY

"STAY HERE!" THE duke strode to the door, opened it, and slipped outside.

Persephone waited until she heard the rumble of voices in the hallway before getting out of bed and donning her dressing gown. Chilled to the bone, she shivered. There was only one reason one of their staff would summon the duke in the middle of the night.

"The twins!"

Dashing to the door, she yanked it open to find Humphries walking alongside her husband speaking quietly to him.

Sensing whatever had happened required silence, she approached them with care before reaching out to touch her husband's back.

He jolted but did not turn around. "I distinctly remember telling you to stay in our bedchamber."

"Have you hit your head on something hard, darling?"

He spun around to face her. "When I give an order—" he began.

"You bloody well expect me to follow it. But you will remember that I do not like being ordered about."

He scrubbed a hand over his face, then raked his fingers through his hair. "You will be the death of me," he growled.

With as much hauteur as she could manage after midnight, she replied, "I do not care for your tone."

"Humphries, escort my wife back to our bedchamber."
Frowning at her, he added, "See that she remains inside while you
guard the door from the outside!"

"Jared, I insist."

He grabbed her arms and yanked her close. "If you value the
lives of our babes, you will do as I say immediately. Is that clear?"

Tears filled her eyes. She had her answer. Their twins were
being threatened…for the second time in a fortnight. Without a
word, she squared her shoulders and lifted her chin. "Crystal."

He let her go but did not watch to see if she obeyed his dictate. He trusted she would. As he approached the nursery,
O'Malley turned toward him.

"Yer Grace."

"Our babes?"

"Sleeping. Mrs. Alexander is with them."

"Excellent." Taking a moment to collect himself, he asked,
"Has anyone entered our home tonight?"

"No one. I'm expecting a report from Garahan shortly. One
of yer footmen advised that the two intruders have been subdued
and are waiting for the constable to arrive."

The duke blew out the breath he'd pulled in. "I need a word
with Mrs. Alexander and to look in on Richard and Abigail.
Persephone would have my head if I returned without having
actually seen them."

"Of course." O'Malley stepped aside and let the duke enter
the room.

"Mrs. Alexander?"

"Your Grace. Is everything all right?"

"I was about to ask you the same. Did anything occur that I
need to tell Persephone?"

Without missing a beat, she glanced at the cradles and then
back. "Just that they are sleeping peacefully. As always, I'll send
word when they wake up hungry."

"I'll just have a look then, shall I? I will not get any rest if I do
not check myself."

She rose and walked beside him. "Careful not to wake them. Her Grace needs her sleep."

The duke nodded. When he stood between the cradles, he stared at them for a moment before turning back to ask, "Why are their blankets covering their heads? Can they breathe?"

"Yes, they can breathe. There's a draft, and I did not want them to catch a chill."

She prayed he would not look too closely because she did not know how long she could keep up the pretense. So much had happened since Mollie confided the plan to hide the babes, she did not recall if the duchess told the duke of O'Malley's plan.

O'Malley opened the door to the nursery to advise, "The constable has arrived."

With a nod to her, the duke strode to the door, closing it behind him.

Gwendolyn sank to the floor between the cradles as the after-effects of lying to her employer hit her between the eyes.

"Gwendolyn?"

Strong arms scooped her off the floor. Though he reassured her everything would be all right, she could not seem to stop trembling.

"Are ye cold?"

She shook her head.

"Worried?"

She nodded.

"His Grace's bark can be abrasive, but 'tis his bite that ye need to watch out for."

That comment had her looking up at him. The worry she saw had her wondering if the situation had not been fully handled. "Has something else happened? Was one of your men injured?"

"Nay," he replied. "'Tis ye I'm concerned about."

"Oh," she whispered. "Not telling the duke the truth—that his babes were upstairs and folded blankets in their cradles, scared the breath out of me."

"Why did ye not tell him the truth?"

"I couldn't remember if he knew of your plans to spirit the babes upstairs with Mollie and Francis."

"So ye lied for the sake of me hide?"

Tears filled her eyes, but she blinked them away to respond, "And to protect you."

"How often have ye had to lie to yer employer?"

She frowned up at him. "Never."

His brows arched up and surprise filled his gaze. "Well now. As it isn't a habit of yers to prevaricate, I'm thinkin' mayhap ye feel more for me hide than ye've admitted."

Tears stung the backs of her eyes, but she refused to give in to them. She could cry later—buckets if necessary. "Mayhap I do."

"I'm not in a position to follow me heart. Even if I were free to do so, I cannot afford any distractions now that His Grace has reinstated me."

Hurt lanced through her as his words sank in. He may be attracted to her, he may have kissed her, but he could not and would not be distracted by her. "I see."

"I do not think ye do. But I'm hopin' ye will soon." He carried her over to the fainting couch, and gently laid her upon it. Then he turned to walk over to the corner and ring the bell pull. "Someone will stand guard outside this door while I fetch Mollie, Francis, and the babes."

"Before the duke returns?" she asked.

Need tangled with desperate desire as his green eyes deepened to the color of the forest at night. "Aye."

A SHORT WHILE later, the maids bustled in with the babes fussing in their arms. "We didn't remember the trick you use to put them to sleep," Francis explained.

"Was it rubbing their cheeks or their ears?" Mollie wanted to know.

Gwendolyn smiled, taking the fussiest of the two—Richard. Cooing to him, she traced one of his eyebrows and then the other, repeating the motion until he quieted. She settled him in his cradle.

Mollie gathered the blankets and folded them, placing them on the chest of drawers beneath the window. "Eyebrows! How could I have forgotten?"

"When it isn't your primary task, it's easy to forget." Gwendolyn reached for Abigail. Using the same motions on the little one, she soon had her soothed and settled her in the cradle.

Francis folded the extra blankets and turned back to face her. "Have you heard anything yet?"

"Not yet," Gwendolyn replied. "Mayhap it would be a good idea to send for Her Grace. She's bound to be climbing the walls right about now."

"I'll go and fetch her," Mollie volunteered.

Francis hesitated. "Aren't we supposed to stay here?"

Gwendolyn glanced from one young woman to the other. "Did Patrick tell you to stay here after you returned the babes to their cradles?"

"No," they answered at the same time.

"Well then, Francis and I will stay here while you go and tell the duchess that the babes are getting restless."

"I'll be right back," Mollie promised as she dashed from the nursery.

True to her word, she returned with the duchess in tow.

"There now, darlings, Mamma is here," she crooned, lifting Richard into her arms. He immediately started to cry.

Gwendolyn was quick to assure the duchess he had only just started fussing as she changed Abigail. Then she lifted the babe into her arms to walk with her. "He always likes to let you know he's hungry and ready to eat. Now Abigail here is quite the little lady. Her cries are much more dignified."

"Would you like one of us to stay with you, Your Grace?" Francis inquired.

"Gwendolyn and I will be fine. Thank you for staying with her while I was impatiently waiting for my husband to return."

"Our pleasure," Mollie assured her.

"Of course, Your Grace," Francis was quick to remark.

The two maids left the room with the promise to return to take over the early morning shift.

The duchess smiled as she settled into her favorite rocking chair. She sighed as her babe made soft little grunting sounds as he greedily ate his fill. She chuckled, brushing the tip of her finger atop his head. "Slow down or you're going to spit it all back up."

"That didn't take long," Gwendolyn noted. "Why don't we switch? I'll walk with Richard and see if I can coax a burp out of him."

"How did I manage without you, Gwendolyn?"

She smiled as she placed Abigail in the duchess' left arm, picked Richard up and placed him against her shoulder. "Probably quite well, though mayhap without as much sleep as you needed."

"Jared and I stumbled about for the first two weeks. Thank goodness for Merry and Constance insisting they take turns with Mollie and Francis. Between the four of us, we managed until the first nanny arrived."

"I'm sorry it has been such a difficult process finding someone to care for your babes."

"It was more difficult than either Jared or I envisioned," the duchess admitted. "Though now that you're here, our babes love spending time with you."

"They've told you, I suppose." Gwendolyn teased.

The duchess lifted her head and smiled at Gwendolyn. "Not in so many words. It's the way they stare up at you as I'm passing one of them off to you during their feedings. Watching their eyes widen when you speak to them in that soft voice you use exclusively for them. The only other person they react that way to is me."

"Your babes are a precious gift. It is my privilege and honor to take care of them for you and His Grace."

"They sense you love them, too."

Persephone's words warmed her heart to the point where she

had to confess. "I do love them. How could I not?"

The duchess lifted Abigail, replete from her meal, to her shoulder and rubbed the little one's back in slow circular motions. When she burped, the duchess smiled. "Time to go back to sleep."

"Why don't you let me put her down? Richard's fast asleep and you look as if you could use some yourself, Persephone."

"I am a bit wrung out, what with Jared dashing off and ordering me to stay put," she mumbled as she handed the babe to Gwendolyn.

Neither one mentioned the fact that the babes had been rushed upstairs to the maids' bedchambers. They were safe and the intruders stopped. "I'll just walk her a bit to see if she has another tiny burp before I put her down."

"What about you?" the duchess inquired. "I know you've been up for some time."

"I'll lay down on the fainting couch. It's quite comfy, you know."

"A cat nap will not replace a good night's sleep."

"Of course not, but it'll do until Mollie or Francis return for their morning shift." The tiny burp had her smiling. "Now I can put little Abigail to bed, and you can seek yours."

"Be sure and wake me if they fuss and won't settle down for you."

"Of course."

The duchess paused in the doorway. "I'm so very glad you're here caring for our babes."

"I love every moment of it. I'll see you in a few hours."

The duchess bid her goodnight and closed the door.

Alone, Gwendolyn admitted to herself that she was so very tempted to trade places with the duchess—if not for the fact that she did not have any feelings for the duke, other than to be wary of him. Now if she was wed to Patrick and these precious little ones were their babes...

"No use wishing for what cannot be, Gwendolyn," she admonished. "Get some rest, your charges will wake and be hungry before you know it."

Her last thought as her eyes drifted closed was to wonder if their babes would have green eyes or amber...

CHAPTER TWENTY-ONE

G WENDOLYN WOKE WITH a start. Richard whimpered in his cradle. Rushing to his side, she reached down to rub his back. His whimpers increased in volume. Afraid he'd rouse his mother when she needed her sleep, Gwendolyn scooped him up into her arms. "Poor babe, what's the matter?"

He started to hiccup and wiggle in her arms. His tiny face scrunched in anguish. Shifting him to her shoulder, she was relieved when he stopped moving and let her rub his back. Cradling his neck and his bottom, she eased him back to look into his eyes. His were wide open and staring at her. "That's better, isn't it, love?"

He smiled and promptly threw up his last feeding…all over her nightrail and wrapper. She shivered as she felt it soak through the layers to chill on her skin. "Poor little thing."

Carrying him over to his cradle, she quickly changed his sleeping gown and nappy, covered him up, and laid him down to blot her chest and shoulders. In her bid to dry off, she hit her toe on the chest of drawers and muffled a groan so as not to wake the babes.

The door opened and Patrick stepped inside. "Is everythin' all right?"

She held one of the spare blankets to her chest and answered, "Yes, thank you." Another shiver wracked her body as she turned around.

"Do ye need me to fetch yer shawl?"

She turned her back on him, embarrassed to the core that her wrapper and nightrail were soaked and practically see-through.

The sound of his footsteps drawing nearer had her heart beating faster. Dear Father in Heaven, not now! She needed to compose herself. She could feel goosebumps breaking out all over her body...and parts of her that should most definitely not be showing were on display for all to see, save for the blanket clutched to cover her bosom.

"Here, now, Lass." His voice was pitched so low that the vibrations soothed her.

He removed his frockcoat and placed it around her shoulders. The warmth immediately surrounded her, enveloping her in his scent. Cold, crisp air, and evergreens entwined with an indefinable scent that was Patrick O'Malley.

"Are ye warmin' up then?"

Need for this man swept up from her toes, shocking her. She had not felt this way in all the time she'd been a widow. *Why now? Why this irritating man?*

"Are ye ill? Do ye need me to fetch Merry or Constance?"

She shook her head. It was obviously not the response he was expecting. He grabbed hold of her shoulders and spun her about to face him. His coat—and the fabulous warmth, started to slip off her shoulders. She grabbed it with both hands, dropping the cloth that hid her near nakedness from him.

Her sharp intake of breath was echoed by a much deeper one.

They stared at one another for what seemed like hours, though it could only have been moments. She watched his Adam's apple bob as he swallowed and cleared his throat. "Did ye spill the pitcher of water over yerself?" His gaze slowly dipped down to her waist and then back to her face. "Is that why ye're soaked to the skin?"

The impact he had on her rendered her speechless. She shook her head and trembled.

"Ah, Lass, ye'll be the death of me." He pulled her against him, wrapping his arms around her. The heat of the man seared her chilled breasts, warming them. His low groan sounded as if he were in pain.

Was he? Mayhap her gown was as icy as it felt.

"I'm sorry to be such a bother, Patrick. Please let me go. I'd hate for Richard's spit up to soak through your waistcoat."

He stiffened and then began to laugh. "Spit up, is it?"

She nodded, relieved when he eased back from her. "I cannot say I've ever had the pleasure of holdin' a half-dressed woman covered in spit up."

Gwendolyn could feel her cheeks flush. What could she say? She had never been in such a position before and had no idea how to respond. She stared at her toes. The last man who saw her in her nightclothes was her husband. That was ages ago.

"There's nothin' to be ashamed of, Gwendolyn," he assured her, pulling the edges of his frockcoat so it covered her completely. "Will ye not look at me?"

She sighed. "I've never been so embarrassed. Please forgive me."

"I cannot see how 'twould be yer fault that one of the babes lost his last meal all over ye."

"It's that…well," she considered. "Not just that. I've never been alone with a man other than my husband dressed like this."

He nudged her chin up. "So ye were accustomed to wearin' yer husband's frockcoat over yer nightclothes then?"

She slowly smiled, realizing he was trying to ease her embarrassment by asking something so silly. So, she agreed. "But only every other night."

"Could start quite a trend, I'm thinkin'."

"Thank you for letting me borrow your coat, it's very warm."

He leaned close, about to say something when he sniffed, then leaned closer and sniffed again. "Lord, I had no idea it'd smell so rank."

Her mouth rounded in shock before she put a hand to her

mouth to cover her laughter. It would not do to wake the babes. Bending her head down, she inhaled and had to agree. "Most babe's spit up smells like this. It's not the first time, and I doubt it'll be the last time I'll end up wearing one of my charge's meals."

His smile had her wishing, not for the first time, that she wasn't a distraction to him. "I'd best ring for Mollie or Francis to relieve ye, so ye can change."

"Actually, it's nearly time for one of them to show up. I don't mind waiting."

When he started to disagree with her, she added, "I'll ask Humphries to have the duke's valet launder yer coat in case the...odor lingers."

He grinned at her. "Ye're certain I cannot ring for someone?"

"I'm fine. Thank you for taking the time, and for worrying about me."

Patrick's eyes deepened to the shade of the forest at night. This was the second time it had happened, and she knew without question that he felt the same pull toward her that she felt toward him.

Though neither of them would act on their feelings, she stepped back from him. The few kisses they'd shared were an aberration and would not be repeated. More's the pity, as her Grandmother O'Toole would say. His beautifully sculpted lips, tempted her as the need to press hers against them nearly overwhelmed her.

"I'd best be goin'," he stalked to the door. "If ye need me before one of the lassies arrive, just open the door. I'll be standin' guard."

"Thank you, Patrick."

He was about to close the door when he felt her hand on his arm. "Lass?"

"Why is it that when you're standing guard, you never have your sword?"

Would he ever understand the complexity of a woman's mind? "If anyone made it past the perimeter and inside, they'd be tryin' to sneak up on me and me kin. A sword isn't of much use when your enemy is close at hand."

She frowned. "I don't understand."

Patrick groaned, the woman was distracting him by standing so close to him. He dug deep to ignore the pull of her to explain. "'Tis better to have a short blade and pistol handy for fightin' in close quarters—though I'd rather be using me fists."

"Then why do people call you The Duke's Sword?"

"Hell if I know. I've only had to use one once or twice protecting His Grace."

The scent of honeysuckle rose above the malodorous spit up and beckoned him closer. "Ye'd best be goin' back inside now. I'm neglectin' me post."

Without a word, she inclined her head, slipped back inside and closed the door.

He stared at the closed door, surprised that it sounded so final. Was he closing the door on the possibility of what may lie between them? Reason quickly returned knowing that Patrick lived the job as head of the duke's guard and could not afford to let anything take his focus away from his duties. Her life revolved around caring for the twins slumbering peacefully behind her—until her next position.

Taking the time to see if there could be more between them was out of the question. But in her dreams, all things were possible. She lay down on the fainting coach, snuggling further into Patrick's frockcoat and sighed. As sleep claimed her, she dreamed she was wrapped in his strong arms, delighting in the press of his lips to hers. Her heart soared with the realization that she could have a second chance and realize her long-suppressed dreams of a home and family…a husband to protect her, provide for her…love her.

Love her as she loved him. Their eyes met and she whispered the words she'd been holding in her heart, "*I love you, Patrick.*"

O'MALLEY STOOD WITH his back to the door. Sweat beaded across his forehead as his body reacted to the lush woman whose very presence just a few feet away beckoned to him. She would have him on his knees begging her if not for his stubborn will not to give in. This nearly uncontrollable need to scoop her into his arms and carry her away slashed through him as he fought for control. Once he had her in his arms, he'd never let her go until he purged this burning desire for her out of him.

With each breath he blew out and drew in, the armor of his control clapped into place, banding around his ribs, his chest, until he could breathe without panting like a madman. His cravat was too tight. He tugged at it to loosen the knot until he no longer felt as if he had a hangman's noose around his neck. It was in that moment, while his gaze swept the area, listening to the household for any hint that all was not as it should be, he came to the conclusion that once he had her where he wanted her—in his bed…he'd never let her leave.

He'd sup from her sweet lips, caress her curvaceous body from head to toe, lighting the fire he knew waited for him to strike the flint and create the spark that would burn them until nothing was left but the ashes of their passion.

And then what? He blinked as his father's voice whispered in his ear. "Da?" Angry with himself for letting his mind wander where he dared not let it go, he reminded himself his father was buried on their family farm in Cork and Mrs. Alexander was out of his reach.

With a quick shake, he brought his full attention back to his duty—protecting the duke's and duchess' infant twins. The flames of desire died down, cooling him. His sweat-drenched shirt stuck to his body, chilling him to the bone. He snorted in disgust at his lack of control. He'd survived many a night in sub-freezing temperatures before. He could handle standing in the cold hallway of the duke's home in a damp shirt.

He curled his hands into fists and clenched his jaw. "It won't be a problem now," he vowed. "She's just a woman who prefers to dress in earth-tones instead of a bold blue to bring out her Irish whiskey-colored eyes and roses to her cheeks."

His mind started to veer off thinking of how he'd like to press his lips to the delicate skin beneath her ear as she tilted her head to one side to give him better access. Her soft moans kindled the ashes of his desire as he gently nipped, then placed warm, moist kisses from her collarbone to the hollow at the base of her throat. He inhaled and was once again surrounded by her unique scent…sun-warmed honeysuckle.

He growled low in his throat, bringing his lust under control. "This *shite* stops now!" Changing his stance until he was on the balls of his feet, ready to spring in any direction at a moment's notice, he finally felt in control. Ready to take on all comers. God, he needed to pound the bloody hell out of someone—make that more than one someone.

O'Malley slowly smiled. He'd have his chance tomorrow when the duke joined their family *discussion*. He couldn't wait to beat the *shite* out of his cousins! If the duke really wanted to spar with him, he'd consider it. Aye, and he may even give His Grace the full force of his uppercut. If the man was still standing after a blow like that, Patrick would drop his hands and let the duke take a swing at him.

The weight of his worries lifted from his shoulders as he imagined what a grand bout they'd be having in the afternoon. Testing his mettle and skills against his cousins always brought a smile to his face—and guaranteed a jab to his gut.

'Twas the simple things in life a man needed. A job he loved, his family surrounding him, and a no-holds-barred bare knuckle bout to vent his frustrations.

A whisper of honeysuckle drifted past his nose. He jolted as he realized the door behind him was open. Turning, he asked, "Is anything the matter?"

She shook her head. "I thought I heard voices."

He sighed. "'Tis me arguing."

"With whom?"

He shrugged. "Meself."

She bit her bottom lip. "I'll…er…let you get back to it then."

His swift nod of agreement was punctuated by the closing of the nursery door.

"Ye're a bloody *eedjit*, O'Malley!"

"Aye, but faith, we love ye in spite of it," Garahan remarked, striding toward him.

"Have ye handled the intruders?"

"Did ye doubt we would?"

"Nay. Been champin' at the bit to be in the thick of things," O'Malley admitted.

"'Twasn't much of a challenge. They were London men…had no idea how to use their surroundings as cover or pitch their voices low so as not to be overheard."

"Flaherty took them out from his perch behind the gargoyles?"

Garahan grinned. "Aye."

"They didn't try to fight ye when ye hauled them to the outbuilding next to ours to wait for the constable?"

"They moaned the entire way. It'd be me guess neither one had been shot before."

"Winged?"

"Aye and shot the pistol out of the other man's hand—got a bit of his hand, too."

"Did anyone patch them up?"

"The stable master keeps a supply of clean linens on hand. He stopped the bleeding before the constable arrived. Although why the man failed to bring a wagon to haul the men away, I've no clue."

"Isn't it the same man who was here when Hollingford and his men attacked?"

Garahan shrugged. "'Twas more than a year ago, and I don't

recall meeting the man."

"Is he waitin' for one of his men to bring a wagon from the village?"

"Nay. The stable master hitched up one of the duke's geldings to one of the supply wagons. Flaherty and I had to help load the men," he shook his head in disgust. "Ye'd think they were dying from the way they wept and wailed."

"Did ye manage to extract any information from them?"

Garahan slowly smiled. "Aye, that was the highlight of me evening."

O'Malley waited, knowing his cousin would take his time telling a tale he obviously relished.

"I may have hinted that neither Flaherty nor I would bandage them up until they told us who hired them."

"Did ye now?"

"And," Garahan drawled, "Flaherty may have interrupted, saying he thought the plan was to let them bleed out."

O'Malley clapped his cousin on the shoulder and chuckled. "Was that when they started wailin'?"

Garahan snorted. "And begging us not to let them bleed to death. I had to step in then and remind them of our terms. Tell us who hired them, and we'd bandage them up."

O'Malley nodded. "Who hired them?"

"Lord Radleigh."

O'Malley's eyes narrowed. "What of the rumor that it was Lady Hampton?"

"King's men have discovered she has a brother..."

"Radleigh?"

"Aye," Garahan agreed.

"If her brother is involved," O'Malley began, "have King's men uncovered anythin' other than the family connection?"

"Apparently rumors are rife through the *ton*."

"And?" O'Malley prompted.

"Lady Hampton has had many lovers among the *quality*."

"The Fifth Duke of Wyndmere was murdered leavin' her

bed," O'Malley stated. "Her husband took his own life after killin' the duke. Given the situation, it would not be surprisin' that she would have to take on a number of protectors to keep her in jewels and gowns."

Garahan agreed. "Her brother has been putting it about that the rumors are untrue."

"Tryin' to salvage their family name," O'Malley speculated. "But why come after the duke's babes?"

"Can ye think of anything else that would slice His Grace to the bone than that?"

O'Malley shook his head. "Radleigh's clever to have thought of it. Though it'll go hard against him when King brings the lord in for questioning."

"What of Lady Hampton?" Garahan asked. "Do ye think King'll question her as well?"

"He may use her as leverage to get Radleigh to confess to bein' behind the kidnappin' plot."

"'Twould be a relief to have him brought to justice."

"Aye," O'Malley agreed. "The duke and duchess have been through hell and back. 'Tis more than time for them to have a reprieve from it."

Garahan stared at his cousin and asked, "Did ye lose yer coat?"

O'Malley shrugged.

Garahan sniffed, then leaned closer to sniff again. "What in God's name is that smell?"

O'Malley sighed. "Spit up."

Garahan's eyes widened. "I beg yer pardon?"

"'Tis a long story for another time."

"Ah, it must involve the lovely Mrs. Alexander."

"It may."

"The lot of us noticed the way ye watch her, 'tis more than just to satisfy yer needs."

O'Malley froze at his cousin's words, insulted on Gwendolyn's behalf. The urge to haul off and plant his fist in his cousin's face nearly strangled him. He drew in a breath to calm down.

"The three of us have talked it over and decided ye best be courting the lass with the intention of marrying her before anyone else notices the depth of yer desire. Sure and His Grace would not approve of yer lusting after a woman in his employ."

"Lust?" O'Malley choked out. "What do ye know of it?"

Garahan snorted out a laugh. "Enough to find comfort away from Wyndmere Hall where the walls have ears."

O'Malley was seldom surprised, but Darby had managed to do just that. "When would ye have had the time when we're workin' day and night guardin' His Grace and his family?"

"I have me ways."

"If ye don't want His Grace findin' out and sackin' ye, ye'll not be headin' into the village on a whim."

Garahan's grin irritated him. "Well now, I wouldn't call the need to lie with a soft woman and spend a stolen hour or two in her arms a whim."

His cousin's words had O'Malley's hands curling into fists. With every ounce of control he could muster, he shoved the need to knock Garahan on his arse aside. "I'll be warnin' ye now, and the others later at our family meeting."

"Care to place a wager, Cousin?" Garahan taunted.

O'Malley ground his back teeth before answering, "Me ma didn't raise any fools."

Garahan shook his head. "Wager or no, I'll get ye to spill yer guts tonight."

O'Malley crossed his arms in front of him and glared at his cousin.

Garahan strode toward the servants' staircase whistling.

Satisfaction flowed through O'Malley. Their meetings always included a bit of bare knuckle sparring. "Ye'll be the first one I'll be punchin'!"

Garahan's laughter followed him down.

CHAPTER TWENTY-TWO

G WENDOLYN STEPPED INTO the copper slipper tub and sighed as the hot water eased the ache between her shoulder blades. Normally, a hot bath was all it took to relieve the aches and occasional stress that came with taking care of her charges.

Though the dried honeysuckle flowers were dear in price, they were the one luxury she allowed herself to indulge in. Stirring the water with her hand, she watched the flowers spinning around and around like they were caught on a breeze swirling around her. Inhaling deeply, she closed her eyes and imagined it was a warm day in late June, one of her favorite times of the year.

A gust of wind rattled the windowpanes, reminding her that it was winter—not summer. With a heartfelt sigh, she leaned against the back of the tub and relaxed. She tried to soak her worries away—most of which revolved around the tall, broad-shouldered, handsome Patrick O'Malley. The honeysuckle floated in a ring. Intrigued, she stared at the pattern and then inside the ring. The light-haired, green-eyed larger-than-life Irishman was not only haunting her nights, but now her days! Slapping her hand at his image to get it out of her mind, she succeeded in getting her hair wet—although it was bundled atop her head and splashing water on the floor.

She'd tarried too long if she was having daydreams about

O'Malley. It was time to finish up. Once she'd scrubbed from head to toe, she slowly stood and reached for the drying cloth next to the tub and wrapped it around her. Careful to brace a hand on the bench by the tub, she eased one foot out and then the other.

The chill falling off the window had her drying off and dressing quickly. Though the view of the wide expanse of snow-covered lawn and snow-packed drive leading from the front of the duke's and duchess' home to the village of Wyndmere was lovely, this was not the time of year to linger in a tub. She laughed to herself. In her experience, as a nanny, one *never* lingered in a tub, no matter the season.

Sitting in the occasional chair next to the lady's desk, she unpinned her hair, careful to place the hairpins in the battered tin cup her father had carried with him during his years in his regiment. The cup and her mother's locket were the only mementos she had...the rest had been sold to pay for her mother's burial.

Taking the time to brush the tangles from her hair, she twisted it into a knot and pinned it on top of her head. Though she always had strands that slipped free from the pins, the overall look wasn't as disastrous as if she tried to braid it and coil it at the base of her neck. That usually ended up getting pulled from the pins by tiny fingers throughout the day.

A glance in the looking glass hanging above the washstand was all she needed to see that she was ready to face the day. She hadn't pinched her cheeks in years, and never had any interest in using lip salve or any of the other cosmetics some women in society used to enhance their looks. Her husband had heartily approved of her natural beauty, and she'd never had a reason to doubt him.

Though she was attracted to Patrick, given his comments about not needing a distraction, which apparently she was, she had no one in her life to primp for. Even if he was interested, she certainly wasn't about to start now.

Interested? Hah! He'd been rendered speechless early this morning when she'd managed to drop the blanket and revealed her nightrail and wrapper were all but see-through after the soaking from the poor little mite's spit up. The intensity in the depths of his glittering green eyes tempted her to see if their earlier kiss was in the heat of the moment and easily forgotten, or perhaps something more.

"What am I thinking?" *Good Lord, did she have attics to let?* How could she possibly look him in the eyes after he'd seen what no other man had since her husband had passed? Though she'd been fully clothed, once the garments were damp, they clung to every curve and left nothing to the imagination. Would he act the part of a gentleman or leer at her the next time he saw her?

Truth be told, he hadn't leered this morning…well, he had been staring intently but, heavens, he was a man after all. Weren't they guided by their baser natures most of the time? Dear Lord, it had been years since she'd felt anything at all for a man. Not that she had been trying to, with Patrick O'Malley it just happened.

What would she do? How should she handle this debacle? Move forward as if it had not happened, or discuss it with him? She shook her head. Best not to bring up the subject if he appeared to be acting normally.

"Yes," she told her reflection. "Act normally." Pretend his seeing her nightrail and wrapper molded to her breasts was a normal occurrence. If he brought it up, she'd wave his comment aside and change the subject. She'd handled herself properly on the two other occasions when a gentleman's comments were far too forward.

She could do this. She was a worldly woman, no prim miss just out of the school room. With a calm she had to work to maintain, she took one last look at her reflection and nodded. Gwendolyn was satisfied her charges would not care one way or the other if she'd dressed in the subtle earth-tones that reminded her of her childhood spent digging in the gardens with her mum, or brighter colors that were more expensive. She swept from the room in search of a bite to eat before returning to her duties in the nursery.

Descending the servants' staircase to the kitchen, she had a feeling it was going to be a very long day, especially if she spent a good part of it trying to avoid a certain member of the duke's guard.

"O'MALLEY?"

He paused, waiting for the duke's valet to catch up to him. "Something on yer mind, Stames?"

"Your frockcoat." Stames held out the coat O'Malley had been wearing just last night before he'd draped it around Gwendolyn's shoulders to warm her.

"My thanks. I'd planned to ask Mrs. Alexander about it this afternoon."

"Merry asked if I would see to the stain…and the unusual odor." Stames' lips twitched as if he fought the urge to smile. "My older brother used to have similar stains and odors on the shoulders of his waistcoats when my nieces were infants."

O'Malley sighed. "Do ye plan to needle me until I tell ye why there was spit up on me coat?"

Stames grinned. "It boggles the mind, O'Malley. So yes, I do believe I shall."

O'Malley shook his head. "I've no time to debate with ye, Stames. 'Tis simple. During me shift guarding the nursery, I thought I heard Mrs. Alexander fall. I helped her to her feet, and noticed the poor woman was shiverin'. I gave her me coat."

The duke's valet prompted, "And that's it?"

"*Shite!*"

Stames shook his head. "I have an excellent sense of smell. It was definitely spit up…not *shite* as you eloquently put it."

"I've a meetin' with His Grace. If ye don't mind."

Stames was still smiling when he replied, "Best not to keep His Grace waiting."

O'Malley wondered what was being said among the staff. He'd never given a thought to the possibility that someone would draw any conclusion other than what really happened. Had Gwendolyn spoken to Mollie or Francis when they came to relieve her early this morning?

Striding down the hallway to the duke's study, he paused, glancing at the staircase leading to the upper floor and wondered if she would shy away from him after last night. The memory slashed through him. Gwendolyn Alexander was a woman to be wary of...a woman who had the power to make him forget his vows to the duke and his family.

She was a woman to avoid at all costs.

He knocked on the study door and entered at the duke's command.

"Ah, Patrick I need to ask—" The duke glanced at the coat O'Malley carried. "I see the rumors circulating belowstairs this morning have a grain of truth to them."

"A grain," Patrick agreed. "But no more."

"Indeed. Just the bare facts, if you do not mind. By the by, a missive from Coventry was just delivered for you."

"Can we set aside the matter of me coat for now?"

The duke nodded, handing O'Malley the sealed note.

Patrick's jaw clenched as his suspicions were confirmed by Captain Coventry. "Coventry confirmed Lady Hampton's brother, Lord Radleigh, has been seen meetin' with a number of men who frequent the docks. Those that ply their trade for a bit of coin, if ye get me meanin'. He's bent on avenging his sister's reputation."

"Bloody hell!" the duke roared. "The woman's reputation should have been in tatters after my brother was shot in the back leaving her *boudoir*!"

"Aye, but the *quality* have an odd sense of right and wrong," Patrick remarked. "I still cannot understand how they would support the woman."

"There were those who shunned her," the duke reminded him. "Though most felt sorry for the woman who'd lost her lover and her husband in one night."

Patrick shook his head. "Those of the workin' class are much easier to understand."

"Like those who would commit a crime for a handful of coins?" the duke challenged.

"Aye. Most men—especially those down on their luck, would do anythin' to put food on their families' tables," O'Malley replied. "Others—like the ones who come out at night on the docks, do it for the coin alone. I understand that as well, and don't believe they should go unpunished."

The duke seemed to calm down as he thought over what O'Malley had just said. "A crime should never go unpunished."

"Ah, there's where we disagree, Yer Grace." Patrick's anger simmered at the injustice he'd witnessed back home in Ireland...and on the streets of London. "'Tis a man's job to see his family fed, clothed, and protected." He challenged the duke, "I'll not be judgin' them. 'Tis between God and the man who commits a crime when his time comes to face Him."

The duke walked to the window facing the stables, clasped his hands behind his back and stood silent. "You're thinking of Smythe."

"Aye, Yer Grace. None of us know the whole of his story. Mute all his life, he had to live by his wits and his fists. 'Tis a credit to yer brother's quick thinkin'—handin' the man a bar to draw his instructions from the treacherous Lady Hampton in the dirt floor, and his compassion that ye've gained the loyalty of another man who would do anythin' ye asked of him."

"Smythe and Garahan saved every horse in my stables the night of the fire."

"Aye. He'll do whatever task is set before him, though he prefers to stay out of the way of visitors and such. He's got the strength of one of me brothers or cousins and a heart just as big."

"Point taken, O'Malley. Did Coventry mention rounding up those who'd been hired by Radleigh?"

Patrick nodded. "Aye and advised there are four men headed to Wyndmere Hall."

"Descriptions?"

"The type that frequent the docks at night. Large men with meaty fists and black hearts."

"Then they'll strike at night," the duke surmised, "as we expect them to do."

"Their size—and position of attack, will give them away."

"All of your men are large with meaty fists," the duke reminded him.

O'Malley grinned. "'Tis a boon to have me men protectin' ye and yer family."

The duke agreed, then slowly smiled. "I'll leave you to your plans and see you after the midday meal…for the *meeting*."

"Garahan and I will be the first to spar," O'Malley informed him.

"Do you decide who you'll be sparring with before your meetings?"

"Only when the occasion warrants it, Yer Grace."

"Patrick!" The duke picked up the forgotten coat and handed it to O'Malley. "I'm looking forward to hearing the truth behind the rumors this afternoon."

Patrick sighed audibly. "Aye, Yer Grace."

He strode down the hallway to the door at the end and stepped out into the chill of the morning air. "Blasted cold. Bloody winter," he muttered, making his way along the path to his quarters. No one was inside—and shouldn't be for another four hours until the change in shift.

He hung his coat on one of the pegs on the wall, closed the door behind him, and strode to the stables to find the messenger and give the man his reply. He located the man quickly, relayed the verbal message for Coventry and directed the man to the kitchen where a hot meal and grog were waiting for him.

Time to check in with the others.

CHAPTER TWENTY-THREE

"I'LL MAKE THE tea, Constance. You have your hands full keeping up with the additional men protecting the duke's home and family."

"I've measured out the tea leaves, all you need to do is add the water. The kettle's hot."

Gwendolyn relaxed, feeling at home in the large kitchen. Constance bustled about the room, all the while keeping an eye on the bread she'd set aside earlier to rise and the large pot of stew simmering on the cookstove. Two scullery maids darted around the cook, following her instructions while chatting amiably with one another.

On a cold day like today, she reveled in the kitchen's warmth as she poured a cup of tea for Constance and one for herself. "Will Merry have time to join us for a cup this morning?"

"She's with the duchess. We can always brew another pot when she arrives."

"Is everyone always this happy?"

Constance brushed a lock of hair out of her eyes and smiled. "Since His Grace came into the title, yes. He's a wonderful master and treats each one of us with respect." Sipping from her cup, she set it down on the saucer and sighed. "It wasn't always thus."

"The previous duke?" Gwendolyn asked.

The older woman sighed. "I never speak ill of the dead."

"Of course not," Gwendolyn readily agreed. "It is such a refreshing change coming here after my last post. Everyone seemed to be looking over their shoulders half the time and ignoring one another the rest of the time."

"One of my previous positions was like that. I'm not one to be told to mind my duties—I know full well what they are. I left that position after being constantly reminded I was not to chat as if I were the lady of the manor."

"That would certainly make for a dismal environment."

Constance agreed. "Now the fourth duke, His Grace's father, was a wonderful man. Wyndmere Hall was run much the same then as it is now."

"Constance," a deep voice boomed from behind her. "Did you save any scones for—" A bear of a man strode into the room and stared before collecting himself. "I beg your pardon, I didn't realize you were entertaining."

Gwendolyn smiled. "No need," she assured the newcomer. "We're sharing a pot of tea before I return to the nursery."

"Ah, Mrs. Alexander," the man bowed. "Thompson, at your service."

She noted his bright red coat and slowly rose to her feet. "A pleasure to meet you, Mr. Thompson. You're with Mr. King's Bow Street Runners."

"Aye. Franklin, Jackson, Greeves, and I are here for a few days."

Surprised that he made it sound as if they were visiting instead of on assignment, she offered, "Why don't you take my seat? I need to get back."

"No, thank you. I'm just passing through on my way to my next post." Smiling at the cook, he added, "And hoping for one of your delicious scones, Constance."

The cook blushed to the roots of her gray-streaked hair. "I saved some for you." She walked to the sideboard and picked up a linen-wrapped bundle and handed it to him.

His dark eyes lit up. "They're still warm!"

"If you have a minute, I've freshly whipped cream and some berry jam."

He sighed. "Mayhap you'll save me a bit for later when I take a break to eat this afternoon."

Gwendolyn couldn't help but notice the man's interest in the duke's cook and wondered if Constance had ever been married. Her cooking was worth raving about, and Gwendolyn couldn't fault the man for paying the cook compliments.

"I'll do that," she promised.

"Thank you." He stared at her for long moments before taking his leave. "Until later." With a smile for the cook, and a nod in Gwendolyn's direction, he walked through the room and out the back door.

"Mr. Thompson must have a sweet tooth."

Constance sighed. "The four of them do, although I must say, Thompson uses flattery to talk me out of scones. The others scan the tabletops to see if there are any before asking."

"He seems sincere," Gwendolyn remarked. "It has been too many years since I spent time in a kitchen baking for my husband. I truly miss that time in my life."

Constance laid a hand on Gwendolyn's arm. "I was married for twenty years to a wonderful man—although there were times when I recall wielding a cast iron pan to get his attention."

"Did you actually take a swing at him?"

The cook chuckled. "Holding it up in front of his face was warning enough. My Theodore was a very smart man."

"You were so very lucky. I only had a few precious years with Jonathan...when he was murdered, the shock of it brought on my labor too early."

The older woman nodded and relief washed over Gwendolyn.

"I lost three babes," the cook confided. "It wasn't meant to be."

Gwendolyn glanced in the direction Thompson had gone and then back to the cook. "Did you ever think of marrying again?"

Constance blushed. "A time or two."

"I never have…is that wrong?"

Constance pulled Gwendolyn into a hug and whispered, "Listen to your heart. It's never wrong." She let go and blew at the hair that kept falling into her eyes. "Would you mind handing me that cup of hairpins. They're in the chipped one on the shelf over the sideboard."

Gwendolyn found the cup and handed it to the woman.

"Thank you. There are days when the pins just don't hold my unruly hair."

"I know the feeling. I keep a few tucked into my apron pocket. Little fingers get tangled easily and get caught if I'm not careful to put my hair up and out of the way. Thank you for the tea and the company."

"Anytime. Will you go for your walk before the midday meal?"

"I think I might. Is that a problem?"

Merriment danced in the older woman's eyes. "No. I like to have the answers ready."

"Answers? For what?"

Constance laughed. "Not what, who. A certain broad-shouldered Irishman with twinkling emerald eyes asks me the same questions every day."

Gwendolyn felt her face heat and knew her cheeks were flushed. "Questions?"

The cook was smiling when she cleared her throat, pitched her voice low, and in a perfect brogue asked, "Have ye seen Mrs. Alexander today? Is she well? Will she be walkin' before her midday meal?"

Gwendolyn's hand went to her mouth as shock arrowed through her. "Never say so!"

"Every single day. That handsome Patrick O'Malley asks the same questions."

Warmth swept from her toes to the tip of her nose. Gwendolyn sighed. "I suppose I should be flattered."

C.H. ADMIRAND

"I would be. The man wouldn't ask after your wellbeing if he did not care."

"I didn't ask to be singled out—to have him pay attention to me," she rasped.

The cook cleared away the teapot and cups, setting them aside to be washed. "It was obvious from the moment you arrived the man was smitten."

Gwendolyn held that comment to her heart. "Was it?"

"Darby Garahan told me Patrick was struck speechless watching you step down from the duke's carriage," the cook advised.

What could she say that wouldn't sound as if she were enamored with the man? Her spotless reputation as a nanny would be called into question if she let herself become involved with one of the duke's staff—or his personal guard. Finally, she managed to say, "He seemed quiet and reserved."

"He can be," the cook admitted. "Though many's the time when I've seen a very different side to the man."

Gwendolyn smoothed her skirts to cover the fact that her hands had begun to tremble as the memory of being pulled flush against Patrick's heat melted the icy cold gripping her heart for far too many years to recall.

"I'd best head up to the nursery," she remarked. "Thank you again for the tea."

"The kettle's always on the boil," the cook reminded her as she was leaving.

She checked her pockets as she ascended the main staircase. Her journal and pencil were in the one, but she'd forgotten to put one of her smaller rock-filled reticules in the other pocket. Moving quickly, she opened the door to her bedchamber and walked over to the mahogany wardrobe. Mindful of the hour, she grabbed one at random and hurried out of the room.

The door to the nursey was open, and she could hear the sound of feminine voices speaking softly. "Have you ever known O'Malley to be so smitten with a woman before?" she heard Francis ask.

188

Pausing out of sight, she waited to hear the response. "Every man in the duke's personal guard is handsome and knows the effect one of his smiles has on a woman's heart."

She silently agreed with Mollie, who she knew had first-hand experience falling for one of the men in the duke's guard. She approached the doorway in time to hear, "I've noticed the look of baffled longing in Mrs. Alexander's eyes when he enters or leaves a room. Do you think she's afraid of O'Malley?"

She cleared her throat and swept into the nursery. "I most definitely am *not* afraid of the man."

Francis and Mollie turned as one, twin looks of horror on their faces. "Mrs. Alexander!" Francis cried. "We didn't see you there."

"The two of you were too involved discussing O'Malley and me to have taken note that I was listening just outside the door."

"We didn't mean anything by it," Francis explained.

"Just speculating," Mollie was quick to add. "Forgive us."

Gwendolyn sighed. "Nothing to forgive. Just please refrain from speculating about another person's life. I can tell you from experience, over the years, I've witnessed more than one staff member being dismissed for doing just that."

Francis looked horrified while Mollie seemed to be digesting the information.

"We will try to curb our natural interest in those we work alongside of day after day," Mollie replied. "In the warmer weather, on my afternoons off, I meet with friends in the village. All are quick to boast about the handsome footmen who work for one of the neighboring squires."

Francis grinned. "They haven't boasted since that time one of His Grace's men were in the village." She paused considering, "Do you remember who it was?"

Mollie frowned. "You know it was Finn O'Malley!"

Gwendolyn sensed this was a sore subject and sought to soothe ruffled feathers. "I suppose he is alike in looks and temperament as his brother and cousin, Eamon?"

Francis sent her an apologetic look while Mollie continued to glare at the other maid.

"Mayhap you should refrain from needling Mollie, Francis. It is so much better to have a companionable relationship with those you work alongside of day after day. Is it not?"

Francis' cheeks flushed with her embarrassment. "Yes, it is." Turning to the woman fuming at her side, Francis apologized. "I'm sorry, Mollie."

"You just wished Finn paid attention to you instead of me."

Francis slowly smiled. "Who wouldn't? The man's looks are lethal to a woman's heart."

"His kisses muddled my head until I couldn't think," Mollie confessed. Tears welled in her eyes, but she wiped them away with the backs of her hands. "I vowed not to fall in love with him…but it happened anyway."

Gwendolyn knew exactly how Mollie felt. The maid turned and asked, "Do you think you'll ever fall in love again, Mrs. Alexander?"

She stiffened at the question. Constance had asked her the same thing not a quarter of an hour ago. Reluctant to answer at first, the sadness in Mollie's eyes and hesitation in Francis' had her responding, "I am not in a position to. I am responsible for maintaining the reputation I have worked hard to build as a nanny. It pays for the rooms I let in London in between positions."

"But what of your heart?" Mollie's voice sounded as if she would begin to weep at any moment.

Gwendolyn shook her head. "I cannot afford to let my heart rule my head. I do not have any family to go to if I were to lose my position here at Wyndmere Hall. The only person I can rely on is myself, and my next position depends upon the recommendation I receive from the duke and duchess."

Mollie and Francis were subdued as they took in Gwendolyn's words. "Thank you for your honesty," Mollie said. "I cannot imagine how hard it would be to rein in my heart if a handsome

Irishman watched me the way Patrick watches you."

Before Gwendolyn could speak, Francis grabbed hold of Mollie's hand and dragged her from the room.

She didn't know whether to follow after them and give them a stern talking to, or admit aloud that she was engaged in a daily battle *not* to fall under the man's spell. From the sounds of their retreating footsteps, they had already reached the stairs.

With Patrick on her mind, and the growing feelings she had for him tucked away in her heart, she pulled the reticule from her pocket and placed it behind the stack of blankets and linens on the chest of drawers.

The babes started fretting and squirming in their beds. "Time to change their nappies." Taking her time to soothe them as she changed them, Gwendolyn felt another tiny piece of her heart break free. She knew she'd never get it back and wondered if one day—in the not-too-distant future, if she'd simply expire because there were not enough pieces of her heart left to her.

Once the little ones had been cuddled, sung to, and tucked back into their beds, she settled in the rocking chair to make a few more notations in the journal she planned to gift to the duchess when she left to take up her next post.

Although she'd enjoyed writing her observations before, this time, she added bits of encouragement, and praise for Persephone who had become a confidante and good friend.

The babes were just starting to work themselves into a good cry when the duchess arrived.

"Ah, I see my darlings must have heard me speaking to Merry." She was smiling as she gathered Abigail into her arms.

The housekeeper motioned to someone in the hallway. A footman entered carrying a large tray laden with a plate piled high with sandwiches and another with scones, biscuits, and teacakes. Another followed with the tea service.

"Her Grace thought you'd enjoy a bite to eat before your midday walk."

Gwendolyn smiled. "I had not planned to," she admitted,

watching as the footmen set the trays on the side table. "But now that it's here, I admit, I'm quite famished."

"I thought you might be. Will you join us, Merry?"

The housekeeper thanked the footmen, sent them on their way and paused in the doorway. "I am running a bit behind schedule this morning and need to get back on task. Thank you for asking, Your Grace."

When the door closed behind her, the duchess settled into one of the rocking chairs with Abigail to her breast.

Richard started fussing and before he could start to cry in earnest, Gwendolyn picked him up and started to sway with him in her arms. He stopped long enough to stare up at her. Smiling down at the precious babe, she started to hum.

"Why don't you rock him?" the duchess suggested. "I need to ask you something and don't want to have to crane my neck around to see your reaction."

Startled, Gwendolyn stopped swaying. "Reaction?"

The duchess laughed. "Yes. Come sit beside me."

When Gwendolyn did as Persephone bid, the duchess sighed. "I heard the most intriguing rumor this morning."

Gwendolyn froze. Richard started to complain, reminding her to continue rocking. He didn't like to be still waiting to be fed. "Did you?"

"Mmmm," Persephone agreed. "It had to do with Patrick's frockcoat and one of his cambric shirts needing to be laundered."

Gwendolyn's stomach flipped over. Ignoring the uneasy, queasy sensation in her belly, she asked, "Do His Grace's men normally do their own laundry?"

"Not at all, although what was brought to my attention was the odd scent attached to his clothing."

Gwendolyn braced for the duchess' anger. Although she suspected she knew what Persephone would say, she asked anyway, "Odd?"

Persephone turned to face her and slowly smiled. "A combination of spit up...and of all things...honeysuckle."

CHAPTER TWENTY-FOUR

O'MALLEY PACED AS he listened to the missive Thompson had just received.

"Radleigh has been rumored to retreat to his country estate at odd times of the year—even when the House of Lords is in session. King noticed those disappearances match times when rumors connected to his sister were replaced by a new scandal."

Thompson's words had O'Malley mulling over what he'd already learned about the man before he replied. "The *quality* is easily bored and not averse to discoverin' the person or persons affected by scandal and either take action to quell the *on dit*—or add to it before passin' it on."

Thompson nodded. "And supply the *ton* with something new to chew on with their morning tea."

"Any word on Radleigh's henchmen?"

The other man glanced about him before responding, "Our contacts advise they lost sight of them for about an hour midday yesterday. A few hours later, they confirmed one of their horses went lame. It took time to replace the horse—"

"Aye, when ye don't plan to *pay* for the beast," Patrick finished the man's statement.

Thompson grunted in agreement. "Any further word from your contacts?"

"Nay."

"What time are you meeting with the duke?"

O'Malley stared at the man before he snorted. "Ye know it's a bit more than a meetin'."

Thompson cracked his knuckles and grinned. "I'm looking forward to it. Jackson, Greeves, and Franklin were grumbling about not being included, but understand that we need them guarding the perimeter with your cousin, Eamon, and the duke's staff."

"Three o'clock, in the outbuildin' by our quarters. We've already cleared the space and set up a feedbag."

"Feedbag?"

O'Malley's grin was lethal. "Aye, hangin' from the rafters. I suggested it to His Grace as he's not had the opportunity to engage in a bout with us...other than a lucky blow one time," he added beneath his breath. "I promised Her Grace nothin' would happen to him. She'd have me head if anythin' did."

The other man's eyes widened. "Bold suggestion. Calling His Grace's bare knuckle skills into question."

O'Malley shrugged in response. "His Grace knows about the promise and agreed to go a few rounds with the bag before takin' on Flaherty or Garahan."

"Why not start with you?"

O'Malley shrugged. "With one recent exception—and I was distracted at the time, I've bested every single one of me cousins."

"I'd be interested in hearing what that exception was."

"Another time," O'Malley grumbled. "I've me rounds to finish before I meet ye at the outbuildin'."

"I'll be there," Thompson promised before he turned in the opposite direction to man his post until the appointed time.

A few hours later, the Duke of Wyndmere opened the door to the outbuilding and stepped into the middle of an argument.

"And I say ye're dicked in the nob!" Flaherty shoved Garahan against the back wall.

Garahan's face lost all expression as he roared and charged his cousin. He hit Flaherty in the gut, lifting him off his feet and into one of the crossbeams.

Flaherty used his right hand to guard his face and reached above his head with his left. Grabbing hold of the beam, he swung his body backward.

The duke watched in amazement as Garahan neatly side-stepped his cousin's move all the while taunting him.

O'Malley noticed the duke as Flaherty dropped into a crouch, preparing to tackle Garahan. "Yer Grace. We didn't see ye there."

Garahan closed the distance between himself and Flaherty and shoved him out of the way as he went to greet the duke. "Glad ye could make it, Yer Grace."

"We were just havin' a bit of fun," Flaherty told him.

"Indeed."

Thompson had been standing on the sidelines watching the two men go at it for the last few minutes, impressed with their skills.

O'Malley shook his head. The duke had no idea what he would be up against. His cousins fought as dirty as he did when the occasion called for it. The need to pound some of his frustration out had him sizing up Garahan, his first opponent— after the duke went a few rounds with the feedbag. A promise was a promise, though Garahan had laughed it off at the time.

He'd be reminding him of it. "If ye don't mind havin' a go at the feedbag hangin' over there." O'Malley pointed to the bag suspended from the rafters in the back corner of the room. "Ye can start there. I don't want Her Grace comin' after me and mine if we injure ye."

"I would not count on coming out the victor," he advised. "Although you are correct in your summation and wise to humor her." He removed his frockcoat and tossed it on the back of a chair leaning against the wall.

"Flaherty will wrap yer hands. 'Tis easy to split the skin on yer knuckles if ye don't protect them from the poundin' ye'll be givin' that bag."

He stood quietly while Flaherty expertly wound linen strips

around his hands. "Can ye flex them, Yer Grace?"

"Aye."

With some minor instruction, O'Malley was pleased with the duke's performance. When the duke dropped his arms and swiped his sleeve across his face. Garahan handed him a towel, while Flaherty held out a cup of water. "Ye'll need to replace some of the sweat ye lost."

The duke tossed back the cup, looked at O'Malley and grinned. "Now then, who do I take on first?"

They drew straws. Flaherty drew the short one. O'Malley could feel the tension around his cousin as he faced the duke. "Remember, Yer Grace," he called out. "None of us plan to spend the night behind bars in the village."

The duke snorted in response, lifted his hands, and waited for Flaherty to do the same. At the last minute, the duke dropped his hands.

Flaherty was quick to call out, "Are ye forfeiting then?"

Garahan laughed.

The duke was quick to explain. "The last time I engaged in a bit of pugilistic pleasure with my brother at Gentleman Jackson's establishment, I was distracted when Jackson kept shouting advice while we sparred."

"I hadn't planned on givin' ye advice, Yer Grace," O'Malley admitted.

"But we tend to get involved in any sparring," Garahan admitted with a shrug. "Mostly insults, if ye must know."

The duke laughed and O'Malley felt the tension slip off his shoulders. "All right then, men, ye heard His Grace. No shoutin' out advice." Turning to Garahan, he frowned. "No insultin'."

"But I always insult ye and Flaherty," Garahan replied. "'Tis part of the pleasure of beating on family."

Thompson chuckled. "Do I get to face off with the winner?"

"Ye have a job to do," O'Malley reminded him. "Ye're the mediator and man to patch up anyone needin' it."

"I would not have agreed to attend if I couldn't at least get a bit of bare knuckle practice in."

"I'd be happy to spar with you, Thompson," the duke stated.

Garahan shook his head. "Are ye willing to place a bit of a wager on that, Yer Grace?"

O'Malley cuffed Garahan on the side of his head. "Are ye daft? Ye don't challenge His Grace to a wager."

The duke shrugged. "If I were still the second son, and not the duke, would you, O'Malley?"

He slowly grinned. "In a heartbeat, Yer Grace. After I finished ye off, I'd have a go at Thompson." Studying the man, he nodded. "I'd take him in five minutes flat."

"You're a cool one, O'Malley," King's man chuckled.

"Faith, don't I know it." Turning back to the duke and Flaherty, he gave the signal and stepped back.

The need to shout encouragement to the duke quickly subsided as he surprised Flaherty with an uppercut. Remembering how his head swam after the duke leveled him with one blow, he realized the duke could more than hold his own.

Flaherty snapped the duke's head back with a wicked right cross, but the duke parried with two quick jabs, one a direct hit to Flaherty's nose.

"Time!" O'Malley called, handing his cousin a wad of cloth to stanch the flow of blood.

"Are you all right, Flaherty?" The duke held a cup of water at the ready, waiting for the bleeding to stop.

He sighed. "Ye've a lethal jab, Yer Grace. I wasn't expecting it."

The duke grinned and in a decent imitation of their brogue, replied, "Faith, don't I know it."

Everyone was laughing as Thompson brought in the pail of snow, scooped some out and placed it in a cloth, handing it to Flaherty. "This will help with the swelling."

"Is it swelling? I can't feel me face."

"Congratulations, Yer Grace," Garahan drawled. "A broken nose—or ribs ends the bout. The one that does the breaking is always declared the winner."

Flaherty started to weave. The duke slipped an arm around him and led him over to the bench against the back wall. "I didn't intend to break your nose, Flaherty. I apologize."

"Accepted. And not yer fault, Yer Grace. Sure and I'd hoped to get a few more punches in…but I wasn't planning on breaking any part of ye."

"Are you three always this amiable?" the duke queried. "The last time I interrupted you sparring—"

"We were fightin'," O'Malley corrected.

The duke frowned at O'Malley. "You said you were sparring."

"We were until we weren't."

"That explains it," the duke mumbled. "Do you always start out sparring and end up fighting?"

Garahan laughed. "Nay. Sometimes we start out fighting and end up sparring."

The duke shook his head. "Will I ever understand you men?"

O'Malley swallowed the answer poised on his tongue, knowing it would not endear himself to the duke. The Irish and the English had a long and volatile history. No sense bringing it up now. They worked together—not against one another.

Before he could answer, the door swung open. Eamon O'Malley locked gazes with Patrick first and then the duke. "Stames is back. Radleigh's men stopped at an inn to change horses."

"How soon will they be here?" the duke asked.

"A few hours at the least," Eamon replied. "More if they're as inexperienced on horseback as we've been led to believe."

"Best prepare to fend them off in a few hours," the duke advised.

Patrick agreed. "Garahan, you'll replace Flaherty as sharpshooter on the roof."

"Aye. I'm a better shot than him any day."

Flaherty shot to his feet and got in Garahan's face. "Are not!"

Eamon growled. "Ye can fight about it later. Right now, from the looks of it, Garahan'll be on the roof."

"Aye," Patrick agreed. "Flaherty, ye can be our man on the inside. The bleedin's stopped and yer nose hasn't swelled as much as last time."

"Don't be reminding me," Flaherty grumbled.

"Ye'll be in charge of handin' out ammunition and loadin' the weapons along with the younger staff among the footmen, undergardeners, and the like." When Flaherty reluctantly agreed, Patrick reminded him, "Ye'll need to be close to Merry and Constance. They've a fine hand with healin'. Ye made need it."

Garahan chuckled until Eamon gave him a shove. "Later," he reminded him.

"Aye, Sorry, Flaherty."

Flaherty grunted.

"Thompson," Patrick began, "ye'll act as the go between."

"Aye, between my men on the perimeter and yours on the interior."

The duke listened to the assignments being handed out and seemed relieved. "You'll be on guard—"

"By the nursery, Yer Grace. As promised."

He reached out and clapped a hand to Patrick's shoulder. "Thank you."

Patrick glanced at his cousins, one at a time. As expected, he received a brief nod from each. They understood he would tell the duke of the intricate plans already in place—and twice already acted upon, for protecting the babes. Patrick alone would accept whatever backlash the duke meted out. "May I have a private word, Yer Grace?"

The two stepped outside and walked toward the stables. "I've something to tell ye that ye may not like."

"About the next attempt to steal our babes?"

"Aye."

The duke rounded on Patrick and demanded, "Tell me!"

"We hatched a plan to protect the babes the moment we

knew Her Grace was expectin'."

The duke clenched his jaw and curled his hands into fists at his sides. O'Malley knew the longer he put off telling the duke, the greater the man's anger would be.

"In the event of an attack, Mollie was to take yer babe to her room on the third floor."

"Wouldn't the kidnappers then search the house if they couldn't find our babe?"

"She was to place a bundle of blankets, shaped like yer babe, in the cradle. At a glance, one would be fooled."

"Wouldn't the kidnappers discover the ruse once they tried to take the babe?"

"Aye, but we'd already be there, and have the attackers bound and gagged. Proof of their bloody plans and all."

"But Persephone delivered twins."

"Aye. We had to adjust the plan after Her Grace delivered not one, but two healthy babes."

"So, the other night when I asked Mrs. Alexander why the babes had their blankets covering the heads…"

"Yer babes were upstairs with Mollie and Francis."

"Why didn't you tell me?"

"We didn't want to run the risk that our plans would be overheard and whispered among the staff."

"Who else knew of your plans?"

"Humphries, Merry, and Constance."

The duke's face flushed a deep red as he proclaimed, "She lied to me!"

O'Malley knew he was referring to Gwendolyn. "She was protecting the babes, ye and Her Grace by keepin' silent."

"She should have told me the truth."

"And risk the lives of Richard and Abigail? Are ye daft?"

"I beg your pardon?"

"She loves those babes and would do all in her power to protect them."

"Would she risk being dismissed to protect them?" the duke

demanded.

"She already has."

Patrick let that sink in before continuing. "Her Grace may suspect," O'Malley advised, "but no one has told her. Not one of yer trusted staff, Mrs. Alexander, nor me men would have one hair on yer wee babes' heads harmed. Ye have to know that."

The duke raked a hand through his hair, glanced down and noticed the bloody linens in the other. Taking his time, he unwrapped them, folded them and put them in his pockets. Finally, he looked at the man standing silent at his side. "You did the right thing. It's not that I doubt your abilities, Patrick, but in the future, you will keep me abreast of any, and all, plans concerning my family."

"Ye have me word, Yer Grace."

The tension between them gone, they continued on to the stables. "Do you think the kidnappers will manage to breech our perimeter guard?"

"They only did the first time because we allowed it. We wanted them to think they would gain easy access to yer home."

"I should have questioned you that night, but my mind was on other things."

"Ye said ye trusted me," Patrick reminded him.

"I do, but don't appreciate being kept in the dark."

"'Twas a risk worth takin'."

They reached the door to the stables before the duke spoke again. "I'll tell my wife."

"Aye, Yer Grace."

An hour later, King's men, the duke's guard, and his loyal staff were ready and waiting.

The anticipated attack did not come early…it came in the middle of the night.

Chapter Twenty-Five

G WENDOLYN HELD LITTLE Abigail in her arms while Persephone held Richard. They swayed as they stood, keeping the babes happy while the women laid out their plans in case of attack.

She could not believe the intricate plans they discussed. Before she could ask, the duchess explained, "Merry and Constance were on our frontlines the last time we were attacked."

Gwendolyn had heard what had happened that night in bits and pieces. She was not surprised both women were proficient with a pistol. Although her curiosity had her asking, "Did you stand beside the duke and the earl?"

Merry frowned. "If they would have handed me a pistol, I could have."

"We were needed here in the heart of His Grace's home," Constance replied. "Humphries stood guard to ensure we stayed inside."

Persephone ran the tip of her finger along her son's cheek and added, "Merry was on hand to organize the lot of us. Constance kept the balance between cooking for the men and keeping the water hot to sterilize threads and to bathe any wounds the men suffered."

"Francis and I helped with the wounded and did whatever task was required," Mollie added.

"It sounds as if you could have used an extra hand or two."

Persephone smiled. "We had three actually. My sister-in-law, Phoebe, and her very good friends, Aurelia and Calliope."

Gwendolyn felt a sense of awe sweep over her. That these women had already had to defend against a madman bent on destroying the duke, the duchess, and their family was beyond comprehension. That only happened in novels, did it not? "And now you're ready to defend against attack again," Gwendolyn remarked. "How do you do it?"

Persephone's brown eyes held a determination Gwendolyn had come to count upon as she replied, *"Aut Vincan, Aut Periam."*

Gwendolyn slowly smiled, interpreting the Latin phrase. "I will either conquer, or perish." She glanced down at the babe in her arms, and then at the one the duchess held. A righteous warmth filled her, spreading from her heart to her head. From her head to her toes. "I'd be honored to stand beside you, ladies. Just tell me what to do."

Persephone began to lay out their plans, assigning tasks.

Merry had Francis scurrying about gathering linen strips, poultices, and salve.

Constance had a pot of hearty soup simmering and two loaves of bread in the oven.

Gwendolyn and Mollie returned to the nursery with the babes. Mollie made up the bundled blankets to be placed in the cradles. Gwendolyn handed her a rock-lined reticule and pointed out the others stashed about in the nursery.

"Do you think it'll stop the attackers from gaining entry into the nursery?" Mollie's worry washed over Gwendolyn.

"It will definitely deter them...although I'm not sure for how long. Depends upon how accurate my aim is."

Mollie's eyes widened before she shook her head. "You are an amazing woman, Mrs. Alexander. There is so much Francis and I could learn from you."

"I'm surprised the both of you don't have a handful of ribbon-wrapped hatpins in your possession."

Mollie snickered. "Lady Phoebe did mention that she thought it was a good idea to have one on hand. We do, in our bedchambers."

"You may want to keep them in your apron pocket," Gwendolyn advised.

"Aye. We might at that."

When the babes began to fuss, Mollie rang the bell pull. Turning back to face Gwendolyn, she asked, "Are you afraid?"

"Without question. Admitting to your fear doesn't make you foolish, it allows you to acknowledge your fear and then move past it to do what must be done to protect yourself and those counting on you."

Francis and the duchess arrived a few moments later.

Persephone announced, "Merry suggested that we rotate duties while we wait to keep us focused on our tasks and not worrying over when the bloody kidnappers will strike!"

Gwendolyn was not surprised at the vehemence in the duchess' words. She applauded the woman's candor. "Where would you like me to go?"

"You and Mollie should report to Constance. Francis will keep the babes occupied while I feed them."

Gwendolyn hesitated in the doorway. "You'll ring if you need me?"

"I will," Persephone promised.

The two were not given a moment to themselves from the time they entered Constance's domain until the time they were dismissed to return to the nursery.

The hours dragged on but the women kept busy, caring for the twins, and switching shifts with Francis and the duchess.

At eleven o'clock, the duchess sent Mollie and Francis to their bedchambers to rest. A quarter of an hour later, O'Malley paused in his patrolling of the floor outside the nursery and took up his position right outside the door.

The first shot sounded as the clock struck midnight.

>>><<<<

MOLLIE AND FRANCIS rushed toward O'Malley a few minutes later.

"We heard the shots," Francis told him.

"Do you want us to get the babes now?" Mollie asked.

The door opened behind him. Gwendolyn's scent grabbed him by the throat as he barked, "Get back inside!"

She poked him in the back. "What should we do?"

"Obey orders," he growled, not bothering to turn around. If he did, the woman would distract him. He was not about to let that happen.

"I made up the new bundles and Francis stashed them in the chest of drawers," Mollie told him.

"We're ready," Francis assured him.

He drew in a breath to keep from shouting at the daft women standing in front of him, while the one behind him dared to poke him again. *Harder this time.*

"God help me, if ye women don't listen, I'll be tyin' ye up and tossin' ye inside the nursery!"

Mollie slowly smiled. "You sound just like Finn."

He reached around behind him, grabbed Gwendolyn by the wrist, and dragged her into the hallway. "What part of get back inside did ye not understand?"

She lifted her chin and glared at him. "I understood every word."

"Then why did ye not obey me?"

The light of challenge in the depths of her amber eyes surprised him.

"It is not my job to obey you, Mr. O'Malley," she drawled.

The sound of more shots being fired galvanized him into action. He pushed the women into the room. "Gwendolyn get the bundled blankets and place them in the cradles. Mollie and Francis take the babes upstairs and do not let anyone but me into

205

the room. Shove the one chest of drawers in front of the door and hide with the babes behind the other!"

When they hesitated, he rasped, "Go! Now!"

The women moved as a team, completing the tasks assigned to them. Once the maids left with their precious burdens, Gwendolyn checked the room to ensure it appeared as if the babes were sleeping in their beds and all was as it should be.

A sound on the other side of the door had her reaching for the reticule in her pocket. *Heavy footsteps…*more than one set. Was it the intruders or the duke's guard? She drew in a breath and held it to better hear.

The explosion of sound reverberated through her. Fists connecting with flesh, bodies hitting the wall. How many men were attacking Patrick? She needed to know! Wanted to help! But she remembered his words to stay inside. She waited.

The sound of a pistol cocking had her springing into action. She opened the door but could not see past the huge Irishman guarding her with his life.

She gasped as a shot was fired, felt his body jerk as he took the pistol ball but did not fall. "The duke will see ye both hang if ye dare to take his babes. Give yerselves up now while ye can."

"The duke won't be handing over the fortune we've been promised," a deep voice rasped.

"Step aside," another voice demanded.

"Make me," O'Malley challenged.

Was the man crazed? She did not want the miscreants to reload and take another shot at the man she loved! Scooting around O'Malley, she swung her reticule with everything she had, connecting with one attacker. Their shock at being attacked by a woman gave her the advantage, she swung again and hit the other man.

Pleased that she'd gotten the upper hand, she gave it everything she had this time, but missed her mark, connecting with the man standing behind her.

O'Malley's groan had her spinning around in time to see his

eyes widen and the blood seeping from the wound in his shoulder before all hell broke loose.

Garahan, Flaherty, and Thompson rushed the men, but Gwendolyn wasn't paying attention to what they were doing. Her only thought was to steady the man she'd hit in the temple with her damned rocks.

"Patrick!"

He held a hand to his head as his eyes cleared. "What have ye got in that damned reticule?"

"Why?"

"Me head aches, 'tis why."

"I wasn't aiming at you," she whispered.

"Well, sure and that's just fine then, isn't it?"

The grayish cast to his face and the yellow-green shade of his eyes worried her. "Lean on me." She wrapped her arms around him, as his legs gave out and he crashed to the floor, taking her with him.

She felt the tears before she realized she was crying. Someone shoved a handkerchief into her line of vision. Not bothering to see whose hand offered the linen square, she mumbled thank you. Folding it in half again, she pressed it against the wound that still bled.

"He's lost so much blood. Are you going to let him bleed out?" She finally looked up into the shocked face of the Duke of Wyndmere.

"Not if I can help it, Mrs. Alexander."

"Forgive me," she whispered, "I meant no disrespect."

"My physician has been summoned, and whether you realize it or not, your quick action keeping pressure on his wound has slowed the bleeding."

She sniffed back her tears and rasped, "Why won't it stop?"

"It will," he assured her.

"But he's lost so much." *How could a man lose so much blood and survive?*

Gwendolyn had not realized she'd asked that question aloud

until the duke responded, "He's a big man…his body holds more blood."

She wondered for a moment if that was true, or if the duke was trying to keep her calm. An irrational woman was not what was needed at this moment. A quiet and controlled one was called for.

Her stomach flipped over, and her head ached. *He cannot die! I will not let him die!*

A large, freckled hand offered another linen square. She thanked Flaherty as she folded it, pressed it to Patrick's wound and handed him the saturated one.

"How did ye know it was me?"

"The freckles. Will he?"

"Will he what?" Flaherty wanted to know.

"Die?" she rasped, concentrating on willing every ounce of her heart, her soul, her very life's blood into the man barely breathing. The man she loved who bled still.

She heard Flaherty clear his throat before answering, "Not on me watch, Lass."

"He's too hardheaded to know when he's run out of blood. He'll not be dying this night," Garahan chimed in.

Gwendolyn looked up, startled to find herself surrounded by an impenetrable wall of contrary Irishmen…the duke's guard. They were protecting their leader. Though not one man voiced the worry that Patrick was fighting for his life, every man knew that he was.

She could not hold back the tears and didn't bother to try. She bent over O'Malley and added more pressure to his wound. Every tear symbolized each time she'd denied the way she felt about the irritating man who was in danger of dying in her arms. How could she have been so selfish, withholding her love from a man who more than deserved it?

He was not Jonathan, but he had captured her heart just as Jonathan had all those years ago. She had vowed the day they buried her husband that she would put one foot in front of the other and keep moving forward. She'd never said anything about opening her heart to love again. Knowing her husband would not have wanted her to live the rest of her life alone had not convinced her to open even the tiniest door to her heart. What had erecting walls around her heart accomplished?

It took the dark and desperate desire swirling in eyes the color of emeralds and O'Malley's confident smile to shake the walls around her heart. Every time he glanced her way with that knowing look in his eyes, as if he knew they would become lovers, she held her growing feelings to herself. Keeping them from him.

What if he had wound fever? What if he did not survive?

Dear God in Heaven, it would kill her!

A large hand appeared in her line of vision. She looked up into the face of a stranger.

"Dr. Fortescue," he said by way of introduction. "I live on the other side of the village and have taken care of the last three Dukes of Wyndmere."

"Mrs. Alexander," she replied. "The nanny." Trying to sort through the names of everyone she knew or had heard the duke or duchess speak of, she finally hit on the name she recalled. "I thought their personal physician was Dr. McIntyre."

The doctor removed her hand and placed a thick, fresh bandage against the wound. "Ah, that would be His Grace's London physician. I never venture that far from home."

The soothing sound of his voice eased the first knot between her shoulder blades until he remarked, "I take it O'Malley was shot at close range."

"Yes. He was protecting me." Her voice broke over the words.

"O'Malley's an honorable man. I would not have expected less from him. How long ago did this happen?"

"Close to an hour," the duke rumbled.

She glanced over her shoulder at the sound of his voice. The duke's face was pale with strain. Lines of frustration and worry creased his forehead.

"We did not want to move him until you arrived to assess his injury," the duke stated. "And as Mrs. Alexander was a bit reluctant to leave O'Malley's side and was keeping pressure on his wound, we felt it best to let her continue to do so."

"Aye," Garahan piped up. "She all but bit me head off when I suggested I'd take over for her."

Her mouth fell open at Garahan's claim. "I did nothing of the kind," she retorted.

Flaherty was quick to agree. "Ye were a bit out of yer head with grief at the time. We let ye have yer way."

"Gwendolyn," Constance said as she reached out her hand. "Let's get you cleaned up. The men need to move Patrick where there is plenty of light for Dr. Fortescue to remove the lead ball."

Her stomach heaved, but she swallowed the bile and forced herself to remain calm as she slowly stood. When her knees threatened to buckle, she locked them into place, and followed behind the cook.

Too weary to do more than nod now and again when Constance spoke to her, she followed as the kindly cook led her back to her bedchamber. All she wanted to do was collapse on the bed and close her eyes, shutting out the blood, the fear, the worry.

"I took the liberty of readying a bath for you."

When Gwendolyn was about to refuse, Constance held up a hand. "I'll brook no arguments from you. Get in that tub. With or without my assistance will be your choice. But you'll wash the blood off and then soak. I'll be back in half an hour. Any longer, and you may fall asleep."

"Thank you, Constance," she whispered.

"I'll send Mollie up to check on you shortly."

Though her limbs felt leaden, her heart ached, and there was a nagging pounding at the base of her skull, Gwendolyn did as she promised. She undressed and stepped into the steaming copper hip bath.

The scent of honeysuckle surrounded her as she sank a bit

lower in the tub. Constance cared enough to add a pinch of the dried flowers to the bath water. The first tear fell, but not the second. She would not allow it. Not until she knew O'Malley was out of danger.

With that resolve first and foremost on her mind, she scrubbed the blood from her hands with a vengeance. Once every trace was gone, she finished her bath, leaned back, and closed her eyes.

Not another day would go by with Patrick wondering how she felt about him. She would share what was in her heart—even if the man accused her of intentionally distracting him, she would not be deterred.

She would tell Patrick O'Malley she loved him with all her heart.

CHAPTER TWENTY-SIX

O'MALLEY DRIFTED IN and out of consciousness over the next few hours. At one point, he caught the scent of honeysuckle and knew Gwendolyn was beside him. The next time he roused, he was being lifted by his cousins and carried.

A deep voice had him fighting to regain consciousness. He did not recognize the voice, but the sensation of behind held down against his will was all too familiar.

"Let go," he roared, "or I'll tear off yer arm and feed it to ye."

Garahan snorted to cover a laugh. "Welcome back, Patrick."

"Don't worry, Doctor," Flaherty assured the man. "He never follows through with those types of threats."

"That we know of," Eamon added.

Patrick opened one eye and glared at his cousin. Not an easy feat, but he put every ounce of energy he had into it.

"Ye'll not want to be opening yer eyes just yet," Eamon warned him. "Ye're a bloody mess to be sure."

"None of us like being held down either," Garahan reminded them.

Patrick groaned then swore again. "Are ye after killin' me then?"

"'Tis the pistol ball," Flaherty explained. "Be still while the doctor digs it out."

He sucked in a breath and slowly let it out. The pain was

excruciating, but he knew it was necessary...to leave the ball in his shoulder could result in lead poisoning. Judging by how long it was taking to remove it, he wondered if his chances were greater that he would end up dying from the poisoning and not the accuracy of the shot fired at close range.

"I've got it!" the doctor exclaimed. "One of you hold this on the wound while I clean it out."

He suffered through the cleansing of the hole in his shoulder. And then he felt the needle pierce his skin. Calling on all the powers of control he had—adding in a prayer to his da that he wouldn't embarrass himself by puking up his guts or passing out in front of his cousins. He bore down and suffered through the stitching.

"Ye're going to have a fine scar, Boy-o." Garahan sounded impressed.

He'd worry about what it looked like later as a familiar scent—one he'd inhaled too many times in the past to count—blood and sweat, filled his nostrils. The stench was probably his own. Then again, his cousins must have been sweating at some point when the kidnappers made their way inside the duke's home under the watchful eye of Gavin King's men and his own. He would rather have captured them before they entered the house, but they required absolute proof of the deed attempted.

He inhaled again...*not a trace of honeysuckle.*

"Where's Gwendolyn?"

No one answered and a feeling of dread filled him. He opened his eyes and focused on the man holding his injured arm still. "Darby, tell me!"

"Do not let him move until I bandage him up," the doctor ordered.

Garahan's look of pity told him all he needed to know. The woman must have abandoned him as soon as he lost consciousness. *Bloody hell! Did he expect a woman to stay with him because he'd taken a lead ball protecting her? Aye, bugger it!*

"Constance took off with her," Garahan said.

"Poor lass was covered in yer blood," Flaherty finished.

"How was she? Was she speakin' or cryin'?"

"Over a little blood?" Eamon asked. "She's made of sterner stuff."

Patrick relaxed. She hadn't been unduly upset by what had happened. Praise God, the nightmares won't be plaguing her. The grisly memory of the first time he'd shot a man still plopped down in the middle of his dreams every now and again.

Dr. Fortescue finished securing the bandage. "If one of you would ring the bell pull, I'd like to speak with either Merry or Constance. I have instructions for O'Malley's care."

Eamon strode over to the corner, gave it a tug, and waited. A few minutes later, the housekeeper appeared with a footman and two scullery maids in tow.

"Ah, Merry," Dr. Fortescue said. "Just the person I need to speak with. I have instructions for you that must be followed to the letter. If not, there is a very good chance O'Malley will succumb to wound fever or lead poisoning."

"I'm very familiar with both maladies, if you will recall," she replied.

He agreed. "That was a dark night, wasn't it?"

She nodded. "I remember as if it were yesterday. The instructions you gave as to wound care, fever, and the chance that one of the men would contract lead poisoning is not one I'll soon forget."

"Excellent." The physician nodded to the footman. "I see you've brought help to move O'Malley while the bedding is changed."

Eamon spoke up. "We'll be moving him, if ye don't mind."

Fortescue nodded, then watched while the men carefully lifted their cousin, propping him up while the scullery maids took care of changing the bed. When the men had carefully placed Patrick back in bed, the doctor stated, "Bed rest for the next fortnight—"

Patrick interrupted the physician, "I'll not be lyin' on me back when there's work to be done."

The physician frowned, then inclined his head, amending his dictate, "A sennight at the very least."

"Aye, Doctor," Garahan agreed.

"I didn't say—" Patrick began only to be interrupted.

"A few days is all the good doctor is recommending. Given the amount of blood loss, ye'd best listen to his advice."

"We're more than capable of protecting His Grace and his family while ye lay about feeling sorry for yerself," Eamon stated.

Patrick knew what his cousins were doing. They were distracting him and placating the doctor so that the man would be on his way. He'd go along with them, at least until the physician left Wyndmere Hall. "Thank ye for diggin' the ball out and puttin' me back together."

The doctor's eyes were calm and clear when he reiterated, "Bed rest and an invalid's diet...for a sennight."

"That was the plan Constance and I were just discussing." Merry motioned for the servants she'd brought with her to follow her with the soiled bedding.

"Aye," Patrick grumbled. *Would the man never leave?*

Dr. Fortescue nodded to the men standing at attention around their leader, before bidding them goodbye.

"I'll see ye out," Eamon offered.

When the door closed, the two men standing on either side of Patrick heaved a collective sigh of relief.

"Never thought he'd leave," Garahan grumbled. "Took forever sewing yer hide back together."

"I'm thinking the doctor was after ye staying in bed only for a few days in the first place," Flaherty confided. "Did ye notice how quick he was to change his tune?"

"Aye." Struggling to sit up, he groaned and fell back against the bed. "I need to talk to Gwendolyn...she needs to understand."

"I'm sure she understands ye were shot," Garahan told him. "Ye aren't going anywhere today."

Patrick tried again. This time, he managed to raise up on his good arm to glare at his cousin. "I'm gettin' out of this damned bed and chasin' down that hardheaded woman!"

Flaherty dared to grin at that comment. "Must be love. We Irish only marry the hardheaded lasses."

Garahan and Flaherty were too busy laughing to notice someone had opened the door and was standing on the threshold.

"Patrick?"

The scent of honeysuckle filled his head, his mind, and his heart. "Lass! Ye're here." He held out his hand and Gwendolyn rushed into the room to grasp it.

"I was so worried," she confessed from his bedside. Placing the back of her hand to his forehead, she murmured, "No fever."

"Takes more than a lead ball to keep one of us down," Garahan scoffed.

Flaherty brought a chair over so she could sit. She thanked him, sat, and took hold of Patrick's hand once more.

He stared at her. The look in his eyes had her wondering, did he think she'd disappear if he blinked?

"I'm not imaginin' ye, am I?"

"No, you're not." Lifting his hand to her lips, she pressed a whisper-soft kiss to the back of it. "I need a cloth to bathe your face."

"He doesn't have a fever." Garahan watched her get up, and take a cloth from the pile on the washstand.

"I know." She poured water from the blue and white china pitcher into the large matching bowl. Dipping the cloth, she wrung it out and returned to O'Malley's side. "I haven't had a chance to thank you."

He watched the myriad of emotions in her warm amber eyes and wondered if she was ready to acknowledge how she felt about him. Oh, he'd told her she was a distraction, but she was far more than that. His heart recognized hers from the moment that she'd stepped down from the duke's carriage.

He'd tried to purge her from his mind with a kiss that backfired on him. The meeting of their lips seared her taste, her scent, and the fiery passion he'd ignited inside them both into his brain and onto his heart.

Time to accept his heart was hers...and had been from the first. To gauge her true feelings for him, he brushed her thanks aside. "'Tis me job. No more."

Garahan's deep chuckle reminded Patrick they were not alone. "Don't ye have somewhere to be? A job to do?"

Flaherty grabbed hold of Garahan and dragged him to the door. Pausing in the doorway, he replied, "One of us will return with a full report. The constable should have arrived by now."

Garahan added, "Thompson and the rest of King's men were standing guard over two of the would-be kidnappers when we followed the other two inside. We'll check with Eamon to see if anyone's supplied the name or names of those that hired them."

"We need to get their confession before King goes after Radleigh," Patrick told the men. "Pinnin' him with all three attempts will help our case against him."

"Aye. Try to rest," Flaherty urged.

"I don't have time to rest."

Garahan smiled. "Won't be the same without ye barking commands at us night and day."

"Don't forget to bring a bottle of the Irish when ye come back!"

With a grin and a salute, his cousins were gone.

"Do they always speak to you like that?"

O'Malley noted only one emotion remained in the warm depths of her eyes—worry. "All our lives."

"Shouldn't they respect you?" Gwendolyn sounded incensed on his behalf.

O'Malley found that he liked knowing she would be. *His* woman should care about all aspects of his life...shouldn't she?

"Gwendolyn—"

"Patrick—" she said at the same time.

"Go ahead, tell me what's on yer mind."

She bit her lip, as if unsure of herself. His mind may be muddled with pain, but he hadn't remembered seeing her as anything but confident…and feisty. He waited patiently.

"I was never going to tell you…"

He shifted on the bed and clenched his jaw against the pain. "Tell me?"

"What can I do to ease the pain? Where do you hurt?"

"What weren't ye goin' to tell me, Lass?"

Ignoring his question a second time, she brushed a lock of sun-kissed hair out of his eyes. "Your shoulder must pain you greatly, but is there anywhere else? Should I ring for Constance or Merry?"

He growled at her. He hadn't intended to, but the woman was making him daft! "If ye won't be cooperatin' answerin' me questions, ye may as well leave."

Her sharp intake of breath had him closing his eyes. "'Tis the pain that's addlin' me wits. Forgive me sharp tongue, Lass."

He heard the swish of fabric and opened his eyes in time to see her opening the door. "Gwendolyn, wait! Don't go."

She didn't turn around, but asked, "Why should I stay when I obviously irritate you?"

"Gwendolyn," he rasped. "Would ye please come back? I'd like to tell ye somethin'."

He wasn't sure if she would leave or stay. Finally, she spun around and marched back over to the chair and stared down at him. He was so glad she'd decided to stay that he didn't smile. O'Malley kept his expression neutral as he held out a hand to her and asked her to sit.

She blew out a breath but took his hand and did as he bid.

Amazed that her hand seemed so small and helpless entwined with his when her personality was so vibrant, so bold…God help him, she intoxicated him.

"Excuse me?"

He noticed the sharp edge to her voice and wondered how he'd vexed her—*bloody hell!* Had he said that last part aloud? His head ached. His shoulder felt as if it had been flayed open and then sewn back together. Was it any wonder he wasn't thinking clearly?

"Did you just say I intoxicate you?"

"My head aches, Lass. I'm not sure what I'm sayin'."

"Then why do you want to talk to me?"

He snorted. "'Tis the truth I have no notion. Ye're a hard woman to talk to."

"You did not seem to have a problem communicating that day in the garden."

He felt the fires of passion ignite in his gut. The flames would eat him alive if he didn't tamp down on them now. "I was surprised by yer bold answer, Gwendolyn. Do ye have feelin's for me?" *Blast!* He had not intended to ask her that. He should *shut his gob!*

She looked away. It was too late for her to dismiss her response when he'd kissed her in the garden. Shaking his head at his inability to hold a simple conversation with the woman, he closed his eyes and lay still while he tried to sort through the morass in his brain.

"Patrick?" She sounded worried. *What of it? Wasn't he worried, too?*

She let go of his hand to scoot her chair closer to the bed. "Patrick, can you hear me?"

She placed the back of her hand to his forehead. Her touch soothed him.

"Oh, Lord! Is he unconscious?"

He heard the chair scrape against the floor. She must have stood up. Deciding to wait to see what she would do, he was flummoxed when he felt the warmth of her sweet lips on his forehead.

He could not hold back the moan of sheer ecstasy. Her lips were plump and soft. He already knew they'd taste of summer sweet berries with a hint of tart. He whispered her name, beckoning her closer as he slowly opened his eyes.

"Thank God, you're awake! I thought you'd fallen unconscious."

"Kiss me, Lass, before I die from wantin' ye."

Her lips were a feast of flavors and texture.

SHE HELD NOTHING back as she indulged in the heady sensation of Patrick's mouth pressed to hers. The firm pressure of his lips. The masterful way he slid his hand to the back of her neck, drawing her closer. She should be telling him what was in her heart, but the need to kiss him trumped all else.

The tip of his tongue traced the rim of her mouth, asking permission to deepen the kiss. She was mindless to all else, save the passion this man awoke within her. Desire swirled in the depths of his emerald eyes, calling to her from the moment their gazes met and held…and time stood still.

They were breathless when he broke the kiss. "Are ye after killin' me with kisses, then?"

The idea was so ludicrous she laughed. "I doubt that is even possible."

"Ye aren't the one sufferin' from fightin' to keep me hands—and other parts to meself. Every time I see ye, I want ye more. Ye're makin' me daft, Woman."

She had no idea what to say to that. Did he want her to want him, or did he want her to leave him alone? *And he said she was making him daft!* Unsure of how to respond, the realization that she owed him the truth had her finally bearing her soul. "I haven't felt like this in so many years, I didn't recognize the feelings rioting inside of me whenever you'd glance my way."

His voice deepened. "Ye don't say."

Uneasy with her physical reaction to him, unable to keep from touching him, she walked over to the washstand and dipped the cloth in the cool water. She wrung it out and returned to his side. Placing it on his forehead, she noticed he was much warmer.

"How do you feel?"

"The same. Why?"

"You're warm to the touch."

His eyes darkened to the color of the forest at midnight. Drawn to the sensual pull that called to her, she leaned against him and let him drive her to the brink of madness with his talented lips and tongue.

"And here ye were worried he was unconscious," Garahan exclaimed.

"He will be if we don't put a stop to things," Flaherty murmured. "He'll be walking back to Cork if the duke walks in and finds yer man here having his way with Mrs. Alexander," Flaherty added.

Gwendolyn sighed as Patrick nipped at her lips before ending the kiss. "Faith, I could get drunk on yer kisses, Lass."

"I think he already has," Garahan grumbled. "O'Malley, we've news!"

Holding a bottle up for all to see, Flaherty chuckled. "We've brought the Irish, though I doubt ye'll be needing it now."

Patrick and Gwendolyn noticed they were no longer alone at the same time. Her cheeks felt as if they were on fire. Patrick didn't seem to be bothered by the intrusion at all. He practically gloated.

Gwendolyn sighed. *Would she ever understand men?*

CHAPTER TWENTY-SEVEN

T HE DUKE PACED in front of his wife. "Did you know O'Malley has feelings for our nanny?"

Persephone evaded the question with a question. "Which O'Malley would that be?"

He stopped in front of where she sat by the fire. "From your answer, one could gather that you know more than you care to divulge."

She sighed. "You would have to be both deaf and blind not to have noticed the spark between Patrick and Gwendolyn."

"I noticed it half an hour ago in the hallway outside the nursery," he bit out. "Is something going on between them? Under my roof?"

The duchess shot to her feet. *"Your* roof?"

"Damnation, Wife! Do not play a game of semantics with me! I demand to know if something illicit is happening between the head of my personal guard and our nanny!"

"It is hard to miss the spark of tension whenever Patrick and Gwendolyn are in the same room together for more than a few moments."

"Is it more than that?" the duke demanded.

"No. Gwendolyn has been alone for a long time, Jared, but she values her reputation as a nanny and would not do anything to jeopardize it. She has no family, her reputation is of paramount importance to her."

"What about O'Malley?"

"His frustration should be answer enough," she countered in a calm tone. "Would he prowl around like a bear with a thorn in its paw if he had been having an affair with all the trimmings?"

The duke squared his shoulders, preparing to do verbal battle with his wife. "Frustration is no indication that he has not been involved with a woman. A man can have a satisfying interlude with a woman and be frustrated five minutes after he leaves her bed."

Persephone's eyes widened before she admitted, "An excellent point. Although the man would have to be foolish to leave the woman's bed if he were still able to walk."

Shock—and the image his wife planted in his brain, took hold as Jared's anger ebbed. She'd done it again, made him lose his train of thought in the middle of a conversation. *He needed to regain control and convince her he was right!* "Ah, my love, but a man bent on protecting the woman he loved would never allow himself to indulge to that extent."

She took a step closer, and challenged, "If the man held a position of power, he would have a host of guards to protect him as he *indulged* behind closed doors."

Jared fought the need to pull his wife to him and plunder. *Damn the woman for distracting him when he was making a salient point!* "What if he had reason to doubt those who guarded his family? He would never forgive himself if anything happened to the woman he loves and the proof of that love—their babes."

Tears filled Persephone's eyes. "You and Patrick have come to an understanding," she reminded him. "You have remedied the issues that led to your relieving him as head of your guard. I implore you to listen to reason—"

"Your version of reason, wife—" he interrupted.

"Yes, my love," she soothed. "Listen to your heart, and if it is silent in this regard, listen to mine."

Persephone took one step and then another, closing the gap

between them. Their eyes met, and her trust in him shone brightly in the depths of her warm brown eyes. His trust in her was unshakeable. He would do as she asked. Pressing his forehead to hers, he inhaled slowly and acknowledged he'd give her anything she needed...she already had his heart. Surely he would not miss his right arm once he'd given it to her.

"I shall do as you ask. Patrick would never betray me in that regard, and from all that I know and have observed of our nanny, she would give notice that she is leaving before she would act in such a manner."

"Then you will cease worrying that anyone under your roof is spending more time in bed with their lover than you?"

The duke barked out a laugh and yanked her against him. "Minx!"

"Tyrant!"

They were smiling as their lips met.

"You wanted to see me?" Gwendolyn hesitated in the doorway to the nursery.

"Gwendolyn." The duchess smiled warmly. "Come in and have a seat. I've something I need to discuss with you."

Her belly clenched as worry filled her. Had the duke relayed what happened earlier outside the nursery, when she spoke without thinking? Her relationship with the duke was tenuous at best. Would he demand that she leave at once?

Persephone rose and closed the distance between them. "What's happened? It cannot be Patrick. I just left the room where he's recuperating, and he seemed fine. Is it wound fever?"

Gwendolyn snapped out of her panic and linked arms with the duchess. "I'm sorry to worry you. Patrick is warmer than before. Constance told me to expect a fever as he'd been shot. I'm sure she's said the same to you."

Persephone sighed. "I do worry about him. He and the men have been a part of our lives since before I married Jared. They are family."

Gwendolyn had noticed the way the duchess and the staff treated the duke's guard. Although the duke was more reserved around the men, there was a definite bond between the men and the duke.

"Merry and I discussed how best to watch over the head of Jared's guard while we wait to see if the fever takes hold."

"They are always worse at night," Gwendolyn advised. "At least in my experience."

"I do recall Merry and Constance saying the same thing, now that you mention it. I'd hoped to avoid the possibility of fever altogether. So much is happening right now. Jared has already spoken with his men. He's meeting with his guard and Gavin King's men shortly. Hopefully, they will have extracted a confession from one or all of the intruders bent on kidnapping our precious babes."

Persephone's worry had Gwendolyn prompting, "The duke's men can be very persuasive."

"They can be if they choose to," the duchess admitted. "If Jared does not have the information he needs by this afternoon, I'll question the bastards myself! No one threatens our family without paying the consequences."

Gwendolyn was pleased to see the fire in Persephone's eyes. Far better to see her ready to do battle than to be overwhelmed by their current circumstances. "I do have a request."

The duchess nodded. "What would that be?"

"I'd like to take turns with Mollie and Francis, sitting with Patrick tonight. I understand it is a direct conflict with my duties—"

"Botheration! Life is full of conflicts and challenges. We should always be ready to bend to meet those circumstances."

"But His Grace—"

"Will not interfere with how I run our household. He has far too many other duties to attend to. I shall speak with Merry and Humphries. I highly doubt any one of us will be getting a full night's sleep until this is over."

Gwendolyn grasped Persephone's hands in her own. "Thank you, Persephone." Releasing her hands, she suggested, "Why don't you go rest now? As you mentioned, you doubt you'll sleep tonight."

"Excellent notion! I believe I shall." The duchess paused with her hand on the door. "You'll ring if the babes wake hungry."

"I promise."

"I do not know what I would do with you, Gwendolyn. The twins are not constantly fussing as they were with the other nannies. I do believe they take after their mother...an intelligent woman who is an outstanding judge of character."

Gwendolyn was smiling as the duchess closed the door.

Word reached her a few hours later that she would have the early evening shift sitting with Patrick.

An hour into her shift, Patrick's fever spiked.

CHAPTER TWENTY-EIGHT

"WHAT HAVE YOU been able to surmise after speaking to the intruders, Thompson?"

King's man shook his head. "Not as much as I'd like to have learned. Apparently, none of the men hired knew of Lady Hampton or Lady H. They only knew there was a bag of coins waiting for them if they kidnapped your twins and passed them off to their contact at the Kent Road Tavern halfway between Wyndmere Hall and London."

"Did you get confirmation that their contact's name is Lord Radleigh"

Thompson glanced at the door to the outbuilding and back. "Not yet, but we agree they're holding back."

The duke frowned as he mulled over the information. In order to pin the dastardly kidnapping plot on the man behind them—Radleigh, and possibly his sister, he needed confirmation of their names. He did not often employ his fists to extract the information he required. He used logic and subtle persuasion.

You broke Flaherty's nose, though not intentionally...mayhap you could encourage the men waiting to be carted off by the constable to give you the name of the bastard with more than words.

Desperate times call for desperate measures.

"I believe I would like to have a word with our...*guests*."

"Of course. Garahan enlisted Smythe to stand guard with

him."

"Smythe more than proved his mettle the last time you were here."

"He's good man to have at your back, as is every man in your private guard."

The duke agreed. "Wisest decision I ever made, hiring on O'Malley and his kin." The two men walked up to the door. Thompson rapped loudly. The door swung open.

"Ah, Yer Grace, Thompson. I gather ye'd like a word with the men who will no doubt be hanged for their crimes…their bodies left to rot at the crossroads before the constable's men arrive to take them away."

The duke held back his snort of laughter at Garahan's description. The four men lined up against the back wall of the building shifted from foot to foot, worry creeping into the depths of their eyes…eyes as black as their hearts.

If he hadn't accepted the mantle of duke, he would slowly, determinedly, beat the confession out of every one of them. But as the duke, he could no longer do as he pleased.

But that did not mean that he could not watch while one of his men used whatever means available to get a confession. His heart was lighter at the prospect of watching Garahan and Thompson slowly—albeit quite possibly painfully, extract the information they required.

He needed that name!

Three quarters of an hour later, he had it…*Lord Radleigh.*

"GWENDOLYN?" PATRICK RASPED as the fever tightened its grip on him.

"She'll be here soon," Mollie soothed, trying to decide if the big man would try to get up and search for Mrs. Alexander again. Should she thank the Lord that the man was weak from blood loss and fever?

He groaned in response. "Got to find her... have to tell her..."

O'Malley was up and on his feet before she could blink. How had he managed that? How could he still be this strong with all of the blood he'd lost?

"Patrick, please!" Mollie begged, trying to grab hold of him and pull him toward the bed. Their legs got tangled and she stumbled onto the bed. Patrick landed on top of her.

The air whooshed out of her lungs and she saw stars. The pain was crushing. Had his elbow broken one of her ribs when it jabbed into her?

"I leave for a few months, promising to return," a deep voice grumbled from the open doorway. "What do I find? Ye've turned yer affection away from me and onto me brother!"

"Finn?" Mollie struggled to shift Patrick's weight off her to no avail. Tears filled her eyes, too many to blink away. "Can't breathe," she gasped.

Finn shifted his brother off Mollie and onto the bed, lifting Mollie into his arms. "Are ye hurt, Lass? Dear God, is that blood?"

Mollie shook her head. She was having a devil of a time speaking as she slowly got her wind back.

"Easy now," Finn crooned. "Ye'll be fine. I've had the wind knocked clean out of me more times than ye can count. Look at me, Lass," he urged. When she did, he nodded. "That's it. Now, close yer mouth and pull in a breath through yer nose."

Mollie managed to follow his calmly stated words, taking in one small breath at a time.

"There ye go. Ye're bleeding," he told her. "Did ye scrape yerself on me brother's knife? I've warned him about carrying it in his belt."

"Not mine," she replied. "Patrick's been shot."

Finn's eyes narrowed to deadly slits of green. "Tell me the man's name, so I can have the body sent back to his next of kin."

Breathing normally at last, Mollie looked up into the face of the man she'd dreamed of every night since he'd left all those months ago. She finally felt whole again now that she was in his arms. Placing a hand to his cheek, she confessed, "I've missed you, Finn."

The light in his eyes shone brightly, and she knew he felt the same. But Finn O'Malley was a man of few words. She doubted he'd do more than grunt or nod.

"I was torn, Lass." His reply caught her off guard. "Between needing to see ye every day, and me duty. Ye're a distraction I can ill afford."

She sighed. "Gwendolyn said Patrick told her she distracted him."

His eyebrows shot up. "Well now, who might she be?"

"Gwendolyn..." Patrick's voice brought them both back to the present and the fact that Finn hadn't set her down yet.

"Yer pardon, Mollie lass." He set her on her feet and urged her into the chair by the bed. "Did me brother harm ye when he landed on ye?"

Mollie lifted her arm and winced.

Finn frowned. "I didn't plan on punching him the first moment I laid eyes on him, but a man has to do what a man has to do."

Mollie got to her feet and stood between the brothers. Frowning at Finn, she told him, "You will do no such thing. He's already lost so much blood."

O'Malley glanced at his brother and then back at her. "Tell me what happened while ye fetch another bandage. This one's soaked."

Concern filled Mollie. "Let me ring for Constance." She walked over to the corner of the room and tugged on the bell pull. "She'll want to see if one of the doctor's stitches came undone."

"Wouldn't be the first time," Finn said. "Won't be the last. Now then, what happened?"

A short while later, Constance entered the room carrying a small bowl in her hands. "Finn!" Her eyes lit up. "I didn't realize you had arrived. Did you come in the side door?"

"Aye. I couldn't find Patrick in our quarters or on patrol with Eamon and Flaherty—by the way, how did Rory break his nose?"

"It's a long story," the cook said as she set the small bowl she carried on the nightstand.

"Always is with a Flaherty." Finn held his brother still while Constance washed the blood away. He wasn't surprised when she found a stitch had indeed come undone.

"I thought something like this would happen," the cook stated. "Fighting a fever is a battle with patients thrashing about. I brought boiled threads with me. Mollie, please bring the bowl I just set down."

Finn blanched when he saw it contained two needles and a coil of threads. "Isn't it better to cauterize the wound than sew it back together?"

Constance selected a needle and threaded it, answering, "Not always, depends on the wound, how deep it is, and whether or not you have the proper supplies at hand."

"We usually have our knives and flint and a bit of cotton handy," Finn mumbled.

"Fortunately, we have everything we need to take care of your brother," Constance assured him. "You don't have to stay. Mollie is strong and can hold him down for me."

"I'll stay. I think he may have injured one of Mollie's ribs when he fell on her."

The cook turned to stare at Finn first and Mollie second. "What happened?"

Mollie sighed. "He keeps asking for Gwendolyn, and I keep having to stop him from getting up and leaving. He's very determined."

"An O'Malley trait," Finn remarked. "We can be single-minded."

"You don't say," Mollie murmured.

He turned toward her and frowned. "When ye're finished, Constance, would ye mind checking Mollie's ribs for me?"

"*I* can ask," Mollie grumbled. "*If* I think I need them to be looked at."

Constance shook her head at the maid. "We cannot have one of our staff injured without having them looked at. The duke and duchess would have our heads if we did not take care of those who work with us."

"Thank ye, Constance." He turned and frowned at Mollie. "Ye'll do as she says, mind?"

"I do not have to listen to you, Finn. You have no hold over me, nor do you have a claim on me."

"There's where ye'd be wrong. I've His Grace's permission to court ye, Mollie Malloy, and I intend to."

"Took you long enough," she grumbled beneath her breath.

Finn chuckled. "I heard that."

"What if I no longer wish to be courted by a man who disappeared right after His Grace gave him permission to?"

His smile was lethal to her heart. "I'm thinking ye do, Lass. Best get used to listening."

Mollie was saved from answering when a soft voice asked from behind them, "How is Patrick's fever?"

"GWENDOLYN, THERE YOU are." Constance pointed to the stack of linens on top of the chest of drawers. "Please bring those bandages. His wound opened."

"What happened?"

"Me brother fell on me intended."

Gwendolyn's mouth gaped open before she collected herself enough to close it. "You must be Finn."

"Aye, and ye're the Gwendolyn he's been asking for."

She glanced at the bed and the man who held her heart. He was so still. His cheeks were flushed, and his temples were damp with sweat. "I'm here for my shift, Mollie. Her Grace asked to speak with you a moment before you return to your duties."

"Of course," Mollie replied, struggling to her feet.

She almost made it to the door when Finn reminded her, "Ye'll need to let Constance have a look at yer ribs before ye leave."

"The duchess needs me," Mollie countered.

"And she'll be seeing ye just as soon as Constance makes sure ye didn't crack a rib."

"Her Grace will understand," the cook soothed. "Now, if Finn wouldn't mind stepping outside for a few minutes, we can step behind the dressing screen, and I'll have a look."

Having cared for those on their staff with injured ribs before, the cook pronounced Mollie's were bruised. She had just finished wrapping them and was buttoning the back of Mollie's gown when Finn barked, "Have ye wrapped her ribs yet?"

"That man is impossible," Mollie grumbled.

"It is clear the man cares deeply for you, Mollie. Answer the man and then go rest."

"I have duties—" Mollie began.

"There are others on the staff who can divide your duties between them while you take the time to heal."

Mollie wrung her hands together. "How long?"

"Mollie Malloy! I'm coming inside. Ye better have had those ribs wrapped, or I'll do it meself!"

The door flung open. Finn O'Malley stood in the doorway, hands on his hips. "Are ye ready to listen?"

The muffled snort coming from the bed surprised everyone. Constance bustled about the room, straightening it, taking the bloody bandages with her while Finn moved to his brother's side. Patrick had roused and was speaking quietly to Finn.

Gwendolyn hurried to the washstand and grabbed a soft linen cloth off the pile by the porcelain bowl. Dipping it in the cool water, she wrung most of it out. Taking the seat the cook had vacated, she gently placed it on Patrick's forehead. Leaning close, she took his hand in hers and whispered in his ear, "I'm here,

Patrick."

He squeezed her hand. "I missed ye."

She put on a brave face, not wanting him to know how concerned she was. His fever could last a few days. In his weakened state, she did not know how he would fare.

"I'll be here for the next few hours. Then I have to get back to the nursery."

When she tried to slip her hand free, he tightened his grip. "Don't leave."

"I won't."

"Promise?"

"I promise to stay until Francis arrives to sit with you. Her Grace needs as much rest as she can get. I cannot neglect my duties taking care of those sweet babes."

"How long will ye be stayin?"

"A few hours."

"Two? Three? More?"

"Three."

"Don't let go," he rasped as his breathing slowed, and he fell back to sleep.

Gwendolyn held tight to his hand until Francis arrived. It was time to get back to her charges.

She brushed her hand across his forehead. He was slightly cooler. "I'll be back, Patrick."

He tightened his grip.

"Richard and Abigail need me."

He sighed and loosened his hold, letting her slip free. "Ye're comin' back?"

"In a few hours."

"Promise me, Lass."

Gwendolyn leaned close and pressed her lips to his forehead. Would he remember their conversation when he woke? "I'll be back. I promise." Exhaustion, from the blood loss and fever, claimed him a few moments later. She leaned close and whispered, "Unless I have no choice."

Her heart ached as she left his side, but duty called. There were babes to care for until their next feeding. Gwendolyn never shirked her duties. She would soldier through until Mollie relieved her to sit with Patrick.

She walked to the nursery with a new purpose...taking care of Patrick for as many hours as they'd grant her. Her heart and her mind in total agreement, it wasn't until she had changed the twins and soothed them back to sleep that it hit her...for the first time in a decade, she'd crossed the line and let her personal life interfere with her job.

Hands shaking, heart aching, she knew what she had to do. In order to save her reputation and continue to earn a living to support herself...*she had to leave.*

CHAPTER TWENTY-NINE

"YER GRACE!" FINN strode to the duke's side.

"I wasn't expecting you until tomorrow," the duke remarked.

"Yer missive was urgent."

"I take it so was the one from Patrick."

"Aye, but knowing me brother—and ye, I thought a bit of time was all that was needed for the issue to be settled."

"I doubt that was the response he expected from you," the duke stated.

"Patrick is used to telling the lot of us what to do. It took a bit of time to make certain everything was in order. There have been rumors that Ruan has been seen at night on the cliffs near Penwith Tower."

The duke was quick to respond. "As to Penwith Tower, you and the men have been doing an excellent job, protecting the workers rebuilding the south wall all the while following leads of smuggling in Cornwall. Coventry and King have been keeping tabs on the Frenchman's contacts at the London docks. They are aware of his latest movements, thanks to information the late Lord Hughes supplied before he was murdered."

"Rumors reported seeing him in and around the caves for a fortnight. The lads will be ready for him to make his move—with or without me."

The duke nodded. "I would not have expected anything less." He paused as if sensing there was more on O'Malley's mind. He prompted, "I understand you've seen Patrick. Rest assured Dr. Fortescue has been here and removed the lead ball from his shoulder."

"Me hardheaded brother pulled a stitch out, trying to leave the room. Mollie was injured when she tried to stop him and the *eedjit* fell on her."

"I hadn't heard any of this. Where is Mollie now? Has anyone spoken to Merry or Humphries in the event we need to send someone to fetch the physician back?"

"I asked Constance to have a look at Mollie's ribs. Me brother jabbed her in the side with his elbow as he fell on her."

The duke winced. "Bruised or broken?"

"Bruised and wrapped. Constance sent Mollie to lie down, said she'd check on her later."

The duke fell silent. "Mayhap we should have one of the footmen sitting with Patrick—they'd be better able to keep him in bed without getting injured."

"Ah, but there's nothing like the gentle touch of a fair lass when ye've been laid low."

The duke agreed. "Anything else?"

"Aye, Patrick needs to have a word with ye."

"Now?"

Finn frowned. "Said it was urgent. I'm thinking it might have to do with the twins' nanny. He's restless whenever the woman's not sitting beside him."

The duke fell silent, digesting the news. "I was about to meet with the men." He glanced at O'Malley and suggested, "They'll be waiting for me in the outbuilding by your quarters. Why don't you go in my place while I speak with Patrick?"

"Aye, Yer Grace."

"Tell the men I'll be along shortly."

Finn strode off to do the duke's bidding while the duke ascended the staircase to speak with Patrick.

The door to the bedchamber where the head of his guard lay recuperating was ajar. A glance had him rushing into the room to help Francis.

"What in the bloody hell do you think you're doing, O'Malley?" the duke demanded.

"I need to speak to Gwendolyn."

"His fever is down," Francis told the duke as he settled O'Malley back on the bed. "He's determined to speak with her."

"Do you plan to tear out more stitches?" Before the man could answer, he sighed. "Ring for Humphries, Francis, and have him send two footmen at once."

"What about Constance or Merry?"

The duke nodded, and she hurried to the corner to ring the bell pull.

"Would you wait outside for Humphries? I need to speak with O'Malley."

"Of course, Your Grace."

"You are supposed to be cooperating while those in charge of your care do their job."

Patrick snorted. "I feel fine. I need to speak to her, Yer Grace."

"Mrs. Alexander?"

"Aye...Gwendolyn. I have to..." his voice trailed off.

"To what?"

He confided, "I've never felt this way before. Me head's been turned a time or two, but me heart has never been engaged."

The duke sat beside O'Malley. "You never saw it coming, did you?"

"How did ye know that?"

"Because I never saw it coming until it hit me between the eyes the night a lovely young woman with hair as black as midnight, fell backward into my arms at the Hollisters' ball."

"Her Grace?"

"Lady Persephone Farnsworth...spectacles askew on her face, dressed in a bilious-colored gown, with the softest brown eyes

I've ever gazed into."

"Ye're a lucky man, Yer Grace."

"I am. What about you? A man deserves to have a life…a wife and family waiting for him at the end of the day. Someone to keep the home fires burning."

O'Malley closed his eyes. "I'll not be neglectin' me duties now that ye've given me a second chance."

The duke frowned. He'd realized and accepted that he hadn't lost O'Malley's trust…by his own doing, he'd lost sight of it. "I thought you accepted my apology and explanation as to why I asked Eamon to serve in your stead."

O'Malley's eyes opened. "Aye, but that doesn't mean I've forgiven meself for failin' to ensure ye had no reason to question that trust in the first place."

"It is time to move forward. If I've learned anything being married to Persephone, it's to listen to my wife. She's far more observant about matters I don't always consider important."

"Such as?"

"The emotional wellbeing of our staff and my personal guard. She mentioned that sparks fly whenever you and Gwendolyn are in the same room…" He paused, then added, "I confess I hadn't noticed."

"It's not part of me duty to let meself be distracted."

"Ah," the duke sighed. "Finn said much the same when he asked to be transferred to Cornwall a few months ago."

Patrick seemed surprised. "Did he now?"

"Indeed. Although I'd given your brother permission to court Mollie, he didn't stick around long enough to do so. I'd thought they'd had a falling out and didn't dig deeper to find out if it was some other reason he felt the need to leave."

"Me brother is a man of few words. Though I knew somethin' was weighin' heavy on his mind."

"According to my wife, he was worried he'd fail in his duties to me as his mind was otherwise engaged."

"Not one of me brothers or cousins would willingly set aside our duties to protect ye and yer family—no matter what happens."

"I know that. What I hadn't considered is that you might one day wish to leave my employ...when the right woman came along and distracted you."

O'Malley sighed. "'Tis the way Gwendolyn looks at me—a mix of wonder and hope with the promise of love."

"I know the look well, though for myself, it was when I dared to touch the rim of her spectacles to straighten them so she could better see."

"Her Grace doesn't wear spectacles."

"It was all part of her guise, borrowed spectacles and hideous-colored gowns so she could blend into the background and not stand out. You see," he explained, "she never intended to marry."

"'Tis obvious she loves ye and dotes on yer precious babes. I'm thinkin' she's glad she fell into ye at that ball."

"Not as happy as I am. From what I know of Mrs. Alexander's background, she's been working as a nanny since she lost her husband and prematurely born son. Mayhap her guise to blend into the background—aside from her curiously earth-toned attire, is putting every ounce of herself into the care of her charges. Keeping the walls intact around her heart."

"What makes you think that?"

"It's what I did. It was the only way I could concentrate on restoring our family name and rebuilding our depleted coffers. To keep myself apart from the society that my father worked tirelessly to aid in the House of Lords and through his good works. The underbelly of that same society coerced my older brother to follow down the wrong path toward a life of excess, deceit, and degradation."

Patrick fell silent as if digesting all the duke had said. "She's had me heart since I first laid eyes on her, Yer Grace."

"I didn't always listen to my heart. With the help of those close to me, I learned to and have been richly rewarded. Isn't it time for you to do the same?" the duke asked. "There is more than enough room on this estate to begin building homes for those in my employ who are lucky enough to meet the other half of their souls."

"I don't understand."

"Listen to your heart. Trust it. Marry her, Patrick."

"What if she won't have me?"

The duke laughed. "And here you've been telling me how single-minded the men in your family are. Use that single-mindedness and go after her until she accepts your offer for her hand."

O'Malley grasped the duke's hand. "I have yer blessin'?"

"To marry, yes. To leave my employ, not yet. Try to get some rest. I'll see about sending Gwendolyn in to sit with you later."

"Thank ye, Yer Grace."

"You're welcome, Patrick."

Leaving the bedchamber, the duke's mind whirled with the possibilities he offered to the head of his guard. Why shouldn't O'Malley and his men marry? He didn't follow the long-accepted standard that servants who married were expected to leave their posts.

On the whole, his staff was happy. Their unmarried, married, or widowed state had no bearing on their excellent service to his family.

It was time to set a precedence that he hoped would continue with his son. He'd speak to Hawkins. The steward would have intimate knowledge of the land surrounding his vast estate. He'd hire an architect, if need be, to begin constructing the first of what he hoped would be many homes for those in his employ—specifically the men who served in his personal guard.

Now that he'd found what he deemed to be a solution to Patrick's and Gwendolyn's situation, he could address the next items on his list. Securing a Special License for Patrick and Gwendolyn—Persephone would most definitely approve. He still had to meet with his men to apprise them of Patrick's condition and find out if any other names had been uncovered in his absence. Lastly, he had to check to see if the constable's wagon had been detained on the way but should be arriving soon.

The duke halted mid-step and turned around. He needed to speak with Persephone and tell her he'd spoken with Patrick. She should be pleased and agree with his plan to start building the first of many homes on their estate for the men in his guard—and the obtaining of a Special License.

Satisfied that he'd more than met the latest challenge presented to him, he smiled, anticipating the approval he'd see in his lovely wife's eyes when he shared his solution with her.

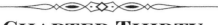

CHAPTER THIRTY

G WENDOLYN FOUGHT AGAINST the tears that threatened as she explained to Persephone that she would be leaving her post before the agreed upon time. The duchess seemed to be taking it in stride. *Why wasn't Persephone angry with her?*

"I understand completely," the duchess assured her.

Wildly, Gwendolyn wondered how the woman could, when in her heart she barely understood her actions in the last hour. "You do?"

"Of course. Your reputation is of the utmost importance securing posts in the future. I would not dream of standing in the way of your doing that."

She didn't know whether to be relieved that the duchess would not argue and beg her to stay or worry that mayhap Persephone did not feel the bond of friendship that had formed so quickly between them. "I was afraid you wouldn't understand."

"I do, completely. While you packed, the duke and I discussed all of the reasons we are giving you a glowing recommendation." The duchess held the sealed note out to Gwendolyn. "I'm certain you will have no trouble securing another position such as ours."

Her throat tightened with emotion as she accepted the note. Reaching into the pocket of her coat, she pulled out the journal she'd been keeping for Persephone. "Before I leave, I wanted to give you this."

The duchess' eyes glistened with tears. She blinked them away, reaching for the book. "Your journal?"

Gwendolyn shook her head. "It's yours. I was writing it for you, in the event you needed to refer back to anything we'd discussed during my time here caring for your darling twins." When the duchess stared at the bound journal in her hands, Gwendolyn continued, "There are many times people hear things they understand and tuck away in the back of their minds to pull out in difficult or trying moments. This journal will ensure that you don't have to worry that you've forgotten all that the two of us discovered about Richard and Abigail in the short time we've spent together."

The duchess beamed at her. "I cannot begin to thank you enough."

"You have that all turned around," Gwendolyn rasped. "I cannot thank you enough for not sending me packing after I nearly let my determination to rush to take care of the twins outweigh my good sense telling me to rest for a few hours before doing so."

Persephone smiled. "Jared would have done just that. He is a man who has an overriding need to fix any problems presented to him. Especially ones that involve the wellbeing of his family. He agreed that it would have been the wrong decision to make at that time. In fact, he and I are in complete agreement that you have been a blessing to our family."

Gwendolyn cleared her throat. "I shall be procuring a room at the inn in the village of Wyndmere for the night and taking the early morning Mail Coach back to London. Thank you for everything, Persephone."

The duchess pulled Gwendolyn into a swift hug. "You will be greatly missed. Thank you for making a difference in our lives."

Gwendolyn held those words to her heart as the coachman assisted her into the duke's carriage. The drive to the village was uneventful, as if a reminder that her life in between postings was the same—uneventful. The only times her life seemed to have meaning were the times she was taking care of her charges. With a deep sigh, she resigned herself to what she would never have...a family of her own.

She smiled and thanked the coachman as he helped her alight in front of the inn. In no time at all, she had arranged for a tea tray to be brought to her room and was ensconced in the small, but private, room at the end of the long hallway. She unpacked the few things she would need for her overnight stay slowly. Stretching out the long hours she'd be spending in her room with not a thing to do except wonder *what if...*

What if she'd been brave enough to stay and shout to the rooftops that O'Malley was the man she loved?

What if he came after her? What would she do?

She'd married the man she'd loved and had been overjoyed expecting their babe. In a heartbeat, it had all been taken from her. The Lord's plans had not fully matched her own. She'd been so happy when Jonathan had asked her to be his wife. The shared joy when she discovered she was going to have their babe. She'd never envisioned the brief time she would live that dream. They were supposed to watch their son grow up into a young man who would have been the image of his handsome father. Neither was meant to be.

But what if...

She shook her head to clear it. She'd been blessed with what few years she and her husband had shared together. Not everyone was destined to be married to a man they loved, let alone share a lifetime together.

Patrick could be that man...

"No," she admonished. "It would never have worked out. I move from position to position every few months. Patrick is in charge of the Duke of Wyndmere's personal guard. His job is to protect the duke and his family. Not following me around from post to post."

What if you took a chance? Maybe you could find the love that would last a lifetime.

"I cannot take the chance," she mumbled aloud. "Even if my heart yearns for a certain Irishman with eyes the color of dew-laden grass and a knowing smile that has my head in a spin and my heart racing."

Her tea arrived while she wrestled with her conscience and her feelings for Patrick. She thanked the serving girl and settled at the small table to have a cup of tea. Her heart ached missing him while her head reminded her that she'd made the right decision. Her reputation and ability to support herself as the years passed would keep the wolves at bay, though they would be cold companions in the endless nights that stretched before her.

CHAPTER THIRTY-ONE

O'MALLEY GRABBED HOLD of his brother's arm. "What do ye mean she's gone?"

Finn shrugged. "Are ye that addled from yer paltry wound that ye don't understand plain speaking?"

Patrick let go of his hold on Finn and shoved to his feet. He wasn't as steady as he should have been, but he'd burn in hell before he let a small thing like being shot—and clocked in the side of the head with a rock-filled reticule, stop him from going after the woman he loved.

"Where in the bloody hell did she go?"

Finn's lips twisted, fighting not to smile. "Why don't ye ask Her Grace? She was the last one to speak to Gwendolyn."

Digging deep, he found the strength to stalk from the room. He'd been shot before but may have lost a bit more blood this time. Patrick gritted his teeth and put one foot in front of the other.

"Where are ye headed?" The laughter in his brother's voice had him steeling against the need to whirl around and punch him in the face.

"Where do ye think?"

"Her Grace is in her upstairs sitting room," Finn added help-fully.

Patrick's head swam, his shoulder ached like a bitch, but he ignored the physical pain he was in. His heart was an open wound, bleeding with each step he took, knowing the woman he loved was gone. Hand to his chest, he staggered down the hall, stopping only when he stood outside the door to the duchess' sitting room.

He knocked and was bid to enter.

"Patrick?" The duchess' eyes widened as she stared at him before she rose to her feet and met him halfway. "What are you doing out of bed?"

"Where is she?"

The duchess glanced at his chest again, not answering fast enough to suit him. He hadn't planned on begging, but if it would get the woman to tell him where his Gwendolyn had gone, he'd do it! "Gwendolyn. I have to find her, speak to her."

"Do you? Why?"

"It's as plain as the nose on yer face," he bit out, then quickly apologized. "Forgive me, Yer Grace, 'tis the wound that has me temper frayin', takin' it out on ye."

She stared at him for a few minutes before the look in her eyes softened. "I doubt that. Aside from Jared, you are one of the strongest men I know. I have a feeling it's the pain in your heart that has you snapping at me."

He started to deny her words, but the truth was as plain as the nose on *his* face. "Ye have the right of it, Yer Grace. I love Gwendolyn and am afraid me life won't be worth livin' if she leaves without me askin' her to stay."

"Is that all you want to ask her?" the duchess prompted.

"I want to ask for her hand...if she'll have me."

"She's already been married and had a son...and lost them both of them hours apart. What could you offer her?"

"Me heart, me two hands, and the strength in me back. I'd work until I drop to make a life for her. She's deservin' of havin' a family."

"Have you told her that?"

"Not yet."

The duchess opened her mouth to speak but he cut her off.

"We're wastin' time while ye blather on about what she needs, askin' what I am goin' to do? Can't ye see me heart will shatter if she leaves?"

She reached for his hand and held on to it. "Our coachman took her to the inn in the village. She plans to take the early morning Mail Coach back to London."

Fear grabbed him by the throat at the thought of so many miles between them. "Not if I have anythin' to say about it." He turned and strode from the room.

"Patrick?"

He looked over his shoulder. "Aye?"

"You may want to finish getting dressed before you ride into town."

He grunted before he left the room with her soft laughter trailing behind him. His mission to track down Gwendolyn, haul her over his shoulder, toss her on his horse, and bring her back to Wyndmere Hall cleared his head and gave him purpose.

Mumbling to himself about a hardheaded woman who didn't know better than to stay where she was needed, nor keep from interfering where her help was not required, he nearly plowed into his brother. Finn's hand shot out to stop him.

"What's yer rush?"

"Forgot somethin'."

His brother's smirk irritated him "Do ye mean this?"

Taking the clean shirt from his brother, he donned it, silently promising to wipe that look off Finn's face later.

"Will ye be wanting yer socks and boots?"

He growled in reply.

Finn's snort of laugher tempted him to punch his brother now. The only thing stopping him was the knowledge that he may need all of his strength reserves to make it into the village, retrieve Gwendolyn, and return.

"Ye're dead on yer feet. Why not let me go in yer stead?"

"Ye don't know what I'm plannin' to say to her."

"I've a good idea."

Patrick shook his head. He didn't have time to argue with his brother.

Finn handed him his frockcoat, pistol, and knife.

He put the knife in his boot, his pistol in his waistband, checked his coat pockets for the pouch with lead balls, a wad of cotton and flint, and made his way to the door.

The hand on his shoulder had him pausing.

"I'm riding alongside ye."

"I don't need—"

"Aye, ye do. We can stand here and argue or get moving. Yer choice."

There was no choice. Finn was as stubborn as he was. "Fine."

He wasn't at full fighting form, but the stitches were intact, and the fever gone. Neither one mentioned the fact that his gait wasn't as steady as it normally would be. None of that mattered. Their mission was their entire focus—find Gwendolyn and bring her back.

Humphries was waiting for them in the entryway. "Her Grace took the liberty of having your horses saddled and ready to ride."

"Thank ye, Humphries."

"Good man." Finn clapped him on the shoulder as they stepped outside.

The cold air revived him the rest of the way. He hated being cooped up and idle—no matter the reason. He swung up into the saddle. "I'll be thankin' ye now, Finn. I may be too occupied when we arrive at the inn."

"She's yer match," Finn confided as they rode out. "*Saoirse* never was."

Patrick grunted in response. Ignoring the dull pain in the side of his head—compliments of the petite firebrand he intended to bring back, he took the lead.

Finn understood and didn't comment when Patrick urged his horse faster. They kept up the grueling pace until they reached the inn, dismounted, and handed their horses off to one of the stable lads.

"Wait here," he told Finn. "This won't take long."

Finn ignored the dictate and followed behind his brother.

The heat of the crowded taproom hit him in the face when he opened the door. His stomach roiled and the ache in his head had yet to let up, but he ignored everything save the need to find his woman. He thought about asking the innkeeper for the key to her room, then decided against it. He'd wasted enough time already and had a better idea. He bellowed her name.

The room fell silent—while his brother cackled like a madman. The startled innkeeper's mouth hung open as he stared at the two huge men standing in the open doorway.

Finn smiled. "We'll only be a few minutes more," he told the proprietor who nodded.

Those gathered in the taproom started speaking quietly.

"GWENDOLYN!" Patrick bellowed louder this time.

Footsteps descending the stairs sounded in the silence. A heartbeat later, she rushed into the room.

GWENDOLYN COULD NOT believe her ears or that the man standing before her had followed her. "What are you doing here? You should be in bed!"

"Ye promised not to leave."

"I promised to stay unless I had no other choice."

"To hell with other choices! Do ye love me?"

Her heart pounded a wild beat. Could everyone in the room hear it?

"Best answer me brother," Finn advised. "He's used to getting his way."

Patrick folded his arms across his chest, widened his stance and glared at his brother first, Gwendolyn second. "Ignore him and answer me question."

He was in obvious pain but ignoring it. She would have to be the first to admit to her feelings. If she had her way, he'd confess his feelings for her before the night was over.

"I may have strong feelings for you."

Finn smiled. "Wrong answer."

Patrick glowered at her, grabbed his brother's arm, and turned his back on her. "I'm wastin' me time. Let's go, Finn."

Fear that she'd never see him again engulfed her, threatening to drag her under. "Wait!" she shouted. Patrick stopped but did not turn around.

Needing to see his face when she told him what was in her heart, she slipped in front of him, tilted her head back to watch his expression and whispered, "I love you."

He leaned closer, his lips a breath from hers. "Me hearin's gone...must be remnants from wound fever or the lead ball I took in me shoulder, *protectin' ye.*"

Finn's rumbling chuckle echoed in the still quiet room.

Her throat felt tight. *What if...?*

"What did ye say?" he prompted.

She fought against the fear holding her captive and dug deep to proclaim what was in her heart from that first moment their eyes met. "I love you, Patrick O'Malley, stubborn, hardheaded Irishman that you are!"

His wolfish grin had her confidence wavering until he spoke. "Well now, Lass, that bein' the case..." he dropped to one knee and took her hand in his. "Will ye marry me, Gwendolyn Alexander? There's so much love inside me for ye...and any babes the good Lord blesses us with."

Tears welled in her eyes, but she didn't bother to hold them back. "What if we aren't blessed with a family?"

"I'd still want ye as me wife, Lass."

She cupped his cheek in her hand. Heart in her eyes, love filling her heart, she answered him, "Yes!"

"The first round's on me brother!" Finn's pronouncement

had cheers and calls of congratulations erupting. "I'll settle up with the innkeeper and follow along behind ye."

"I need to grab my bag—"

Patrick's mouth crushed against hers, silencing any protests she might have as she melted into his embrace. When he ended the kiss, the bemused look on her face had him grinning. "Finn, fetch me the bride's bag."

"I am perfectly capable of retrieving my things."

He frowned at her. "Easy or hard?"

She glared at him in reply.

"Hard it is." He swept her off her feet and tossed her over his shoulder.

"Are you mad? Put me down!"

He laughed. "I've got ye now, Gwendolyn. I'm not lettin' ye go until me ring's on yer finger."

She squirmed against his shoulder. "It takes three weeks for the banns to be read."

"Not necessarily," he remarked.

"Need a hand?" Finn called out.

"Nay. I've handled fractious fillies before."

Her sharply indrawn breath had him chuckling as he walked past the innkeeper and nodded. "Pleasant night."

The old man smiled. "I have a feeling it will be, O'Malley."

He paused to correct the man. "Just as soon as we're wed."

"Mayhap I've changed my mind," Gwendolyn huffed. "I cannot think clearly hanging upside down like this."

He walked outside and whistled for one of the stable lads. The young man gawked at the sight of the couple but ran to fetch O'Malley's horse.

"You cannot intend to carry me across your shoulder all the way back to Wyndmere Hall!"

Patrick eased her off his shoulder and set her on her feet. "We don't have time to fetch yer coat." He slipped out of his. Ignoring the sharp slash of pain in his shoulder as the stitches pulled, he helped her into it. "It'll keep ye warm."

"Thank you."

He mounted the horse, bent down, swept her off her feet and placed her onto his lap. "Ye'll be more comfortable ridin' back to Wyndmere Hall on me lap."

She leaned against him. "You won't always get your way."

He laughed. "Watch me."

As they rode through town, she peppered him with questions. "What will the people at the inn think?"

"That ye're a lucky woman."

"I've never been in this type of situation before…ever! My reputation—"

"We're gettin' married tonight. Between the duke's staff, and the vicar, the whole of the village of Wyndmere will be hearin' the romantic tale of it within the hour."

"Impossible!"

"Not for the duke."

"What does His Grace have to do with it?"

"Cease yer questions, Woman!"

"When you start to make sense."

"Faith, I love ye even when ye're irritatin' me."

She fell silent.

"Are ye finished?"

"Finished?"

"Aye, irritatin' me."

When she didn't answer him, he shifted her in his arms and brushed a tender kiss across her sweet lips. "Yer lips taste like faery nectar, Lass." He coaxed her lips to part for him and indulged in a longer, deeper kiss. "Legend has it a man could get lost for a hundred years once he's sipped from a cup of faery wine."

Gwendolyn tightened her arms around him. "Kiss me like that again, and I'll follow you to the ends of the Earth…or into the realm of the *Fae*."

"*Mo ghrá*," he rasped, nipping her bottom lip.

"*Mo chroí*." His tongue soothed the fullness before he feasted on the heady flavor of her mouth.

"*Go deo,*" he whispered against her lips.

"My grandfather O'Toole used to call my grandmother *Mo ghrá*. What does it mean?"

"My love."

She sighed. "And the rest?"

"My heart…forever. Ye'll have both. 'Tis me pledge to ye," he rasped as they approached the duke's estate.

"I was so afraid to let myself love you, Patrick."

"But not any longer?"

"O'Malley!" The stable master waved to them as they approached the stables. "His Grace is expecting the both of you."

"Thank ye, Winters."

"Whose carriage is that?" she asked as Patrick dismounted before helping her down.

"Visitors," the man answered with a twinkle in his eyes as he set her on her feet.

"Are ye ready, Lass?"

She beamed at him. "As long as you are by my side, I'm ready for anything."

"Then brace yerself, Lass. There's a bit of a surprise waitin' for us."

The pounding of horse's hooves sounded behind them. Patrick glanced over his shoulder. "Just in time, Finn!"

Patrick held out his arm to her. "Shall we?"

"Shouldn't we wait for your brother?"

"He'll catch up. I'm to escort ye to Her Grace. She's waitin' to speak to ye."

"What could she possibly have to say to me after I resigned my post?"

"She has somethin' she wishes to talk to ye about before we meet with the duke."

Gwendolyn sighed. "Very well."

He pressed his lips to her temple. "Don't worry, ye'll like the surprise."

CHAPTER THIRTY-TWO

C ONSTANCE AND MERRY were waiting for them. The moment Gwendolyn and Patrick walked into the kitchen, they whisked Gwendolyn away, reminding Patrick, "Meet us in the downstairs sitting room in one hour."

Desire for her glittered in the depths of his brilliant green eyes, the tautness of his jaw, the flare of his nostrils. When he yanked Gwendolyn into his arms, she went willingly.

She inhaled his scent—a combination that was uniquely Patrick's: cold crisp air, evergreens, and pure male. Surrounded by the strength of his arms, held against the massive breadth of his chest, she braced for another of his mind-bending kisses. Prepared to meet passion with passion, she was undone by the tender way he cupped her cheek as if she were a bone china teacup.

His gaze held hers captive. Was he trying to decide if he'd plunder her lips as he'd done before, or kiss her forehead and leave her wanting more? Unable to control her reaction to this man, she trembled in his arms. He slowly smiled and feathered kisses along the line of her jaw, ever closer to where her lips tingled in anticipation.

His lips touched the corner of her mouth as she imagined the brush of faery wings would feel upon her face. With a sigh of complete surrender, she melted in his arms.

"Her Grace is waiting," Merry reminded them.

Her emotions tangled, her body still singing from his touch. She marveled that Patrick had battered her senses with tenderness when she'd expected gut-churning passion. He'd touched her face as if she were a delicate young woman to be treasured...not a widow who'd lost her premature babe and husband hours apart. She was short in stature, but the wind would not knock her off her feet with her full-blown figure...a figure that had only captured the attention of two men in all of her twenty-eight years—Jonathan Alexander and Patrick O'Malley.

Cradling her against him, he whispered, "I'm pacin' me-self...for later." He lifted her hand and pressed a kiss to the back of it. "Until then, Lass."

He nodded to the women and strode from the room.

"Will I ever understand that man?"

Constance smiled. "It'll take time, patience, and understanding. Mayhap in ten or twenty years."

"Come, Her Grace is waiting," Merry repeated.

The duchess greeted her with open arms. "Gwendolyn! I'm so relieved that you came back. Patrick O'Malley is one of the best men of my acquaintance. You will never regret your decision to marry him."

A small part of Gwendolyn's fears began to evaporate. "Why aren't you angry that I left before the agreed upon time? Is the duke angry with me?"

"We don't have much time. Turn around. I'll unfasten your gown." The duchess gave her a gentle shove toward the dressing screen. "Do you need help undressing and getting into the tub?"

"I wasn't expecting any of this. I do not deserve your kindness after leaving you in a lurch."

Persephone was laughing when she tugged on Gwendolyn's arm and pulled her behind the screen. "Hurry up! Mollie's bringing your gown, then Francis will put the finishing touches on your hair. Merry will be right back. She has to check that everything is in place."

Gwendolyn gave in with a laugh. "I will under protest, but I still think—"

"You're wasting precious time." Persephone pointed toward the steaming copper tub, "Get in!"

"Yes, Persephone."

The duchess smiled and walked around to the other side of the screen. "I wish there was enough time to share a cup of tea, but Patrick took longer than we anticipated."

Gwendolyn eased into the fragrant water and sighed as the heat seeped into her limbs, relaxing her for the first time since she'd stepped into the coach that carried her away from the man she loved—the babes she adored, and the people she'd come to think of as family.

Unsure of how much time had passed since she'd heard Persephone remind Patrick to meet them in one hour, she hurried to finish her bath. She had just begun to dry off when someone knocked on the door.

"Don't get dressed yet," the duchess ordered. "Mollie is here with your gown."

"I didn't leave any of my gowns behind."

"Wrap the drying cloth around you, we're coming in!"

Mollie helped slip a chemise of the softest cotton batiste over Gwendolyn's head and fastened the trio of buttons at the back.

The duchess nodded to the maid who handed Gwendolyn her stockings and garters. As she put them on and stepped into satin slippers that matched the gown, Persephone continued, "Mollie and I conspired to have a gown made for you. While you were caring for Richard and Abigail, she took the measurements off one of your gowns."

"When would you have had the time?" she asked the maid.

"Right after you shared your story with me," Persephone replied.

Mollie held up a gown the color of sunlit evergreens.

Her eyes welled with tears, but she blinked them away. "I haven't worn gowns in any color other than earth-tones since I came out of mourning for my husband."

Persephone confided, "I had no wish to marry. My mother suffers from color blindness. I had no desire to marry and used her affliction to my benefit, wearing bilious-colored gowns."

Gwendolyn giggled. "Did you really?"

"It put off almost all of my suitors. Greenish-yellow does not enhance one's complexion as you might well imagine."

Gwendolyn sighed as the gown slipped over her head. She smoothed her hand over the exquisite, whisper-soft fabric, fighting the urge to curl her fingers into it. "I thought it best to blend in with my surroundings, not to attract attention to myself. There were other nannies that I'd heard were dismissed from catching the eyes of their employers. I chose colors that reminded me of the time I spent with my mother digging in her gardens. No one ever noticed me," she confessed.

"Patrick did."

She slowly smiled. "At first glance, he's so intimidating. His height, the breadth of his powerful chest, the width of his strong shoulders…and then?"

"Then?" the duchess echoed.

"I noticed how his emerald eyes deepened in color the longer his gaze held mine. I was shocked at first."

Mollie answered the knock on the door, admitting Francis who carried a small container of hairpins.

"Francis. You're just in time," Persephone told her maid before turning to answer Gwendolyn. "I would imagine so.

Mollie fastened the back of her gown. Gwendolyn turned around and caught the light of approval in the duchess' eyes. "No peeking until we've put your hair up. Sit!"

Gwendolyn obediently sat while Francis fussed with her hair, fashioning it into a knot on the top of her head. When she started to stand, Francis shook her head. "Let me pull a few strands free to frame your face."

Uneasy, worried, and wondering what Patrick would think, she fidgeted until the duchess told her to stand. "You look beautiful."

"Like a princess," Francis told her.

"A faery princess," Mollie added.

She walked slowly over to the looking glass that hung on the wall and stared at the stranger looking back at her. The hesitant look in her eyes was familiar, but the blush on her cheeks, upswept hair, and sumptuous gown of the deepest green had her staring. "I don't look like me."

Persephone put an arm around her and told Gwendolyn, "The first time I dressed in one of Mother's gowns, I did not recognize myself either. It had been so long since I'd worn a flattering color. It was a bit of a shock."

"It's hard to change," Gwendolyn whispered.

"It takes courage," Persephone remarked. "Neither one of us lack courage. Now, what do you think?"

Turning back to face the women, Gwendolyn answered, "I love the gown but I'm not sure about the color. Do you think he'll like it?"

"I'm certain of it," the duchess remarked. "We must hurry. Patrick is waiting for you."

"You've gone to so much trouble. I cannot thank you enough. I'll be sure to return the gown to you after we've eaten."

Persephone smiled as if she knew a secret and led the women from the room.

PATRICK PACED IN front of the fireplace until Finn grunted at him. "Ye're making me dizzy."

"Don't watch."

"They'll be here any moment now," his brother remarked.

"Are ye sure she hasn't changed her mind?"

The worry in Patrick's voice carried to where the duke stood speaking with the vicar. "She accepted your proposal. She'll be here."

"She doesn't know we're to marry tonight," Patrick reminded him.

"I thought you said her response was that it was impossible for the two of you to marry tonight," the duke stated.

"'Tis the truth she did."

"She'll have to admit she was wrong," the duke told him.

"What if she balks?"

"She won't," Flaherty rumbled as he entered the room.

"'Tis the truth," Garahan agreed, walking in behind his cousin. "She only has eyes for Patrick."

Humphries cleared his throat to capture everyone's attention. "Her Grace, the Duchess of Wyndmere, and Gwendolyn Alexander."

Finn nudged his brother. "Told ye, she'd be here."

Patrick rushed to her side and offered his arm. When she linked arms with him, he rasped, "Ye remind me of home, Lass. Yer gown's the color of Ireland's rolling hills, yer hair the color of peat…and yer eyes the color of the finest Irish whiskey."

She stared at Patrick until he shifted from foot to foot. "Is me cravat tied wrong?"

She slowly smiled. "It's the first time I've seen you wear anything but black."

He straightened his shoulders and lifted his chin. "'Tis me good coat. The black's the uniform the duke supplied the lot of us with when he hired us on as his personal guard."

"You are an imposing sight wearing black." She smiled at him. "The green of your coat matches your eyes."

"Does it now?" He winked at her.

"I'm thinkin' it's a bit darker than me eyes."

She snuggled against his side. "Not when you get that look in your eyes."

He leaned close to whisper, "That look?"

She was held captive by the intensity simmering in his eyes and could not look away. Finally, she was able to clear her throat and respond, pitching her voice low so as not to be overheard.

"Aye, one I have come to recognize as the prelude to your kiss."

Garahan glanced at Flaherty and patted his coat pocket.

His cousin mimicked the move and turned to glance at Finn who chuckled and patted his own pocket. They were ready if Patrick needed a wee drop of courage…if not, they'd save it for the toast—or later.

The vicar walked toward the couple standing in front of the fire. "If you'll take your places, we can begin the ceremony."

"Ceremony?" Gwendolyn squeaked, gripping Patrick's arm as if it were a lifeline.

He bent to reply, "Ye didn't believe me when I told ye we'd be marryin' tonight, did ye?"

"No…but—"

"Is there a problem?" the vicar asked.

Patrick grinned at the man. "Faith, me intended is overcome with gratitude, marryin' a man such as me."

His brother snorted, and his cousins joined in the laughter.

The duke walked over to stand in front of the couple. "I thought you accepted O'Malley's offer of marriage?"

"I did."

"Then what is the problem?"

Had her wits gone begging? She struggled to respond. "I thought we were going to have dinner."

The duke's knowing smile changed his countenance from serious to sincere. "We will most definitely be dining—*after* the vicar marries you."

Her mouth opened and shut—twice, before she found her voice. "I see."

The duke queried, "Having second thoughts?"

She stole a look at the man still holding her to his side and noted the lack of expression on his face. Was he expecting her to leave…again? "No. Just surprised."

Patrick's chuckle eased the worst of her nerves. "I told ye there was to be a surprise."

She shook her head and softly laughed. "You most certainly

did. I wouldn't have missed this surprise for the world. Though before we say our vows, may I ask a question?"

"Aye," he replied.

"May I have dessert first?"

Patrick's eyes bulged and his face flamed. "Best make it the short version, Vicar."

Laughter filled the room as Patrick and Gwendolyn pledged their lives and their love to one another before the witnesses gathered. The duke and duchess beamed as they congratulated the couple.

When it was Finn's turn to do the same, he leaned close and rasped, "His Grace asked me to handle yer duties for the next few days."

"Thank ye, Finn."

His cousins waited behind his brother and took turns shaking his hand. Flaherty kissed Gwendolyn on the cheek. Garahan swept his arm around her, dipped her backward, and kissed the breath out of her. With a nod to his cousin, he strolled over to stand beside Mollie.

The duke was smiling as he and Persephone returned to speak to the couple. "I've arranged for you and Mrs. O'Malley to stay in one of the vacant tenant farmer's cottages until the house I'm having built for you is completed."

Patrick's eyes widened. "Ye don't have to build us a home, we can make do—"

The duke grinned. "I'm not sure your wife would be comfortable living in your current quarters."

"I wouldn't mind!" Garahan said with a grin.

Patrick tightened his hold on his wife. "Remind me to punch Garahan later."

"I'd be happy to," Gwendolyn replied.

Persephone motioned for Constance who held out a large basket to Patrick. "My darling duke and I thought you may wish to dine alone tonight."

"Thank ye, Yer Graces."

"We've instructed one of the footmen to deliver your meals for the next few days, until you return to your duties," the duke added.

Patrick's voice broke as he asked, "How can we thank ye?"

"By forgetting about your duties and enjoying this time alone getting to know your bride."

Persephone leaned against her husband. "Sound advice, my darling duke."

Mollie and Francis hurried over to wrap a cloak around Gwendolyn's shoulders as everyone bid them goodbye.

"I hope ye didn't go to a lot of trouble with the weddin' feast, Yer Grace—seein' as how we won't be attendin'."

Persephone laughed. "We didn't plan on either of you joining us," she retorted. "See you in a few days."

Patrick grabbed hold of Gwendolyn's hand and grinned. "Are ye ready to begin our adventure, *mo ghrá*?"

"I'm ready."

"Brace yerself, Lass."

Chapter Thirty-Three

P ATRICK HANDED GWENDOLYN down from the carriage and waved to the duke's coachman as he drove off. Setting the food basket down, he opened the door and swept her into his arms and carried her over the threshold.

He noted the fire in the hearth and simple but homey touches inside the cottage. There was a single rose in a glass jar on the sturdy oak table by the window. Two chairs where they could enjoy a meal together while looking out over the fallow field. The view was framed by white lace curtains. Along the opposite wall, a bed was draped with a colorful quilt.

"The duke and duchess thought of everythin'."

"It's a lovely cottage. So unlike the room I let in London."

"London has never been to me likin', but 'tis where me brothers, cousins, and I found enough work to send money home to our families."

"Do you still send money home?"

"We all do, it was part of our arrangement when we left home to find work to help feed our families."

"You and your family are men of honor. I'm proud to be your wife."

He hesitated before telling her, "There may be a time or two in the future when you'll be wonderin' why ye married a man such as me."

"I'm certain you will wonder the same about me."

"Are ye hungry, Lass?" His deep green eyes bored into hers, waiting for her answer.

She slowly smiled.

Her incandescent beauty magnified by the firelight had him fighting to keep from striding over to the bed, tossing her on it, and…he shook his head.

"What's wrong?"

He reined in his need to make her his and gritted his teeth. "Not a thing, Lass."

She sighed and kissed his cheek. "Would you mind setting me down?"

"I'm thinkin' I'll be keepin' ye right here against me heart for the next little while, if ye don't mind."

"I don't want you to have a relapse."

"Ye don't relapse from gettin' shot," he corrected. "Ye recover. Ye relapse when ye've been ill, Lass."

She shook her head. "You had a fever."

"'Tis gone."

"But it could come back if you tire yourself out."

He snorted in laughter. "By all that's holy, what do ye think I plan to be doin' tonight instead of sleepin'?"

Her mouth hung open. With the tip of his finger, he helped her close it. After a few moments, she found her voice and replied, "I couldn't possibly say."

Unsure of how to ask but needing to know if he should go slowly and take his time reinitiating her to the art of lovemaking, he asked, "How long have ye been alone?"

She stiffened in his arms. "Ten years last month."

"Ah, Lass. I'm sorry for yer loss, but I had to ask."

She wiggled until he set her on her feet, walked over to the window and stood with her back to him.

Approaching her with care, he breathed her name as he set his hands on her shoulders. "I wouldn't hurt ye for the world, Gwendolyn. I've a powerful need to lie with ye…to take ye in me arms and make ye mine."

She shivered. He slid his hands over her shoulders, down the length of her arms until he grasped her hands. "But I can bank that need and take me time warmin' ye up."

She shrugged. "I'm not cold."

His sharp bark of laughter filled the small cottage. "Ye missed me meanin'."

With a grumble, she spun around and glared at him. "Why are you dancing around whatever it is you need to say? Just ask me!"

"Fine, then!" he growled. "When was the last time ye made love?"

Her face blushed a lovely shade of rose. "I…well, that is…it's been a long while."

"Now who's dancin' around the answer? Last month, last year?"

Shock had her mouth hanging open for a heartbeat while she stared at him. She snapped it shut and rushed to the open door. He beat her to it, snatched the basket inside, set it on the floor, and closed the door. His hand held it shut as she tried to yank it open.

"Ye'll not be leavin' this cottage until ye answer me, Wife."

"If it's so important, why didn't you ask me before you married me?"

"I'm not suggestin' ye'd been with other men, Lass. The answer will tell me how slowly I have to go after I undress ye." He slowly smiled. "I'm goin' to drive ye to the brink of madness with me mouth and me hands before I bury meself in yer softness and plant the seeds of our babe so deeply ye'll quicken this night."

Her eyes widened in shock.

"The look on yer face is answer enough."

"I've never spoken of such things."

"Not even with yer husband?"

She shook her head. "He wasn't as uninhibited speaking about such things as you apparently are."

"Ye'll get used to it and come to appreciate me plain speakin' in time, *mo ghrá*."

She licked her lips and he stared at her mouth. "I've been cravin' a taste of more than yer sweet lips, Lass. Will ye lie with me?"

She nodded. He scooped her into his arms, surprising a squeal out of her. He was chuckling as he eased her onto the bed. "We're both a bit overdressed, but I can fix that."

She watched him, her eyes burning with desire for him. He shed his frockcoat with a wince, tossing it over the chest at the foot of the bed. Next came his cravat, waistcoat, and cambric shirt. Instead of shedding his trousers, he surprised her by sitting on the bed to take off his boots and socks.

"Now then, Lass, your turn." He wiggled his eyebrows. "Need me help?"

She sat up and scooted off the other side of the bed. "I can manage…if you'd please turn around."

"I'm thinkin' I'd rather watch me wife undress…after all, ye watched me."

GWENDOLYN THOUGHT SHE'D expire on the spot from embarrassment. It took a considerable amount of courage to lift her chin up and remove her cloak before turning her back to him. "Would you please undo my buttons?"

"With pleasure."

He did as she bid and asked, "Do ye need me help takin' off yer gown?"

She bravely turned back to face him, stealing a glance at the power and beauty of his heavily muscled chest and arms. His physical presence overwhelmed her. "If you don't mind, I don't want to wrinkle the fabric. It's been a long while since I've had a gown this fine."

He eased the fabric over her head and held it out to her.

"Thank you." She folded it carefully and draped it across his clothing atop the chest. She scooted back to the bed and was about to slip under the covers when his voice stopped her, "Haven't ye forgotten somethin'?"

"Have I?"

His tender smile melted the chill of unease she'd been feeling when he'd started asking her intimate questions. "Yer chemise. I can help ye with that as well."

"But it's still light outside."

He nodded. Rounding the end of the bed, he closed the distance between them. "Ye won't be entirely without coverin', ye know."

She thought he meant the quilt until his eyes gleamed with devilment. "I'll be all the coverin' ye need tonight."

"You are a rogue!"

"Ye'll come to love me for it, Lass."

She sighed and gave in to him, shivering as he slid the soft cotton from her body. Unable to look him in the eyes while he still had his trousers on and not a stitch of clothing covered her, she stared at her toes.

"I'll treat ye like me ma's finest china teacup, Lass, if ye'll let me."

The tender way he looked at her nearly undid her. "You're still dressed," she reminded him.

"Mayhap ye can help me with that."

Digging deep for courage, she reached for the placket on his trousers. With trembling hands, she undid the buttons. "Can you manage the rest?"

He slid them down over his lean hips and stepped out of them.

Her eyes rounded with awe, staring at the sculpted beauty of the man before her. He was handsome fully dressed...standing in front of her, in all his naked glory, the man rivaled the ancient high kings of Ireland. In the time of gods and heroes, Patrick O'Malley would have been a god!

"If ye keep starin' at me like that, I won't be goin' slowly."

"I...I'm sorry. I've never..." her words trailed off as he slowly reeled her in. When her breasts met the warmth of his rock-hard chest, she quivered in his arms.

When he stroked a hand the length of her spine from neck to waist…and lower, she moaned. "Ye've the body of a goddess. I'm thinkin' it'll take me most of the night to touch ye everywhere I've been dreamin' of."

"You've dreamed of me, too?"

"Aye, Lass, let me show you."

He picked her up and laid her in the middle of the bed and slipped in beside her. In one swift move, he rolled her beneath him.

She noticed his wince. "Your shoulder?"

"'Tis nothin', I've had worse."

"Have you?"

"Aye," he said as he nudged her legs wide and settled between them. The warmth of his skin, the power in his muscles, intoxicated her. She wanted him closer…as close as they could be until they were joined together as one.

SHE MOANED HIS name, and he bent his head to take her lips. Desire building with each meeting of their lips, he plundered what he'd been craving since that first decadent taste of her.

Inhaling her scent, he let his tongue burn a trail of fire from beneath her ear to the hollow at the base of her throat. "Ye taste of honeysuckle."

He captured her lips again and plumbed the depths of her sweet mouth, while his hands explored every generous curve of her lush body. Tracing, teasing…tasting every inch of her until she was mindless, writhing in his arms.

"*Mo ghrá*, look at me."

Her eyes slowly opened, and his heart tumbled the rest of the way into love. "Make love with me."

His reply was swift and sure as he buried himself to the hilt. Surrounded by her softness, he could not hold back any longer. His groan of ecstasy echoed her own as he withdrew only to bury himself again and again. With each thrust, she lifted her hips to meet him, offering herself to him with a passion that arrowed through his heart into his soul.

She came apart in his arms as he thrust home, planting the seeds of their family deep, praying one would take hold this night. Tucking his leg around hers, he rolled them over until he was on his back, and she lay with her curves filling the hollows of his body.

A peace, such as he'd never known, enveloped him, lulling him to sleep.

HE WOKE WITH a grunt as her elbow dug into him too close to his *bollocks* for comfort. "Have a care, Lass," he grumbled. "Else ye'll emasculate me."

"I'm so sorry." She scooted to the edge of the bed.

He pulled her back, tucking her close to his side. "Are ye all right?"

She sighed. "Mmmm. I haven't felt this relaxed in years."

"If ye aren't too sore," he rasped. "I'm more than ready to lull ye back to sleep."

"Again? So soon?"

He rolled onto his back and filled her with a swiftness that stole her breath. Words were no longer necessary as they caressed and stroked one another, building the fires of passion to a conflagration. He grabbed hold of her hips, anchoring her to him as he thrust inside her again and again, lifting them off the bed in a frantic rhythm until she arched back and screamed his name. His echoing battle cry of triumph erupted as he followed her over the edge of madness into oblivion.

Hours later, they lay awake, replete in one another's arms. He'd unlocked an untapped passion he never would have guessed lay dormant waiting for him to release it. Holding her to his heart, he marveled that Gwendolyn was his *wife*. The need to share what was in his heart filled him. "I love ye, Lass."

Her sharp intake of breath told him she'd heard his words. The need to hear her echo his words filled him. *Would she say them back?*

"I never thought to marry again. I never imagined I'd be blessed to love again." Pressing her lips to his heart, she eased back to gaze into his eyes. "*Mo ghrá, mo chroí, go deo,* Patrick—you have my love, my heart, forever."

Limbs entwined, bodies tangled together, the lovers drifted off to sleep.

EPILOGUE

"AMERICA?" PATRICK COULD not believe the turn of events in the few days since he'd last been on duty. "I thought King's evidence would be enough to convict the man."

The duke frowned. "Apparently, Radleigh and his sister, Lady Hampton, were spirited away just hours before King arrived to escort them to Bow Street to answer the charges levied against him."

"Connections in high places?" Finn wondered aloud.

"I'm wondering," Garahan mused, "if they booked passage before the last kidnapping attempt."

"Knowing they would not succeed," Flaherty added.

Patrick took in the solemn faces of the men gathered in the duke's study and slowly smiled. "From what we hear from our kin that have made the crossin', the weather this time of year makes for a difficult voyage."

"If he dares to step foot on English soil," the duke added, "there will be a reckoning."

"Lord willin', we'll be there to witness King clappin' him in irons," Patrick added. "Has King uncovered anyone else behind the kidnappin' attempts?"

"No," the duke replied. "Coventry advised he and King consider the matter closed. Though they'll both be keeping an ear to the ground in case there's scuttlebutt." He nodded to Patrick and said, "It's good to have you back."

Patrick slowly smiled. "'Tis glad I am to be back. Though faith, I could use a bit of a rest. Think I'll start with patrollin' the perimeter. Me wife expects me home for supper."

"Marriage has put a gleam in yer eyes," Garahan acknowledged as he followed Patrick out the door.

"'Tis the lack of sleep, I'm thinking," Flaherty remarked, following behind his cousins.

Eamon elbowed them aside to call out, "Ye're a lucky man."

"And well I know it," Patrick said with a grin. "She's the world to me, lads."

"We'd best let ye get on with yer duties, then," Finn told him. "Ye've more work to do after supper."

Patrick paused mid-stride. "I do?"

"Aye," Finn replied. "I'm thinking a niece or nephew would be a welcome addition to our family."

Garahan and Flaherty were laughing as Patrick paused to consider his brother's words. "What's the wager?"

Finn grinned. "Three to one ye'll have a daughter."

Eamon was quick to add, "Come the fall."

Patrick knew in his gut that Gwendolyn already carried their babe. "She'll have hair the color of peat and eyes like the finest Irish whiskey."

"Well now," Garahan rumbled, "odds are she'll have yer ugly mug."

"And Gwendolyn's fine eyes," Flaherty added.

Patrick was laughing as he shoved his cousins out of his way. "Ye're just jealous, lads. Go find yer own women."

Finn was quick to boast, "I'm thinking it'll take me a week or so to convince Mollie to marry me."

"Ye won't regret it," Patrick told him as the brothers made their way down the hallway to the side door.

Garahan sighed. "Do ye think we're missing out not having women in our lives?"

Flaherty glanced at their cousins' retreating forms before

responding, "Mayhap we are."

"What do ye plan to do about it," Garahan asked.

"I think I'll let Fate lend a hand," Flaherty replied.

Eamon snorted. "Ye're asking for trouble, lad."

"Ah, but Fate was kind to our cousin. I'm thinking she may have a bit of luck left over to split between us."

"Well now," Garahan grinned. "I'll take that bet."

"Faith, I knew ye would."

NINE MONTHS LATER... Patrick and Gwendolyn welcomed a beautiful daughter, and the duke's guard added one more to their ever-growing list of those they'd protect with their lives...or die trying.

About the Author

Historical & Contemporary Romance "Warm...Charming...Fun..."

C.H. was born in Aiken, South Carolina, but her parents moved back to northern New Jersey where she grew up.

She believes in fate, destiny, and love at first sight. C.H. fell in love at first sight when she was seventeen. She was married for 41 wonderful years until her husband lost his battle with cancer. Soul mates, their hearts will be joined forever.

They have three grown children—one son-in-law, two grand-sons, two rescue dogs, and two rescue grand-cats.

Her characters rarely follow the synopsis she outlines for them...but C.H. has learned to listen to her characters! Her heroes always have a few of her husband's best qualities: his honesty, his integrity, his compassion for those in need, and his killer broad shoulders. C.H. writes about the things she loves most: Family, her Irish and English Ancestry, Baking and Gardening.

Sláinte!
CH

C.H.'s Social Media Links:
Website: www.chadmirand.com
Amazon: amazon.com/stores/C.-H.-
Admirand/author/B001JPBUMC
BookBub: bookbub.com/authors/c-h-admirand
Facebook Author Page: facebook.com/CHAdmirandAuthor
Facebook Private Reader's Page ~ C.H. Reader's Nook:
facebook.com/groups/714796299746980
GoodReads: goodreads.com/author/show/212657.C_H_Admirand
Instagram: c.h.admirand
Twitter: @AdmirandH
Youtube: youtube.com/channel/UCRSXBeqEY52VV3mHdtg5fXw

www.ingramcontent.com/pod-product-compliance
Lightning Source LLC
Chambersburg PA
CBHW061519280925
33286CB00014B/1519